Arabella had grown to like the handsome Marquis of Meridale. Although she resisted, she felt safe and happy when he was around. But was it wise to entrust him with the terrible secret that burdened her heart?

Listening in the shadows of a doorway she heard Gentleman Jack making plans. Her breath stopped. The Marquis was in dire danger. Now she had to tell him the truth—had to warn him and save his life.

Quickly she turned toward the stairs, and stopped! In the darkness was a man—his hat drawn low on his forehead, a pistol in his belt . . .

Also in Pyramid Books

by

BARBARA CARTLAND

THE
SECRET
FEAR

Barbara Cartland

PYRAMID BOOKS • NEW YORK

THE SECRET FEAR

A PYRAMID BOOK

Copyright © Barbara Cartland 1970

Pyramid edition published May 1971
Tenth printing, June 1976

Printed in the United States of America

Pyramid Books are published by Pyramid Publications (Harcourt Brace Jovanovich). Its trademarks, consisting of the word "Pyramid" and the portrayal of a pyramid, are registered in the United States Patent Office.

PYRAMID PUBLICATIONS
(Harcourt Brace Jovanovich)
757 Third Avenue, New York, N.Y. 10017

One

THERE was a sound of footsteps in the hall and a small figure sped silently across the thick carpet to hide behind the long, velvet curtains framing the window.

A second later the door of the Library was opened and Arabella knew that her stepfather had entered the room.

She heard him throw his riding-whip down on the desk and then, with a feeling almost like sickness, realised she had left a book open in the armchair.

She could almost see his sharp eyes under the dark bristling eyebrows glance towards it, and he would notice the rosewood library steps below the place in the cabinet from which the book had been extracted.

She held her breath, feeling that at any moment he might suspect her presence in the room and start to look for her. Then, with a sense of relief, she heard her mother come in.

"Oh, there you are, Lawrence," Lady Deane exclaimed in her soft, low voice. "I thought I heard your horse outside. Did you have a good ride?"

"Arabella has been here!" Sir Lawrence announced dramatically, his harsh voice seeming to echo round the room. "I understood she was too indisposed to leave her room."

"Indeed, she is still far from well," Lady Deane said hastily, "and I am sure she cannot have come downstairs."

"Do you see that book?" Sir Lawrence demanded. "If I've told my stepdaughter once, I've told her a thousand times, I will not have her reading my books. Many of them are not fit for a young girl and, besides, too much learning is not good for the young. But she has disobeyed me, as she has disobeyed me so often before."

"Now, Lawrence, pray do not distress yourself," Lady Deane begged. "I will speak to Arabella . . ."

"I will speak to Arabella," Sir Lawrence thundered.

There was a moment's silence before Lady Deane said agitatedly :

"I do beg you not to be incensed with her ! And if you are thinking of whipping her as you have done before, she is not well enough. Indeed, Lawrence, she is too old for that sort of thing."

"She is not too old to misbehave !" Sir Lawrence retorted. "And if she does what she has been told not to do, then she must take the consequences."

"Lawrence, I beg of you . . ." Lady Deane began, only to be interrupted by her husband . . .

"We will speak of this no more. You will send Arabella to me first thing tomorrow morning. There is not time now, we leave for the Lord Lieutenant's at five o'clock."

After a pause, as if Lady Deane was forcing herself to cease the argument, she said in a low voice which trembled :

"Do you really consider it wise that I should wear the diamond tiara tonight, Lawrence, and my other jewels? All the county knows that his party is to take place and I am convinced that terrible gang of highwaymen will be lying in wait for the guests."

"Everything has been taken care of, my dear," Sir Lawrence answered loftily. "You will wear your tiara and not perturb yourself about these cut-throats."

"But Lawrence, you remember the last time ! I lost my ruby parure, and the villains even dragged the rings from my fingers! I have never suffered such fear or such humiliation!"

6

"Nor I!" Sir Lawrence said frankly. "But what could I do? I was unarmed and there were six of them. And that damned felon, Gentleman Jack or whatever he calls himself, had the effrontery to jeer at me. One day I shall watch him swing for that! I swear to you, Felicity, it will be the happiest day of my life!"

Sir Lawrence spoke with such venom in his voice that Lady Deane gave a little cry of protest.

"No, no! You must not speak like that, Lawrence! It frightens me. These men are all you say they are, but their crimes, abominable though they may be, must not inflame you until you would be as brutal as they are."

It seemed that her words softened Sir Lawrence's fury because, when he spoke again, his voice was more gentle.

"All woman, aren't you, Felicity? And not a bad thing to be, either. I cannot abide these hard-swearing, hard-riding, modern young females, who pretend they have no need of masculine protection. But all the same it is a disgrace that two years after the war with Bonaparte is ended, we cannot have more soldiers to deal with this scourge upon our countryside. Why, His Honour the Judge himself was waylaid on his way back from the Assizes. They took his watch and his ring and fifty guineas that his Marshal carried, in gold, to pay for their lodging on circuit."

"The Judge!" Lady Deane exclaimed. "Will nothing deter them?"

"It's just sheer incompetence that they have not been apprehended before now." Sir Lawrence stormed. "In the last century highwaymen terrorised the whole countryside; but today, in 1817, we should have thought out new methods to bring them to justice. What we need is a company of Dragoons, and I shall tell the Lord Lieutenant so myself this very evening!"

"That is if we ever reach the party," Lady Deane said apprehensively. "Oh, Lawrence! Pray do not make me wear the tiara. It is so conspicuous!"

"It will be quite safe," Sir Lawrence assured her, "and you would feel sadly inconspicuous if you appeared without it. There is a chance—but only a chance, mind you—that His Royal Highness will be present."

"His Royal Highness? You mean to say the Regent will be there this evening?" Lady Deane cried.

"Well, Lady Hertford has accepted an invitation, and we know full well where Lady Hertford goes, Prinny will follow," Sir Lawrence said. "So put on your best bib and tucker, Felicity. I would not have you put out of countenance by any lady of the Carlton House set. They may be all the crack, my dear, but they cannot hold a candle to you when it comes to looks!"

"Lawrence, you flatter me!" Lady Deane said softly. "But you are right. Of course I must wear my jewels. I am thankful now I ordered a new gown from Bond Street for this very occasion, though indeed it was wretchedly expensive."

"I want to be proud of you," Sir Lawrence said. "Damn it all! Those who wondered why I chose to marry a widow rather than a fresh-faced maid shall have their answer tonight. You are in good looks, my dear!"

"I will try to do you credit," Lady Deane answered sweetly. "And now I had best go and prepare myself."

"Have no longer any fears for the safety of either yourself or your tiara," Sir Lawrence said. "I have made special arrangements for the journey. We drive in convoy."

"In convoy? What does that mean?" Lady Deane enquired.

"Colonel Travers will start first and drive the short distance to The Towers, where Lord and Lady Jeffreys will be waiting with their coachman and footman, both armed, and also two outriders. The carriages will proceed here and we shall join then. I am arranging that there will be two footmen on our coach and both grooms will come on horseback. That way we shall have seven armed men and six outriders. What think you of my clever scheme?"

"It is indeed clever," Lady Deane enthused. "Only you could have organised it so thoroughly. Dear Law-

8

rence, how fortunate I am to be the wife of a man with a brain."

"Between us we have both beauty and brains, Sir Lawrence said with satisfaction. "Run along, my dear. We must not keep Her Ladyship waiting.

"No, indeed," Lady Deane agreed, moving towards the door.

"And do not forget to tell Arabella," Sir Lawrence went on, "that I will speak with her tomorrow morning."

Lady Deane paused.

"There is something I have to tell you, Lawrence," she said, "and I hope you will not be incensed. I have arranged to send Arabella away."

There was a moment's silence, and then, with a note of ominous irritation in his voice, Sir Lawrence said loudly:

"You have arranged to send her away without consulting me?"

"Naturally I was going to speak with you about it," Lady Deane said. "When Doctor Simpson was here today . . ."

"Simpson? Who the hell is Simpson?" Sir Lawrence shouted.

"He is the new doctor," Lady Deane replied. "You recall that our old physician, Doctor Jarvis, has retired. He had a stroke and I fear he will not recover. Well, Doctor Simpson, a younger man, has taken over the practice."

"Some nit-witted whippersnapper who thinks he knows everything, I suppose!" Sir Lawrence growled.

"He seems intelligent," Lady Deane said, "and he was perturbed to find that Arabella was so thin and weak after her illness. Scarlet fever can be very lowerring, Lawrence, as you well know."

"Arabella is well enough to come downstairs, stealing my books," Sir Lawrence muttered.

"Doctor Simpson had a suggestion," Lady Deane went on bravely, ignoring the interruption. "He told me he was extremely anxious to find a companion for

9

Beulah Belmont, and he suggested that Arabella might go to the Castle for a short visit to give her a change of atmosphere, and perhaps be of some help to poor little Beulah."

"Poor little Beulah, indeed! A help to poor little Beulah!" Sir Lawrence guffawed. "Why the child's an addle-brained idiot from all accounts ! What good could Arabella do to her?"

"It's Doctor Simpson's idea that the child needs companionship. After all, as we all well know, there is no one at the Castle except her governess and all those old servants."

"While the Merry Marquis amuses himself in London, eh?" Sir Lawrence exclaimed. "Upon my soul, you can't blame the man. Who would want to put up with that ramshackle old place? It ought to have been pulled down long ago."

"Oh, Lawrence, how can you say such a thing? It's just been sadly neglected since Lady Meridale died. Doctor Simpson feels that little Beulah may be retarded because she has never had the love of a mother."

"Sickly, sentimental tosh !" Sir Lawrence growled. "The child's said to be half monster! If young Meridale wants someone to look after his sister, he should come home and arrange it himself. And as for Arabella going there, I have never heard such a nonsensical notion in the whole of my life. You've spoiled her and the girl is out of hand already. Wasting her time at the Castle won't do her or anybody else any good. And I'll tell Doctor Know-All so myself when I meet him!"

"We'll talk about it tomorrow," Lady Deane said soothingly. "I must hurry now or, indeed, you will blush with shame at my appearance. And, besides, I do not wish to play the wallflower while all the most attractive women in the room cluster around you, Lawrence!"

The flattery brought a smile back to Sir Lawrence's grim countenance. Nevertheless, when his wife left the room, he walked across to the chair and picked up the open book where Arabella had left it.

He stood looking down at it pensively, then slapped

10

it shut. There was still a faint smile on his lips but it was very different from the one which had been evoked by his wife's compliments. Indeed, there was something unpleasant and a little evil in the manner in which, while his eyes narrowed, he set the book down gently beside his riding-whip on the desk.

For a moment he contemplated the two objects. Then with a little sound like a faint laugh he went from the room, closing the door behind him.

It was some moments before Arabella dared move. She was well aware that her stepfather, with his often uncanny perception where she herself was concerned, might have closed the door to let her think he had gone, and remained inside the room to watch her emerge from her hiding-place.

But she heard his footsteps cross the marble hall and only when they had died away did she come from behind the curtain.

She was small-boned with delicate, etched features, but now she was unnaturally thin from the illness that had kept her in bed for over five weeks. It made her violet eyes seem enormous in her tiny, pointed face, and as she moved silently across the floor she looked little more than a pathetic waif that needed feeding and cosseting back to health.

She opened the door a mere inch, saw that the hall was empty, and sped swiftly as a fleeting shadow not up the front staircase, but down a side passage which led to the back stairs.

Only when she reached the sanctuary of her own bedroom did some of the fear and tension go out of her face, and she sat, gasping for breath, on a stool in front of the dressing-table, But a knock at the door brought her swiftly to her feet again, her eyes wide and apprehensive.

"Who is it?" Her voice was hardly audible.

"'Tis me, Miss Arabella," a voice replied.

"Oh, come in, Lucy."

"Her Ladyship wants ye," Lucy announced in broad Hertfordshire accents.

11

She was an apple-cheeked young girl from the village who was being trained in the duties of fourth housemaid and found it exceedingly hard to remember all she had to do.

"I'll go to her at once," Arabella said, and added anxiously, "Is she alone, Lucy?"

"There be only Miss Jones with her," Lucy replied, understandingly. "The Master be in his own room."

"Thank you, Lucy," Arabella said, moving swiftly towards her mother's bedroom, which opened off the landing at the top of the staircase.

Lady Deane was sitting in front of her mirror and her lady's-maid was arranging a sparkling tiara on top of her elaborately ringleted hair.

"Mama, that looks lovely!" Arabella exclaimed spontaneously as she entered the room. "I adore you in your tiara. When I was a child I thought you looked exactly like a fairy queen and I always expected to see wings sprouting from your shoulders."

"How are you, darling?" Lady Deane asked. "I pray you have not over-tired yourself? Doctor Simpson said you were not to do too much the first few days you were out of bed."

"I promise you, I have done very little," Arabella replied.

She wondered if this would be the right moment to admit that she had been hiding in the Library downstairs and decided against it. She knew only too well what awaited her tomorrow and how deeply it would distress her mother.

"I am nearly ready, Jones," Lady Deane said to her maid. "Will you wait outside and tell me when Sir Lawrence goes downstairs? I want to talk to Miss Arabella."

"Very good, Milady," Jones replied.

She was a middle-aged women, who had been with her mistress for over ten years and knew all the difficulties and crosscurrents that beset the household. With a sympathetic glance at Arabella she went from the room, closing the door behind her.

Lady Deane turned impulsively to her daughter.

"Listen, dearest," she said, "we have not much time and there is so much I have to impart to you. I want you to leave here tomorrow morning early."

"To go to the Castle?" Arabella asked quickly.

Lady Deane looked up into her daughter's face.

"You were in the Library," she said. "I half suspected it."

"I do not think he knew I was there," Arabella replied: "in fact, I am sure of it. If he had known, he would have ferreted me out when you left."

"No, I am sure he was ignorant of your presence," Lady Deane said. "But how could you have been so foolish as to leave the book behind?"

"I was not expecting him back so soon," Arabella answered. "No, that is not the whole truth, Mama. I just became enthralled with what I was reading. You know how I forget everything, the time, the place . . . and even my stepfather, when I am reading."

"You will have to leave before he punishes you," Lady Deane said miserably. "You are not in a fit state to endure it. And I know that I could not stand by and see you suffer, as I have done in the past."

Arabella was very still.

"It is not that I mind his whipping me," she said in a low voice. "It is when he is . . . pleasant that it is unbearable. Oh, Mama! How could you have married him?"

"He is kind to me, Arabella. And you forget that dear Papa left us completely penniless."

"All that mad gambling!" Arabella said bitterly.

"He enjoyed it so much," Lady Deane sighed, "and he was always so penitent when he lost. And when he won, what fun we used to have!"

"I know," Arabella said. "I remember how he used to come home and call for a bottle of champagne. You used to give me a tiny sip and we would all laugh, and it seemed like the most wonderful party in the world. Then he would carry you off to London. Once I said to him, 'What are you going to do, Papa, when you get

13

to London?' He picked me up in his arms and swung me above his head and replied, 'Your Mama and I are going to spend money and be gay, Arabella. That is what life is for—for laughter, wine and gaiety. Not all this grumble, grumble about bills.' "

Lady Deane laughed.

"That sounds exactly like your father," she said. "How he used to hate the bills and the grumble, grumble about them. And now he has not to worry any more."

For a moment Lady Deane closed her eyes, as though she would shut out everything but her memories. Then she said quickly :

"It is no use, Arabella. We cannot live in the past. I assure you that I am content with Sir Lawrence. It is only where you are concerned that I cannot control him."

"I am sorry, Mama," Arabella said.

"Oh, it is not your fault," Lady Deane replied. "You are going to be very beautiful, Arabella, and beautiful women are always a disturbing influence where men are concerned."

"I hate men!" Arabella cried. "I hate all of them! I hate the way they look at me. I hate the greedy, possessive expression on their faces, the way their hands go out towards me."

She shuddered.

"Oh, Mama ! I don't want to grow up ! I want to remain a child."

"That is exactly what I want you to pretend to be," Lady Deane answered.

"What do you mean?" Arabella asked curiously.

"Doctor Simpson has only seen you in the last week since he took over Doctor Jarvis's practice," Lady Deane answered. "You have been in bed, you have appeared so thin, small and very young, Arabella. He thinks you are still a child."

"Is that why he has asked that I should go to the Castle?" Arabella asked.

Lady Deane nodded.

"I imagine he believes you to be about twelve or thirteen. He inferred that and I did not contradict him."

"Why not tell him the truth . . . that I shall be eighteen in a month's time?" Arabella asked.

"If I had," Lady Deane replied, "he would not have made the suggestion that you visit the Castle. It is not what I should want for you, Arabella, but you must get away from here."

Arabella moved forward to play with the silver brush on her mother's dressing-table.

"I did not think you had noticed, Mama," she said quietly.

"Of course I noticed," Lady Deane said. "I saw you growing prettier and prettier, Arabella, and I knew, too, that your stepfather was jealous of you where I was concerned. He always has been, and it gave him an excuse to punish you severely and cruelly at every possible opportunity. But as you grew older . . ."

"Do not let us talk of it, Mama," Arabella begged in an anguished voice. "We understand, both of us, and as you say, I must go away."

"I was wondering what to do . . . I have been wondering for a long time . . ." Lady Deane said, "and when Doctor Simpson suggested you might be a companion for poor little Beulah, I knew it would give us time to think. I have thought that perhaps you might visit your godmother in Yorkshire, or your father's aunt who lives in Dorset. It is just that I have lost touch with both of them. But now I will write to them and find out how they are, what are their circumstances, and if there is any possibility of their offering you hospitality for a long period. But tomorrow you must go to the Castle."

"I am a little vague about the Castle and who lives there," Arabella said.

"The Marchioness of Meridale died soon after her daughter, Beulah, was born," Lady Deane said. "From all accounts, the child is not normal. She must be about seven or eight years old. But Doctor Simpson seems to think that if she were treated differently from the way she has been in the past, her mental faculties might improve. He appeared to think she was neglected at the moment."

"Poor child," Arabella exclaimed.

"I gather," Lady Deane continued, "that the Doctor has made a study of these unfortunate chidren and being young and enthusiastic he wants to try out his ideas. It won't be very entertaining for you, Arabella, but I promise that I will try to move you from the Castle as soon as possible."

"Do not fret, Mama!" Arabella said. "It might be quite interesting. Who is the Merry Marquis?"

"The present Marquis of Meridale is, of course, Beulah's brother," Lady Deane replied. "I am afraid he has not a very enviable reputation. He was a soldier during the war, and these last two years everyone expected him to come home and make some improvements to his property. The farms are tumbling down. The tenant farmers grumble. The land wants money spending on it. But I gather his Lordship prefers his amusements in London where he is a member of the Carlton House set."

"He sounds odious!" Arabella exclaimed. "But I shall not be troubled by His Lordship, it seems."

"No, indeed," Lady Deane agreed, "but do rest, Arabella, and try and get some colour back into your cheeks. Your hair . . . it used to be so lovely . . . looks lank and limp. But Doctor Simpson says that is always the result of a high fever. Anyway, please play the part that is expected of you, until I can make other arrangements. Oh, darling! I shall miss you so!"

Lady Deane held out her arms and drew her daughter close.

"You are all I have left of Papa," she murmured almost inaudibly. "It is not easy to part with you, Arabella. But I know I am doing what is right. It is just that the house will be so empty . . . so very empty without you."

"I love you, Mama," Arabella said, "but I know you are correct in thinking I must go away."

She found she could say no more, the words were choked in her throat. Then there came a knock at the door.

"The Master has gone downstairs, Milady," Jones said in a low voice.

"Then I must not keep him waiting," Lady Deane said, disentangling herself from Arabella's clinging arms and rising to her feet.

"He will be angry tomorrow, Mama," Arabella warned. "He will not be pleased that his prey has escaped so easily!"

"I can handle him," Lady Deane replied confidently. "In his own way, he loves me. The carriage will be waiting for you by the kitchen door, Arabella, at eight-thirty. Jones will help you pack. If I do not see you to say 'goodbye', you will know that I shall be thinking of you. I shall also be praying for you."

"Do not worry about me, Mama," Arabella said bravely.

Almost as though she could not bear to look at her daughter again, Lady Deane went from the room, the gems in her tiara sparkling in the light from the tapers.

The room seemed curiously dark when she had left it. Arabella stood still, listening. She heard her stepfather's voice in the hall and then the sound of carriage-wheels drawing up to the front door.

Arabella went to the window. Below her she could see three coaches with their painted panels, each drawn by a pair of well matched horses, the silver on their harness sparkling in the light from the setting sun. The outriders with their powdered wigs and livery-caps all carried pistols which she knew were loaded. The footman on the box of her stepfather's coach had a blunderbuss across his knees.

"At least the tiara is safe for tonight," Arabella thought with a little smile. The six highwaymen who had been terrorising the whole countryside would not dare attack such a formidable adversary.

The cavalcade moved off and Arabella watched them until they had moved out of sight down the drive. Then

17

she turned back into the candle-lit bedroom. Jones was snuffing out the candles.

"Her Ladyship will outshine them all," she said.

"I only wish I could see her at the party," Arabella said. "Do you think the Regent will really be there?"

"If the party's grand enough, he will be," Jones answered. "But there's more things to be done in this country, Miss, than the giving of parties."

"You are right, Jones," Arabella agreed. "You would think he would want to see what was being done about the men returning from the wars—if they have homes to go to, and pensions for those who were wounded."

"His Royal Highness leaves that sort of thing to the politicians," the lady's-maid said sourly. "And from all accounts, they're only jostling for power."

Arabella gave a little sigh.

"I wish I knew more about what is taking place. I wish I could go to Parliament and listen to the speeches at Westminster. I wish I could talk to someone really seriously about these things."

"That talk is not for females," the maid said tartly. "Now, come along, Miss Arabella, we've got to decide what clothes you're to take. Her Ladyship said I were to pack all the dresses you were wearing years ago and nothing which makes you appear your real age. You've lost so much weight, you'll get into them all. 'Tis a blessing I kept 'em."

"Oh, dear ! I thought I had seen the last of those baby muslins," Arabella sighed.

"Her Ladyship gave me her instructions," Jones said primly.

"Very well, then. It is no use asking me, Arabella replied. "Pack what you wish. I do not expect to be at the Castle long and anyway there will be nobody to look at me. At the same time, it will be rather an adventure."

She went to bed thinking about the morrow and was awake long before Lucy came to call her with a cup of hot chocolate.

Arabella only sipped the chocolate and dressed herself quickly in the clothes that Jones had left ready. She could not help smiling at her appearance when she had finished.

The dress, full and falling from a high yoke at the shoulders, made her look exactly the age that Doctor Simpson had thought her to be, if not younger. The soft, heel-less slippers over white socks were very suitable for a child and so was the broadbrimmed hat, trimmed with pale blue ribbons and large, artificial daisies.

She parted her hair down the middle and let it fall on either side of her face. Once it had been like living gold, with fiery lights in it, in vivid contrast to the magnolia white of her skin. But her illness had dulled the gold and now the heavy tresses only seemed to accentuate the sharpness of her little chin and the tired lines under her large eyes.

"Well, one thing is certain," Arabella thought to herself, "not even Sir Lawrence would look at me like this!"

It was as a woman that she had most feared him . . . as a child she had merely hated him for his brutality.

Ready, she said goodbye to Lucy, and ran downstairs and through the kitchen quarters. As her mother had arranged, the carriage was waiting outside, and she got into it quickly, half afraid at the very last moment that her stepfather would come bellowing round the corner to prevent her escape.

They drove sedately down the back drive and out through the North Lodge onto the dusty road, which led away from the village and down ten miles of narrow, twisting lanes towards Meridale.

They passed through a small hamlet with its village green on which stood the stocks, then Arabella had her first glimpse of the Castle. She could see its castellated turrets over the tops of the trees, long before the drive, winding between an avenue of oak trees, led her to the full sight of it.

Then, as it came into view, she gasped. She had expected from her stepfather's description something ancient and crumbling. Instead she saw a magnificent,

19

awe-inspiring edifice of grey stone, set high on a hill but sheltered by a forest of dark trees.

It had originally been a Norman fortress, Arabella thought, and though succeeding generations had enlarged it, the additions had increased, not diminished, its magnificence.

As they drew nearer, she saw below the Castle there was a lake, the water blue in its reflection of the sky above, and on it floated several white swans.

They passed over a bridge, under which flowed the stream which fed the lake, then the coach drove onto a wide gravel sweep in front of an imposing nail-studded door, with a flight of stone steps leading up to it.

Arabella stepped out of the coach to stare about her, looking up towards the Castle which towered towards the sky. It must have been in the reign of Queen Anne, she thought, that the arrow slits had been replaced with tall square-paned windows.

After so much magnificence it seemed somehow incongruous to see in the doorway an old, very decrepit butler, rather untidily dressed, instead of a resplendent individual in keeping with the building.

"Good morning to ye, Miss. The Doctor told us ye were a'coming," the butler said in a surprisingly countrified voice. "But we didn't expect ye so early."

"I am sorry if it is inconvenient," Arabella said quickly.

" 'Tis not inconvenient to Oi," the butler replied. " 'Tis Miss Harrison Oi be a'thinking of. Her baint one for getting up early. But never mind, George'll take ye up. Ye must excuse Oi, Miss, for not accompanying ye mysel'. M'legs ain't what they used to be."

"No, of course not, I quite understand," Arabella assured him.

George was an equally uncouth footman, she thought. He was in his shirt-sleeves, wearing a dirty striped waistcoat with crested silver buttons which badly needed cleaning.

George was also unshaven and she thought how

outraged Sir Lawrence would have been if any of the footmen at home had dared to appear in such a guise.

"Take th'young lady upstairs to th'schoolroom, George," the butler admonished, "and ye should have put yer coat on!"

"It be in the pantry," George answered.

"Never mind then," the butler said testily. "Oi dare say ye'll be excused."

Arabella said nothing. She was beginning to see that the absence of the Master of the Castle had a deteriorating effect. It was not only the farms that had gone to waste.

The dust was thick on the polished chairs and she thought it must have been a long time since anyone had thought to clean the windows. There was also a smell of damp, as though no one had bothered to air the place for a long time. As they climbed higher, things got worse.

The schoolroom was on the second floor and they passed along corridors and landings, set with fine furniture and magnificent pictures. But they were all grubby and unkempt.

Arabella thought how her mother's house always smelt of beeswax and lavender; the windows were open; the sunshine streamed in. Here the very air was stale and she felt her spirits droop long before they reached the second floor.

George stopped and knocked on a door. There was no answer and he knocked again.

"Oi doubt if her'll be up yet," he said.

"It is after nine-thirty," Arabella said, who had noted on the last landing a grandfather clock which was actually going.

George did not bother to reply, but opened the door and by the light of a partially pulled back curtain Arabella could see that she was in a large, very comfortably furnished room.

There was a fire burning in the grate, so somebody must have been there before them—perhaps the same

21

housemaid who had pulled back one of the curtains so that she could see what she was doing.

But the room was empty and George glanced towards a door on the further side.

"Ye'd best wait here," he said. "Her may be asleep."

"Please do not disturb Miss Harrison," Arabella said quickly.

"Oi weren't a'going to," George said laconically and walked off, leaving Arabella standing in the centre of the room.

It was a curious welcome, but she felt that the fault lay in the expediency which had made her leave home so early. No one could be expected to anticipate visitors at nine-thirty in the morning.

Then a strange sound made her start.

She was not certain what it was. But when it was repeated she realised it came from under a large, round table in the middle of the room, which was covered by a fringed cloth reaching to the floor.

The sound came again, and now Arabella, overcome with curiosity, moved forward, lifted the edge of the cloth, and peeped underneath.

There, sitting on the floor, was a child. She was in her white nightgown and in her arms she held two small kittens. Two others were on the floor beside her, drinking from a saucer of milk.

"Hush!" the child said, in a funny, lisping voice. "Beulah . . . not . . . wake . . . her."

"I thought you must be Beulah," Arabella said. "I am Arabella and I have come here to play with you."

Two small eyes, almost like blue marbles, stared at her.

The child had a strange appearance. Her head was too big for her body, her face was round, expressionless, almost moonlike. She was not exactly ugly or repulsive, but her hair, cut short and standing almost on end, made her look unnecessarily queer.

"Ara . . . bella," Beulah repeated, hesitatingly.

"That is right," Arabella smiled. "Why do you not come out so we can talk?"

"Beulah . . . not . . . wake . . . her," the child replied. She repeated the words in a slow, staccato manner as if she had learnt them like a parrot.

"Do you mean your governess?" Arabella asked. "No, of course not, that would be a mistake. Are those your kittens?"

Beulah nodded and held the animals in her arms even tighter, as if she thought Arabella would take them away. One of them miaued and clawed at the child's nightgown.

"They are very pretty," Arabella said gently. "But I will not touch them as they are yours."

Beulah's round, marble eyes stared at her. Then impulsively she held out one of the kittens.

Arabella did not take it, she merely stroked it.

"You keep it," she said, "it belongs to you."

Beulah seemed satisfied with this. Then she said in a low whisper:

"Beulah . . . know . . . secret. Beulah . . . not . . . tell secret . . . Beulah . . . promised!"

"That is right," Arabella said "If you have a secret you must, of course, keep it to yourself."

There was the sound of a door opening.

"What is going on in here? Who is talking?" a querulous voice asked.

Arabella got quickly to her feet.

From the bedroom appeared a youngish woman wearing a negligée trimmed with lace. Her dark hair was curling over her shoulders and Arabella could see she was pretty in rather a coarse way.

"Oh, it's you!" the woman ejaculated. "The child the Doctor was telling me about. Well, I certainly didn't expect you as early as this."

"I am sorry to have come at an inconvenient hour," Arabella apologised.

"I don't suppose you could help it. So I shan't blame you," the governess replied. "Now, let me see, your name's Arabella, isn't it? Doctor Simpson did tell me."

"Yes, that is right," Arabella smiled.

"I'm Olive Harrison," the governess said. "Miss Harrison to you, of course."

"Yes, of course," Arabella said respectfully.

The governess went to the window and tugged back the curtains.

"I don't have these pulled when the housemaid comes to make the fire," she said. "All that rattle and jangle wakes me up. Now, I expect you would like some breakfast."

"Thank you, but I am not hungry," Arabella answered.

"If you aren't, you ought to be," Miss Harrison said. "You look as though a square meal would do you good! Never seen such a skinny little creature! But I remember, you've been ill, haven't you."

"Yes, I have had scarlet fever," Arabella replied.

"Never mind, we'll soon put a bit of flesh on you here. I will say one thing for this place, the food's good. I've always said I would never stay anywhere where the food wasn't."

Miss Harrison finished pulling the curtains back from the four windows, then going to the fireplace, she tugged at the bell-pull.

Far away in the distance Arabella heard a faint sound.

"The housemaids will be waiting for that," Miss Harrison said cheerily. "Someone will be along to dress Beulah, and they know I'll be ready for my breakfast."

She gave a large yawn as she spoke, making no effort to put her hand over her mouth.

Now that the daylight flooded into the room, Arabella could see how voluptuous the governess was. Her negligée was strained over her full breasts, her skin white, her lips red and seductive. She had large blue eyes, fringed with dark lashes.

"Angels above! I've a head bursting at the sides!" Miss Harrison exclaimed.

She walked across the room, opened a cupboard and brought out a bottle. Pouring some of its contents into a glass she drank it quickly. Even before she smelt the

24

spirits which seemed to pervade the room, Arabella knew what it was.

Brandy for breakfast! This was indeed a strange governess!

"That's better!" Miss Harrison said with satisfaction. "And now, dear, come and sit down by the fire and tell me all about yourself."

Her tone was far more genial than it had been before. As she settled herself in a big armchair she put out her hand to gesture to Arabella that she should sit in the one opposite. But Arabella was staring at the fat, white hand and something that flashed on its little finger.

For a moment she was unable to move and could only stand there, staring. For on Miss Harrison's hand was, unmistakably, a ring which had belonged to her mother.

Two

ARABELLA lay sleepless in a small four-poster bed with a frilled canopy. She was tired, but her brain kept turning over and over the events of the day, and after a time she gave up the pretence of trying to sleep. She had been exhausted by the time Miss Harrison sent for a housemaid to put Beulah to bed, but now she felt wide awake.

"You had best run along too, little girl," Miss Harrison had said, but Arabella had known it was not because the governess thought of her as a child that she was so solicitous, but because she was planning to entertain the Head Housemaid—Miss Fellows. An unopened bottle of brandy had been taken from the cupboard and was set ready with two cut-crystal glasses on a table together with a pack of playing cards.

Arabella had not been in the Castle more than a few hours before she realized that Miss Harrison had taken upon herself the role of mistress. The servants hurried to obey her commands, and Arabella noticed that a number of very elegant pieces of furniture had found their way to the schoolroom.

After luncheon at midday, Beulah was put to rest in her small bedroom which led off the schoolroom, on the opposite side to a large room occupied by Miss Harrison. Beulah slept by herself, except for her kittens which had a basket at the foot of the bed.

"She won't be separated from them," Miss Harrison

explained lazily, when Beulah cried for her pets and Arabella asked if she was to collect them.

It was obvious that Miss Harrison was prepared to take the line of least resistance where her charge was concerned. Anything was allowed so long as it did not interfere with her own comfort.

It was not difficult for Arabella to understand Doctor Simpson's anxiety that Beulah should have someone to play with, and if possible to instruct her. Miss Harrison did neither. She never spoke to the child except to tell her to come to the table or go to bed, and she seemed completely indifferent as to what Beulah did with her time or whether anyone or anything contributed to her happiness.

Miss Fellows was a thin, spiteful-looking woman, who seemed to have nothing better to do than to sit in an armchair as close to Miss Harrison as she could so that they could gossip with each other hour after hour.

They spent most of the morning in that position and after lunch was finished—an enormous, well-cooked meal, served by two footmen—Miss Harrison settled herself comfortably on a day-bed with a number of cushions behind her head and a fur rug over her feet. In addition to the large amount of wine she had imbibed at lunch, one of the footmen set a decanter of brandy on the small table beside her.

Knowing that Miss Harrison was not interested in her movements Arabella slipped away, but, instead of going to her own chamber, she went down the stairs towards the main rooms of the Castle. The Grant Staircase with its carved banisters was impressive and the walls were hung with gilt-framed family portraits. It was difficult for her to see the glories of the Salon because the furniture was disguised with holland covers and the wooden shutters were closed and bolted over the long windows. But the room smelt musty and damp and Arabella felt depressed as she closed the door behind her.

An adjacent room seemed less interesting and Arabella passed on until she opened two large double doors.

Then she stood still and gasped. She had found the Library!

There were shelves of books from floor to ceiling. Books bound in leather which made the wall even in the dim light a kaleidoscope of color. Arabella ran to the windows, drew back the closed curtains, and flung wide the latticed casements to let in the air and sunshine.

Books! Books! More books than she had ever seen and more than she could hope to read in a lifetime. Books! And she was certain there would be nobody in the Castle to say "Reading is not for women!", as her stepfather had said so often, invariably adding "No man wants a damned brain-box for a wife."

There was the smell of very old leather in the Library and there was dust everywhere. The books on the shelves were thick with it. As Arabella touched them with her fingers she promised that she would clean and care for them, restoring them to the proud beauty they had once known.

The high ceiling was painted with mythical figures of gods and goddesses, and over the mantelshelf there was a huge mirror with a carved and gilded wood frame, in which the books were reflected. Arabella gave a little sigh of utter happiness. Here she could go on educating herself. Here she could continue to read the classics.

She had been instructed in Greek and Latin by the Vicar of their little village. He was an erudite man with a deep love of knowledge and he taught well. Her father had insisted that, as he had no son, she should have a boy's education.

"Why should women always be treated as fools?" he had asked.

"I am no scholar," her mother answered. "Do you consider me a fool?"

He laughed at that and putting his fingers under her chin, turned her face up to his.

"It's only when they are as beautiful as you, my love, that they have no need of brains," he said softly. "Ara-

28

bella will never rival you, so let us give her something else to rely on besides a pretty face."

Her mother had accepted her husband's decision as she accepted everything he wanted. But when she had married again, Sir Lawrence had quickly put a stop to what he called "those damn-fool lessons."

"Teach the chit sewing," he said harshly. "It's comfort her husband will want—if she ever gets one—not arguments."

The old Vicar had been dismayed.

"If only you were a boy you would have won many honors at a University."

"If only I were a boy!" Arabella repeated. "Don't you know how much I loathe being female? I hate to be ordered about, controlled, commanded, and forced to obey another's wishes."

"My child, you must accept God's will in these matters," the Vicar said quietly, but his eyes were sad and she knew he understood how much she suffered.

And now unexpectedly, and when she least had thought it possible, the door of knowledge was opened to her once more. Books. She threw her arms wide as if she must embrace all of them.

Her eyes were shining as she took one book after another from the shelves, until finally she chose three to take back to her room.

Suddenly she realised that she had been a long time in the Library. Quickly she turned to the window, closed the casements and drew the curtains again. Then she walked back towards the Great Hall. She had just reached the foot of the Grand Staircase when a young housemaid, her cheeks pink and her white mobcap askew, came hurrying along the corridor.

"Ah, there you are, Miss Arabella!" she exclaimed breathlessly. "I've been a'running round a'looking for you everywhere. I thought you must have hid yourself."

"I was looking round the Castle," Arabella explained. "Does Miss Harrison want me?"

"No, not her," the housemaid replied. "She be asleep

29

until she rings for her tea. Has it like a lady she does. No, 'tis Miss Matherson who wants to see you."

"Miss Matherson?" Arabella queried. "Who is she?"

"Come this way, Miss," the housemaid said, leading the way up the stairs. "She'll be a'wondering why I've been so long a'finding you."

"Who is Miss Matherson?" Arabella repeated. "And has she a position here?"

The young housemaid looked up the stairs nervously as if she thought someone might be listening. Then lowering her voice she replied:

"'Tis a bit difficult to explain to you, Miss. Miss Matherson used to be personal lady's-maid to the late Marchioness, his Lordship's mother, afore she died, and for a short time after her Ladyship's death she ran the Castle. Then there be trouble."

"What sort of trouble?" Arabella asked curiously.

The housemaid looked embarrassed.

"'Tis not for I to say, Miss, and not to a child like yourself, but I knows there were trouble."

"It is difficult for me," Arabella said gently, "to come to the Castle not knowing who anyone is, or what authority they have. I am sure you can understand."

The young housemaid—she could not have been more than sixteen, younger in reality than Arabella—gave her an impish grin.

"I knows how you feels," she said confidentially. "It seemed very strange here when I first comes to the Castle nigh on five years past. Miss Harrison now, she be the head of the Castle, in his Lordship's absence. Her gives the orders and Miss Fellows carries them out. They hates Miss Matherson and they have done everything to be rid of her. But she wouldn't budge, not her! And no one can dismiss her save his Lordship and as he never comes home, her stays."

"So what happens?" Arabella asked.

"Miss Matherson has withdrawn," the girl replied almost triumphantly, as if it had been a tactical victory. "She has her own rooms and her doesn't speak with Miss Harrison or Miss Fellows. We waits on her and she makes us keep things up to scratch. We daren't disobey her, however much Miss Fellows says we should."

"It all sounds very uncomfortable," Arabella commented.

"It be funny at times," the young housemaid replied with a giggle. " 'Tis my belief there be something queer a'going on, but it don't do to ask questions. I gets a fair wage, and plenty to eat. Not much to complain about, and there be half-dozen girls in the village willing to come here if I should leave. The work bain't hard."

"I can see that," Arabella murmured, thinking of the dusty Library and the lack of cleanliness apparent all over the Castle.

"When Miss Matherson were in charge, they says the place was that spick and span," the housemaid murmured, "the King himself couldn't have asked for better."

They reached the first floor, and walked along a broad corridor with high mahogany doors on either side of it.

"That were her Ladyship's room," the housemaid whispered, pointing, "and that his Lordship's. Of course, I never seen them, but they all tell what a good Master he were, kind and generous to everyone."

When they reached the end of the corridor, the housemaid knocked on the last door and a quiet voice said:

"Come in."

"I found Miss Arabella, Ma'am," the housemaid said.

The girl opened the door and Arabella entered.

"Thank you, Rose," Miss Matherson replied. "You can go now."

She got up from the chair where she had been sitting sewing by the window. Arabella saw a short, elderly, grey-haired woman, wearing a neat black dress with a black satin apron over which hung a gold chatelaine.

"How do you do," Miss Matherson said respectfully.

Arabella held out her hand. As she did so she saw that her fingers were covered in dust.

"I am sorry my hands are dirty," she apologised,

31

"but I have been in the Library. I hope it will not be amiss but I have borrowed two books to read."

"And discovered how dirty they are," Miss Matherson said bitterly.

She took the books from Arabella and set them down on a table. Taking a duster from a drawer she began to wipe the books, making a disapproving noise with her lips as she did so.

"Perhaps, Miss, you would like to wash your hands?" Miss Matherson suggested when she had finished.

She led the way through another door, through a room fitted with wardrobes, to a bathroom. The curtains were drawn back, and Arabella gazed about her in delight. She had never seen a bathroom like this before. There was a marble bath sunk into the floor, so that the bather entered it down a flight of steps. The floor was marble too, and against one wall there was a wash stand set with a basin, ewer and dishes, all in exquisitely polished silver.

"How beautiful!" Arabella exclaimed.

"The Charles II set," Miss Matherson said with pride. "His Majesty stayed here after his Restoration and this was one of the gifts he presented on his departure. But the bath is a copy of one Her Ladyship saw in Rome when she visited Italy."

"It is marvelous!" Arabella enthused.

"I doubt if there is another like it in the length and breadth of the land," Miss Matherson said proudly. "It used to take the footmen nigh on twenty minutes to fill it with big cans of boiling water from the kitchen. Do you mind washing in cold water, Miss?"

"No, of course not," Arabella replied.

The water in the silver basin was scented, and so was the soap, while the towel which Miss Matherson held out to her was of finest linen edged with real lace.

"I kept everything ready in case the rooms should be wanted," Miss Matherson said quietly, speaking as if she answered Arabella's unspoken question. "I'm sure you would wish to see Her Ladyship's bedchamber."

She opened another door and Arabella stepped into

the most beautiful room she had ever seen or imagined. The sun was shining through the open windows to reveal a great four-poster bed, with silken embroidered hangings. There were mirrors surmounted with cupids, furniture carved and gilt, and a carpet soft as swansdown. There were fresh flowers on the dressing-table and Arabella felt the room was waiting as if its owner might at any moment walk in and take up her life again where it had left off. It was like a shrine to the past and Miss Matherson its only dévotee.

Almost as though she knew what Arabella was thinking, Miss Matherson said quickly:

"Let us go back to my sitting-room. I hope you will excuse me, Miss, for asking you to visit me, but I was so anxious to meet you. We get few visitors to the Castle."

"Doctor Simpson thought it might be good for Lady Beulah to have a companion," Arabella said.

"I heard about his suggestion of bringing another child here," Miss Matherson said, "but no one expected him to find one so swiftly."

"There were reasons why I came at once," Arabella explained turning her face away so that Miss Matherson should not see her embarrassment.

"These rooms get all the sun," Miss Matherson said as they reached her sitting-room. "I did not sleep here, of course, when her Ladyship was alive: I was on the second floor. But I thought now it was best to be near her apartments."

"And to keep them so beautiful," Arabella said. "It would be a pity . . ." She paused.

"If this room became as the rest of the Castle!" Miss Matherson finished for her. "Once it was fine and elegant, now it is a sad disgrace."

"Does the Marquis never come home?" Arabella enquired.

"His Lordship was abroad with his Regiment until two years ago. Now I understand he is very preoccupied in London. Meridale House in Berkeley Square is, of course, open, and sometimes we hear news of the social world when they send for a servant or a horse."

"It seems a shame!" Arabella exclaimed—then stopped. It was not good manners for her to criticise her host, even though she had never met him.

"I am glad you are here for Lady Beulah's sake," Miss Matherson said. "She has no one to care for but her pets. But now, Miss, if you will forgive me for suggesting it, Miss Harrison will be expecting you for tea. I would not have her enraged because Matty had detained you."

"Matty? Is that what they call you?" Arabella asked.

"I've been here many years," Miss Matherson explained, "and Matty is the name his young Lordship gave me when he was but a tiny child. Her Ladyship also adopted the name, I like to think, as a term of endearment."

Miss Matherson's eyes were misty.

"What is the Marquis like?" Arabella enquired.

"Handsome and headstrong," Miss Matherson replied. "But who wants a man not to have spirit or willpower of his own?"

"And you love him?" Arabella asked softly.

"When he was a boy of course," Miss Matherson replied quickly, "but I have not seen his Lordship for over eight years. What he is like now nobody knows. Perhaps one day we shall find out."

"May I come and see you again?" Arabella asked. "I would love to hear what the Castle was like in the old days. Did you have big parties? And could you perhaps tell me about the Marquis when he was a little boy? I never had a brother. I always wanted to be a man."

"Why should you want that?" Miss Matherson said with a smile. "Soon you will be a young lady and have the gentlemen courting you."

"I have no wish to be courted," Arabella replied in a hard voice. "Because I am a woman I hate men, yes hate them! They are beasts, every one of them!"

She spoke vehemently without thinking and only realised the effect of her words when she saw the astonished expression on Miss Matherson's face.

"I am sorry," she said quietly, "I should not have spoken like that."

"I understand," Miss Matherson said gently. "Now, do, pray, take your book and run along, Miss. But come back when you will, there is always a welcome for you in this room."

"Thank you," Arabella smiled. Then, as she reached the door, Miss Matherson added:

"Be careful, I do beg of you to be careful. I can see that you are not as young as was expected. You are safe only if you are very young and very stupid."

"What do you mean?" Arabella asked.

"Nothing. I cannot explain!"

Miss Matherson crossed the room and almost pushed Arabella out of the door. Impelled by a sense of danger she did not understand, Arabella reached the schoolroom just in time. One footman was carrying in the tea on a big silver tray bearing a large silver tea-pot, a silver kettle on a candle-heated stand, and a locked tea-canister. Another footman was setting the table with a fine linen cloth.

Rose had been speaking the truth when she said Miss Harrison had her tea like a lady. This was no ordinary schoolroom meal, and only the nobility and the wealthy drank tea—which was monstrously expensive—every day.

Arabella entered the room and heard Miss Harrison give a large snore as she woke.

"Tea!" she exclaimed, "just what I'm needing. My throat is as dry as a Good Friday sermon!"

She flashed her eyes at the footmen as she spoke, waiting for their response to her witticism, and obligingly they laughed.

Beulah was awake, sitting up in bed holding in her arms three struggling kittens. Her large round face was expressionless, but her eyes were bright with a glimmer of intelligence in them.

35

"Gently," Arabella said. "The pussies are so small. You forget how strong you are."

"Beulah's . . . all . . . Beulah's," the child said, speaking in a thick voice and slurring the words as if each one was an effort.

"Yes, of course," Arabella answered. "But you mustn't hurt them, they are only babies."

She noticed that Beulah had the cunning not to play with the mother cat who could use her claws, but confined her attentions to the defenceless kittens.

She put on the child's dress, tidied her hair, and led her into the schoolroom.

Miss Harrison was already seated at the table. She was wearing a flamboyant red satin gown and was ladling the precious tea in generous teaspoons from the unlocked caddy into the silver pot.

"Would you like tea?" she asked Arabella. "Beulah has milk."

"Chocolate . . . want . . . chocolate," Beulah cried.

"Pull the bell," Miss Harrison said to Arabella. "Drat the servants! Why can't they ask the child what she requires before they leave the room?"

Arabella looked at the plates of cakes, scones, biscuits and wafer-thin bread and butter, but she was not hungry. She had already eaten more than usual at luncheon.

"I have my dinner at six," Miss Harrison announced with satisfaction, as she spread thick golden butter on a scone and topped it with honey from a comb set in a cut-glass crystal dish. "Beulah goes to bed at half after five of the clock."

Arabella was thankful when Beulah was taken to her bedchamber struggling because her kittens were left behind, and the governess suggested she should go to her own room.

"Goodnight, Miss Harrison," she said politely with a perfunctory curtsy.

"Goodnight, Arabella," the governess replied, then added:

"I suppose you have no knowledge of piquet?"

36

Arabella hesitated, then before she could answer Miss Harrison added:

"No, of course not! It was just a thought, because Miss Fellows is such an inconsequential player. But there, as I always say, one is born to cards or one is not."

"I supose so," Arabella agreed.

She did not add that she was a good piquet player, having been taught by her father. She had no wish to stay up late in the company of Miss Harrison and Miss Fellows. The former seemed preoccupied with her own thoughts and had made no effort at conversation during tea.

Arabella found it hard to keep from watching the fat white hand wearing her mother's ring. It shone in the sunshine—two hearts interlocked, one heart fashioned from a large diamond, the other a ruby. She remembered her father giving it to her mother.

She must have been six years old at the time. She had been sitting on her parents' bed opening the presents which Father Christmas had brought her, which she had found at the foot of her own little bed when she woke. Her father reached under his pillow and brought out a small velvet box.

"For me?" her mother asked.

"For you, my darling," he replied, "because I love you and because this is going to be the best Christmas we have ever spent together."

Her father had a deep note in his voice which made Arabella look at him wide-eyed. He had leaned towards her mother and kissed her mouth.

"Nothing I can give you is good enough, my love." Her mother had laughed at him.

"Not in front of the child, dearest. Let me open my present."

She took the box from him, opened it and gave a cry of sheer delight.

"It is wonderful! The prettiest ring I have ever seen!"

"Let me put it on your finger," Arabella's father sug-

37

gested. Her mother had held out her hand and he slipped the ring onto her wedding-finger.

"I love it, but it's crazy, we cannot afford such extravagance, as you well know!"

"I couldn't resist it," he replied. "These are our hearts—yours and mine—so close that nothing can separate them."

It seemed to Arabella then that their happiness filled the room with a golden glow.

Now with a forced indifference she made herself say casually:

"What a pretty ring you have, Miss Harrison!"

The governess spread out her fingers.

"Indeed it is very pretty," she agreed.

"Did somebody very special give it to you?" Arabella asked.

There was a pause, then Miss Harrison seemed almost to snatch her hand away and put it quickly into her lap.

"Finish up your tea, Beulah," she said sharply. "Arabella, you haven't eaten enough to keep a mouse alive. You look like an unfledged sparrow."

She got up from the table and walked to the window.

"Tomorrow," she said with her back to them, "you children had best get out into the garden."

Lying in her bed Arabella wondered over and over again about the ring. She felt a surge of anger that an overdressed, comfort-seeking governess, who drank too much and made no effort to teach, should wear her mother's jewels, and yet what could she do about it?

She could, of course, tell her mother; but, even if Lady Deane knew where the ring was, it would be difficult to accuse the governess of wearing stolen goods. Miss Harrison could say someone had brought it from London and if she refused to reveal the identity of the donor, what could anyone do? What was more, if she herself fell out with Miss Harrison, it would mean she must return home.

Arabella thought of Sir Lawrence and shivered. It was not his anger of which she was afraid, or even the

38

whip he used so frequently. It was something very different, something which made her clench her hands in the darkness.

She must have dozed for a little, because she awoke with a start to hear the clock in the distance strike five. Already the dawn was breaking. She had a sudden longing for some fresh air. The dust and dirt of the house seemed to have crept up into her nostrils so that she felt heavy and headachy.

She slipped out of bed, washed in cold water and dressed herself, taking as protection against the morning chill a shawl which she draped round her shoulders. She guessed that the servants without supervision had grown lazy and would not rise early and therefore she was unlikely to encounter anyone as she moved silently like a small ghost down the corridors and stairs.

She thought it best not to try to open the heavy oak front door, but to go down the passages which led to the kitchen-quarters. On badly washed flags she passed the pantry, the huge kitchen with its rafters heavy with hams, the sculleries, the still room and the dairy. Finally she reached the door into the yard.

There was a big key to turn but fortunately only one bolt where she could reach it. The door creaked open and with a sense of relief she smelt the clean, fresh morning air. There were shrubs and several apple trees in blossom. Beyond them she saw a path leading towards what was obviously the stables. With a sense of excitement Arabella walked towards them.

She had ridden since she was three years old. This was another thing which her stepfather denied her, saying that he could not afford to keep her horse as well as those which he required for himself and the carriages. When her horse was sold, Arabella wept all night into her pillow, but she would not let her stepfather know how bitterly he had wounded her. Instead she had sat stony-faced while he lectured her about the impropriety of girls riding recklessly over the countryside.

She had known that he had sold her horse merely to humiliate her and because she would not acquiesce in his authority. He knew she hated him and he was determined to break her spirit. She was equally determined to defy him.

It became a relentless battle where neither opponent gave any quarter. Sir Lawrence would beat her at every possible excuse. Books and horses, which he knew instinctively were her delight, were forbidden. That Arabella took books from the Library became an excellent excuse for punishment and more punishment.

Now the hope of seeing fine horseflesh made her quicken her speed. It was still not yet completely light. The first pale fingers of the sun were sweeping away the darkness of the night, but the stars still twinkled overhead.

Arabella reached the curved archway which was the entrance to the yard. The stables were very large, in fact they could have housed a hundred horses. The loose-boxes stretched away in a long line, the majority of them closed. Suddenly at the very far end, where the yard curved a little, Arabella saw something move.

Instinctively she shrank back into the shadow of the archway. A horseman was riding into the yard. A stall was open and ready.

As he reached it the rider jumped down and led his horse inside. He was followed by another horseman and yet another, each going to an open box, each moving slowly and without speaking. There could only be heard the faint clatter of the horses' hooves on the cobbles. The doors closed behind them, and then there was silence.

Five men, five horses. Arabella wondered who they were and why they were there. Suddenly, making her heart jump in her breast, a hand gripped her arm.

"Who the devil are you and what are you doing here?"

She was held so tightly, fingers biting into her flesh, that she almost cried out in pain. She looked up into the face of a man. He was middle-aged, with hard lines running from nose to mouth, his dark eyebrows almost meeting across his forehead. He was handsome in a sardonic, rather sinister way, but his face was cruel and frightening under the raffish angle of his top-hat. He was elegantly dressed in riding-breeches, highly polished hessians, and he wore a grey whipcord riding-coat. Surprisingly his cravat was black, but skillfully and fashionably tied.

Arabella tried to back away from him but her movement only tightened his clasp on her thin arm. She felt she was as helpless as a rabbit in a retriever's mouth. Something in his face told her that she was in danger—in a desperate, terrifying danger which she did not understand.

"Answer me!" he repeated harshly, but his voice was cultured. "Who are you and what the hell are you doing spying on my men?"

Arabella drew in her breath and knew what she must reply.

"I am Arabella," she said in a high child's voice, "and I am looking for Beulah's kitty which is lost."

"Beulah!" the man said. "What has that loony to do with it?"

"I am staying here at the Castle to play with her," Arabella answered.

She felt the grip on her arm loosen a little and with a quick twist of her body she managed to free herself.

"Kitty? Kitty? Kitty?"

She ran towards the house, calling for the imaginary cat. She knew that the man was watching her and when she reached the shelter of the kitchen door, she bent down as if to pick something up. Then pretending to carry a kitten in her arms she opened the door.

She ran up the stairs as if pursued, and her breath was coming fitfully by the time she reached the schoolroom. She told herself she was being imaginative, yet she felt she had escaped from some menacing danger. Who was the man who had spoken to her and who resented her entering the stables?

Outside the schoolroom one of Beulah's kittens was struggling to get back through the slightly open door through which it must have escaped. It was mewing

41

piteously. Arabella picked it up automatically, crossed the room and opened the door of Beulah's bedchamber.

The child was asleep, her moon-face quiet and impassive in the dim light. She looked gnome-like but very young and very vulnerable. Arabella felt a sudden compassion that she had not experienced before. Poor little Beulah whom nobody loved! Perhaps Doctor Simpson was right, she might become more intelligent if she had companionship.

"I will try to help her," Arabella whispered silently. As she closed Beulah's door she heard footsteps coming down the passage. They were heavy purposeful footsteps and, almost without thinking, she looked round, wishing to hide herself as she had done so often from her stepfather.

The footsteps drew nearer and just as they reached the door Arabella dived under the table where she had found Beulah hidden the day before. The long tasselled cloth hid her completely. The footsteps crossed the room.

"Olive?" a male voice called. She knew the man who spoke was the one who had threatened her in the stable-yard.

"Olive?" he repeated as he opened the door of Miss Harrison's bedroom. Inside the room a candle was lit, the golden glow streaming through the crack in the door which the man had left ajar.

"What in God's name is going on here?" Arabella heard him ask angrily.

"Oh, there you are, Jack!" Miss Harrison exclaimed, her voice thick and sleepy. "I must have dozed off, I expected you hours ago."

"We were delayed," the man called Jack replied. "Wake up and answer my question! I found a child in the stable-yard. Told me her name was Arabella and that she is staying here."

"Yes, that's right," Miss Harrison replied. "But what could she be doing in the yard at this hour?"

"She told me she was looking for one of Beulah's kittens," Jack replied. "Now I've told you, Olive, that I won't have any blasted strangers here—whatever age they may be—it's dangerous, as you well know."

"It wasn't my fault," Miss Harrison said plaintively. "The new physician, Doctor Simpson, said he would find a child to come here and play with Beulah. How could I refuse? And before I knew what was happening Arabella arrived. She's a quiet little creature and shouldn't give any trouble."

"Why did she leave home?"

"I understand," Miss Harrison replied, "that she didn't get on with her stepfather."

"Who is he?" the man enquired.

"Sir Lawrence Deane. Do you know him?"

There was the sudden sound of laughter—harsh, cynical laughter.

"So that's who the brat belongs to!" The laughter stopped suddenly. "But it's dangerous. Get rid of her!"

"What excuse can I give?" Miss Harrison asked weakly. "She won't do any harm, she won't really, and if she helps Beulah . . ."

"Beulah! Nothing can help her!" the man exclaimed. "She should have been suffocated at birth. Nothing so monstrous should be allowed to live. As I have told you, Olive, so often, it would give me pleasure, yes pleasure, to strangle the puling mooncalf with my bare hands. And once again listen to my ultimatum—one word from anyone in this place and Beulah dies!"

"Oh, don't be so violent, Jack," Miss Harrison pleaded. "Beulah does nobody any harm. Besides, have you thought that if Beulah wasn't here I shouldn't be here either."

"I'm not going to be strung up for any turnip-top with an attic to let," the man said savagely.

"Stop worrying!" Miss Harrison cried. "Arabella is no danger to you at this moment. Come to bed, my love, you're tired. I've been waiting too long for you."

"Sure of yourself, aren't you?" he answered surlily.

"I'm only sure of one thing," Miss Harrison replied, "that you're tired, cold and like a bear with a sore head. It's warm in here with me, and everything will seem better after a few hour's sleep. Come on, Jack, I'm waiting! And you'd best lock the door."

The door of the bedroom was slammed to. Arabella sat very still, then slowly she put up her fingers to her lips as if to prevent herself from screaming. She knew now who the man was—Gentleman Jack, the most dangerous, most hated, the most feared highwayman north of London.

Three

"DAMNATION!" Lord Lowther cried plaintively, pushing his chair back from the card-table. "I owe you five thousand guineas. My pockets are to let. I can't plunge any deeper!

The man sitting opposite him at the table shuffled the cards with his long, thin fingers. Then he remarked sneeringly:

"Chicken-hearted, Lowther!"

There was a moment's silence and several members of Crockfords who were standing round the table seemed to stiffen. Lord Lowther rose to his feet, his boyish face flushed with anger.

"Curse you!" he exclaimed angrily. "You shall not accuse me of being a coward."

Before Sir Mercer Heron could reply, a voice from the doorway interrupted.

"I should think not, indeed. And if you had seen him at Waterloo, Heron, you would not suggest for a moment that he was anything but a hero."

Sir Mercer Heron turned his head to see who was speaking and his lips tightened before he remarked icily:

"So, it is you, Meridale. Why should this matter concern you, if I may be so bold as to ask?"

"Tony Lowther and I have campaigned together," Lord Meridale replied, moving forward until he stood against the green-baize table. "One experiences a certain *camaraderie* in the field which is not likely to be under-

45

stood by the gentlemen of England who lie abed and do most of their fighting when they are in their cups! It takes a brave man to say he has lost enough money, and I commend Tony for his bravery. Are you prepared to argue with me, Heron?"

The Marquis had never raised his voice while he was speaking; in fact, he almost drawled his words. Yet there was a hint of antagonism beneath them which was very obvious to those who listened.

"If His Lordship wishes to retreat, then that, of course, is his choice," Sir Mercer said surlily.

The Marquis's easy, indolent attitude suddenly changed. He drew forward the chair from which his friend had risen, sat himself down opposite Sir Mercer and said sharply:

"If you are so anxious for a game, Heron, let me take you on. Last time you engaged me, if I remember right, it was you who retreated, in some discomfort!"

Sir Mercer Heron rose from the table, his sharp features contorted by an irrepressible anger, his narrow eyes glinting.

"I have no desire to play with you, my Lord Marquis," he said. "Your insolence does not make for pleasant companionship."

"Chicken-hearted, eh?" the Marquis gibed, in a voice that could be heard all over the room.

For a moment Sir Mercer glared at him, then turning walked quickly towards the door.

The Marquis of Meridale threw back his head and laughed.

"If ever there was a bogey-man, it's Heron," he remarked. "You see, Tony, a frontal attack can be very successful."

"If you ask me, you surprised him in the rear!" the Duke of Wellington chuckled from one of the big, leather armchairs.

"Anyway, he is vanquished for the moment, Your Grace," the Marquis said cheerily. Then in a lower voice to his friend:

"How could you be such a fool as to play with that outsider, Tony?"

"He challenged me and I did not like to refuse," Lord Lowther explained.

"He picks them when they look milk-fed and vacant," Lord Meridale said with a smile.

"Damn it! You are not going to talk to me like that!" Lord Lowther retorted. "I may be young but I am not so bird-witted as not to recognise a double-shuffle when I see one. But a gentleman has certain obligations."

"Not to the tune of five thousand golden guineas he hasn't!" the Marquis declared. "Come and have a drink. We have to figure out how you can find the money within a week."

Lord Lowther looked very pale, as if suddenly he felt physically sick at the magnitude of his debt.

"Excuse me," he said, a little unsteadily, and went from the room while the Marquis stood staring after him.

"That was decent of you, Meridale," a deep voice said from behind him.

The Marquis turned to see one of the older members of the club, a retired Judge, respected and liked by even the young, more irresponsible members.

"I cannot think why you allowed Heron to become a member," Lord Meridale said. "He's not up to snuff! You know he deliberately picks out the bad players and invariably takes off them more than they can afford."

"This is not a nursery, Meridale," the Judge said quietly.

"No, I know," the Marquis replied. "But Tony is a decent chap, except that he wants to cut a dash and show he's a Corinthian."

"Send him back to the country," the Judge suggested. "I know his mother. She's eating her heart out with fear of what mischief her only son will get into, among a lot of gay blades like yourself."

"I doubt if he'd go if I asked him to," Lord Meridale said.

"Why not? The country's pleasant at this time of the

year. You might all of you try fresh air instead of champagne; a gallop over the parkland instead of chasing the Fashionable Impures round the brothels, or listening to the Regent in that gold-fringed and gold-tasselled travesty of what was once Carlton House."

The Marquis threw back his head and laughed.

"I almost wish I had been up before you when you were on the Bench, Sir. You have a turn of phrase which makes me laugh."

"But I am serious," the Judge persisted. "Young Lowther is not the only person who is making a cake of himself. From all I hear, the grass is growing high at Meridale Castle."

The Marquis stiffened.

"Who told you that?"

"I have many friends in Hertfordshire," the Judge replied. "Why not see for yourself? An absentee landlord cannot expect anything in the rafters but woodworm. You surely know that."

The Marquis gave him a stiff little bow.

"Obviously, Sir, you know more about my possessions than I know myself," he said quietly, but with an underlying anger in his voice.

He walked from the room, through the hall and down the steps. A linkman called his coach and when he had entered it, he told the footman to drive to Carlton House.

He had earlier intended to go there, having been commanded by the Regent to one of the huge receptions with which the *beau ton* was becoming increasingly familiar.

Now the Marquis wondered why he had been such a fool as to go into Crockfords on the way and get himself involved in an argument with Sir Mercer Heron and an uncomfortable conversation with the Judge.

He now regretted the impulse that had taken him there, but at the same time he was honest enough to know that it was the Judge's words that had got under his skin; that it had, in reality, amused him to annoy

Sir Mercer and save Lord Lowther from what might have ended in a senseless and perhaps tragic duel.

"The grass is growing high at Meridale!" He had a sudden vision of it as it must be at the moment, with the wonder of Spring making the gardens a panorama of color and beauty: the lilacs, white, mauve and purple; the peach and almond blossom, pink against the sky; the daffodils cresting the park with trumpets of gold. And beyond them the Castle itself, grey and impregnable. An unassilable fortress and yet a home, which for twenty years he had loved to the exclusion of all else—before there had come disaster.

The coach drew up with a flourish, the door was flung open by a flunkey wearing the Royal uniform. There were lights blazing on the white columns. Then passing through the crowd of attendants and servants, he was inside Carlton House.

Blue drapery embroidered with golden *fleur-de-lys,* fluted pilasters solidly gilt, pelmets of pure gold surmounted by white ostrich feathers; rose satin festooned with garlands and a frieze of Sphinxes encircling a bust of Minerva, were all passed as the Marquis moved from room to room looking for his host.

Women swayed towards him, their voices calling him, their gloved hands outstretched in welcome. In their high-waisted, pastel-hued gowns of satin, gauze or damped muslin, they were like a multi-colored bouquet of flowers. And their beauty was amplified by the pictures the Prince had collected from all over the world, a collection as yet unpaid for!

There was no sign of the Regent. Then a voice called "Julius!" imperatively.

The Marquis turned to see an exquisite figure in a dress of transparent silver gauze, which revealed more than it concealed of a slim, sinuous body. A huge necklace of emeralds adorned the Vision's long, white neck.

"Julius! I swear I thought you were not coming. You assured me you would be early."

"Forgive me, Sybil," the Marquis replied, raising

49

her gloved hand to his lips, "but I was unavoidably delayed."

"At White's or Crockfords?" Lady Sybil Sheraton asked.

She was a strikingly beautiful brunette and her dark curls framed what should have been a classically lovely face, had not her eyes turned upwards at the corners, giving her a slightly oriental expression. Her red lips parted as she added:

"No, do not answer me. It is enough that you are here. Will you take me home?"

"I shall be greatly honored," the Marquis replied gallantly.

Nevertheless her face turned to his and her eyes looking at him so compellingly made him feel a little uncomfortable.

He had told himself often enough that he was not concerned with the gossips, but at the same time he had no desire to fall foul of those patrons of Almacks, who, while permitting themselves a Royal licence where morals were concerned, were only too quick to deplore any laxity in other people.

"Where is His Royal Highness?" the Marquis asked.

"Flirting somewhere with the indefatigable Lady Hertford," Lady Sybil replied sarcastically. "Have you heard the latest *on dit?* Lord Grey has referred to her as a 'pestilential secret behind the Throne'."

"Hush!" The Marquis felt embarrassed at his companion's indiscretions. Such things were not said aloud in Carlton House, even though the speaker lowered her voice. At the same time his eyes twinkled. All London was bored by the coy archness of Lady Hertford, and her hold over the Regent was the subject of endless anecdotes.

"I must find him," the Marquis said.

"I will come with you," Lady Sybil offered, and they moved together through the crowded rooms.

Lady Sybil Sheraton was a widow, whose husband had been killed on the Peninsula, and it was said that his death only preceded the inevitable end of their marriage. Before he died, Lady Sybil had found the Prince of Wales's set at Carlton House very much to her liking.

Her only trouble was that, having married because of a wild infatuation for a good-looking officer in the Guards, she had not considered how she was to live without the wealth to pay for her endless extravagances.

Her father had died in debt and her brother inherited what was left of the family possessions. They had all expected Sybil to make a good marriage, by which they had hoped she would find a rich and generous husband. But Sybil had let her heart rule her head.

The War had mercifully saved her from the inevitable consequences of her imprudence. She did not intend to make the same mistake again.

The years of marriage and of widowhood had taught her that she needed two things to continue comfortably in the life she enjoyed. The first was position; the second, money.

She was convinced that she had found what she sought when she met the Marquis of Meridale. Moreover after they had been together for a short time she had discovered that she wanted him not only for his title and his possessions but also because he attracted her almost as passionately as her husband had done.

The only difficulty was that the Marquis showed no sign of making their *liaison* into anything more permanent. Never at any time had he suggested marriage and, though Sybil had told herself she might have been wiser not to have succumbed so easily to the fiery desire which had driven them, almost on first acquaintance, into each other's arms, she had the uneasy feeling that had she played hard to get he would have ridden away in search of someone easier.

"Julius!" she said now to attract his attention as they perambulated the Conservatory.

This was the Regent's pride, built in the pseudo-Gothic manner of a diminutive cathedral! From pillared arches a glazed trellis spread upwards and fan-

51

wise to a perforated roof. There were curtains of crimson, windows emblazoned with heraldic arms, and as they passed through an arched doorway into the garden, where by day the Regent's peacocks preened their feathers and strutted on the smooth lawns, there was a conflagration of fairy lamps and Chinese lanterns twinkling in the warmth of the windless night.

"Julius!" Lady Sybil repeated imperiously. "You have not told me how I look tonight!"

"Very beautiful!" the Marquis replied. But it was obvious that his answer was automatic and his thoughts were elsewhere.

"There is something wrong," Lady Sybil said.

"No, not really. I'm but a trifle perturbed," the Marquis answered.

"About what?" Lady Sybil asked, rather apprehensively. She felt for a moment as though a cold hand had been laid on her heart. Supposing, just supposing, someone had been tittle-tattling to the Marquis. She had been so careful and yet . . . one never knew.

"It would not interest you," he said evasively.

"I want to know . . . I must know," Lady Sybil urged.

They stopped still while the Marquis looked over the garden to see if he could perceive the Regent.

Lady Sybil put her hand up to tug at the lapel of his blue satin evening-coat.

"Look at me, Julius!" she insisted. "Look at me! I cannot bear you so indifferent!"

"I am not indifferent!" the Marquis protested, looking down at her, his voice warming a little. "You are in great looks tonight, Sybil, as well you know. Those emeralds become you. I am glad you persuaded me to buy them."

"It was a wonderful present." Lady Sybil's voice was soft and seductive. "Remind me to thank you for them . . . once again."

There was an invitation in her words and her eyes flamed a little beneath her mascaraed eyelashes.

But the Marquis was not to be drawn.

"Ah! There is Prinny!" he exclaimed.

At the upper end of the Conservatory there was a circular *buffet,* laden with gold plate, decorated with flowers and over-hung by a medallion, draped in pink and silver, bearing the initials "G.P.R."

The Marquis saw the Regent, a glass in his hand, stout and florid but nevertheless mightily imposing, with the Ribbon of the Garter and its Star ablaze upon his chest, move from the *buffet* towards the supper tables. These stretched out into the garden and under several great marquees.

Even above the noise of the bands—there were four of them—the chatter and the laughter, the Marquis could hear the popping of corks. For a moment the noise reminded him of the guns in France, then he pushed the memory aside and strolled towards his host.

"Meridale!" the Regent exclaimed as he saw him. "I thought you had forgotten that I had invited you here this evening!"

"No indeed, Sire," the Marquis replied, bowing. "I was not likely to forget such an honor. Besides, I have been here some time. But Your Royal Highness was so deeply engaged that I did not like to intrude."

He glanced towards Lady Hertford as he spoke and she gave him her hand to kiss, simpering flirtatiously as she did so behind her fan.

"I have always told His Royal Highness that you have an instinct and a delicacy," Lady Hertford smiled. "Unlike some people we know."

The Marquis knew she was referring to those who had tried to prevent the Regent's infatuation for her being so intense or, indeed, so expensive.

"Your Ladyship is most kind," the Marquis murmured. "And perhaps you will intercede for me in a special request I would make of His Royal Highness?"

"Special request?" the Regent asked hastily. "What is this?"

He had a dislike of people asking favors of him, especially at a moment when, having dined and wined with indiscretion, his judgment was not always to be relied upon.

"It is but a small request, Sire," the Marquis said, "that you will permit me to decline the gracious invitation that I should accompany you to the races in two days' time."

"Decline? Why should you wish to decline?" the Regent demanded.

If there was one thing he disliked above all else, it was not to have all his friends around him. He was middle-aged, but he still liked to think of himself as a dashing blade and the leader of the Corinthians.

When he went to the races, it pleased him to be in the company of all the young bucks. It made him feel young. It made him forget that, since the doctors had commanded him to take off his stays, he found it easier to sit than to stand.

"Perhaps you have a better engagement," he said sarcastically, before the Marquis could speak.

"That would be impossible, Sire," the Marquis replied. "I am just asking Your Royal Highness for leave to visit my home. I understand there are things there to which I should give my attention."

The Regent's frown vanished.

"In that case," he said benevolently, "you have my permission not to accompany me on Wednesday. We shall miss you, Meridale. Do not be away too long!"

"My visit shall be accomplished with all possible speed," the Marquis promised.

"Good boy!" The Regent's fat hand rested for a moment on his shoulder and then he passed on, Lady Hertford twittering on his arm, to the supper table. There a miniature fountain flung high a sparkling cascade which flowed in a continuous stream between banks of moss spanned by four fantastic little bridges.

As the Marquis watched him, Lady Sybil returned to his side.

"I heard what you said," she whispered. "What has happened at your home?"

"That is what I am about to find out," the Marquis replied.

"Then I will come with you," Lady Sybil announced. "I vow I am bored to tears with the Season already. After all, it is nothing but a round of parties, each one very much like the last."

"You would certainly be bored at the Castle!" the Marquis declared. "I have not been there since my m . . ." He paused, then added, ". . . for seven, nearly eight years."

"As long as that?" Lady Sybil exclaimed.

"I was abroad most of the time," the Marquis explained, speaking more as if he made the excuse to himself than to his companion.

"So you have no idea what has been happening these past eight years?" Lady Sybil asked. "How exciting! It is almost like a new world to discover! Besides, I have heard how magnificent Meridale is and I should like to see it."

"You cannot come with me unchaperoned," the Marquis demurred.

"Who is to know?" Lady Sybil enquired. "Certainly no one in London need learn of it and unless you have announced your arrival, the stuffy County notabilities will not be expecting you. But if you feel you need chaperoning, dear Julius, let us by all means take Richard with us!"

"No, Sybil, listen," the Marquis began, but already, impetuously, Lady Sybil had called out to the tall, good-looking young man standing amongst the banks of flowers in the Conservatory.

"Richard!" she cried.

He came towards them, a smile illuminating his rather pale face. There was no doubt that he was a buck of the highest pretensions, with his exquisitely tied cravat, diamond tie-pin and jangling fob.

"Your servant, Ma'am," he said to Lady Sybil, and then to the Marquis:

"Where have you been, Julius? I have been looking all over the place for you."

"We have a plan," Lady Sybil said, before the Marquis could speak. "Julius has to visit his Castle. You will hardly credit it, but he has not been home for nearly eight years! I intend to go with him and you are to come because Julius is afraid to be alone with me and compromise his spotless reputation!"

"I said nothing of the sort," the Marquis interposed.

Captain Richard Huntington laughed.

"It is a splendid suggestion. It is going to be hot for the next few days. I have just been talking to one of those boring old fellows who believes he is a weather-prophet, but I am sure he's right. And, Heaven knows, the heat here is enough to give one a spasm!"

"Let's get out, then," the Marquis suggested. "Have you spoken to Prinny?"

"I've done all the things," Richard Huntington answered, "and kissed enough hands to make my lips sore. Let's go back to your house and get drunk."

"There's no time. I shall depart early tomorrow morning," the Marquis objected.

"Why this sudden decision?" Richard Huntington asked.

"I just had the idea I should go home," the Marquis replied.

"But I thought you had special reasons for not doing exactly that," Richard said. "I may be wrong, but I remember once when we were in France you said that even if you weren't killed—which at the time we thought we were all going to be—you had finished with ancestral possessions, the Castle and all that trumpery."

"Must have been bosky!" the Marquis replied. "It sounds a cork-brained sort of thing to say, doesn't it!"

"Thought you must have been a bit queer in the nob," Richard Huntington replied. "Stands to reason that, with a home like Meridale, you would want to go there."

"Yes, of course," the Marquis agreed.

There was something in his voice which made Lady Sybil glance at him sharply.

"There is always some mystery about him," she

56

thought. Even in their most abandoned moments of passion she always felt that he kept a curb on himself. There was something which held him back, something which she could not probe, could not understand. Perhaps the Castle would reveal the secret to her.

Anyway, when she had him alone in the country, it might be easier to elicit a proposal from him.

She thought of the pile of bills that filled two drawers of her escritoire. She thought of the creditors who were getting increasingly more importunate. He had got to come up to scratch in the next month!

"We will convey you to Stanhope Street," the Marquis said to her, and though she longed to insist that she should come to Meridale House so that they could discuss their journey further, she was wise enough in the ways of men to know that tonight, at any rate, the Marquis was not particularly interested in her.

Nevertheless, his lips lingered for a moment on her ungloved hand as she said "goodnight", and despite the fact that Richard and the servants were there, she laid her cheek against his.

"Goodnight, my love!" she whispered. "I shall be ready for you."

"Do you really wish to accompany me?" the Marquis asked. "I warn you that you may not be very comfortable at the Castle."

He spoke as though that was in fact an improbability, and Lady Sybil knew it was but an excuse for him to go alone.

"No, no! You must not be selfish!" she replied. "Richard and I would only fret if you were away and we were not certain in what mischief you had become involved. Send your coach for me at ten o'clock, or had you planned to go in your High-Perch Phaeton?"

She knew the answer without waiting for the Marquis to confirm it.

"Very well, the Phaeton," she sighed. "But the wagon must call for my baggage and my maid early, for Heaven knows what the sun and the wind will do to my countenance!"

As the coach carried the Marquis and Richard from Stanhope Street to Berkeley Square, Richard Huntington said tentatively:

"Are you wise, Julius?"

The Marquis did not pretend to misunderstand his question.

"To take Sybil with me?" he asked. "No, of course, it's damnably stupid! But she insists and if she desires to behave in an outrageous manner why should I stop her?"

"She intends to marry you," Richard said. "You know that, of course."

"I shall never marry anyone," the Marquis asserted in a surprisingly firm voice. "I have never spoken of this before, Richard. I do not intend to speak of it again. But for reasons which I shall not divulge there is no question of my marrying Sybil or anyone else."

"But why? Why?" Richard asked.

"That is my secret," the Marquis said, "and, Richard, it would greatly oblige me if you would not accompany us tomorrow. It was Sybil who gave you the invitation, if you remember. Not I! I have a wish to go to the Castle alone. If Sybil insists on accompanying me, that's her choice. But for once I am not proffering you my hospitality."

"Oh, well, if it's like that . . ." Richard said almost huffily.

"No, do not misunderstand me," the Marquis begged. "You are my oldest friend, Richard, and there is little I would not share with you, but tomorrow I wish to go home alone."

"And with Sybil!" Richard said.

The Marquis shrugged his shoulders, and then he smiled . . . a smile that had no humour in it.

"Perhaps it is not a bad idea for Sybil to come, after all," he said. And Richard could get no more out of him.

The day dawned fine and warm and Lady Sybil was almost mollified, when she emerged from her house in Stanhope Street, to see the High-Perch Phaeton, which had been built for speed, with its yellow wheels and tandem of perfectly matched chestnuts.

The Marquis, wearing a many-tiered driving-coat and a conical beaver hat, which he swept from his head, watched her come down the steps, her face very lovely despite the lateness of the hour when they had gone to bed.

"This is an adventure!" Sybil said, with a provocative glance from under her eyelashes. She certainly looked alluring in a huge chip-straw bonnet trimmed with ribbons which were tied under her chin and cascaded down over her strawberry-coloured driving-coat.

As they turned into Park Lane, the Marquis thought it was a good thing that it was too early for those who belonged to the social world to be abroad. Otherwise there would certainly have been malicious tongues wagging, to the effect that the Marquis of Meridale and Lady Sybil Sheraton had eloped together.

There was a grim smile on his lips this morning, as though he enjoyed some bitter-sweet, cynical joke which was known only to himself, and his eyes were dark and hard as though the journey held little pleasure for him.

"Where is Richard?" Lady Sybil asked.

"He's not coming," the Marquis replied. "I preferred that we should be alone."

Sybil made a little movement of pleasure and for a moment one of her hands fluttered towards him.

"That's what I wanted, too," she answered, "but I was afraid that you would disapprove."

"As I have already told you, it is not comfortable for you to accompany me," the Marquis said. "If anyone should hear of it . . ."

"They will not learn of it from me," Lady Sybil replied. "I have told the servants to say that my grandmother is indisposed and I, perforce, have to visit her. You will find, strangely enough, that no one is remotely curious. Besides, most of the smart young females who cast such languishing glances in your direction will be delighted to be rid of me! They will hope that you will return alone and they can get their claws into you!"

"You flatter me," the Marquis rejoindered.

"Julius, let us enjoy ourselves!" Lady Sybil urged. "It is not often we are alone. Tonight you can tell me about yourself—a subject, I might say, on which you are extremely reticent."

"It's not a topic I find very interesting."

There was something in the Marquis's voice which told Lady Sybil he had no desire to discuss it further.

They had a light meal at midday at a little village inn about fifteen miles outside London.

"I do not intend to change horses," the Marquis told his groom. "But rub them down and let them rest. We have not much further to go."

"Very good, Milord," the groom replied.

The Marquis sprang down from the Phaeton and assisted Lady Sybil to alight. She was taken by the inn-keeper's wife to a bed-chamber where she could wash and tidy her hair which had strayed from under her bonnet.

When she rejoined the Marquis, he was sitting in the private sitting-room which had been allotted to them. He did not hear her approach and she was astonished at the look on his face as she entered the room.

"What is wrong, Julius?" she asked involuntarily.

He got to his feet and she knew that whatever was the trouble he had no intention of divulging it.

"The landlord says there is hot lark and oyster pie," he said, "or a cold collation of mutton, pigeon, pigs-head and ham. Which do you prefer?"

"I would rather have something cold," Lady Sybil answered, "a little ham will do. Please pour me some of that wine, Julius. The dust has got into my throat."

She went out of her way to amuse him while they ate, telling him stories of what had been said before his arrival at the party the night before, of the latest outrage committed by the Princess of Wales, who referred to her husband as "The Great Mohammet", and

60

how Mrs. FitzHerbert was deeply hurt at the Regent's present indifference to her, when previously she had been treated as his wife in all but name.

"You can expect no gratitude from princes," the Marquis remarked.

"But one sometimes receives it from ordinary mortals," Lady Sybil said softly. "Do not forget, I have promised to thank you once again for my emerald necklace."

"Does it mean so much to you?" the Marquis enquired.

"But of course! I am entranced by it," Lady Sybil declared. "And you should have seen the glances of envy that were turned on me last night. If my so-called women friends could have dragged it from my neck, scratching me in the process, they would have done so!"

For some extraordinary reason the Marquis seemed almost relieved by her answer.

"I must give you earrings to match," he said. And with Sybil's enthusiastic thanks ringing in his ears he rose from the table.

"Come! I feel better fortified to encounter what lies ahead," he said.

"You sound apprehensive," Lady Sybil remarked with unusual perception. She had noticed that he drank deeply during the meal, something he seldom did. And now, when he had donned his riding-coat and taken his hat in his hand, he reached for yet another glass of wine.

He downed it with a swift gulp, and then surprisingly, for his manners were usually impeccable, he walked ahead of her down the passage and out into the stable-yard.

The horses were waiting. He helped Lady Sybil into her place and, taking the driving-seat, he picked up the ribbons.

He was a noted whip, but Lady Sybil had never known him to drive so fast or so furiously. There was no sign of tiredness as the horses responded to his insistence. It seemed to her that the wheels flew over the white, dusty roads, till suddenly they turned into the great, stone-flanked gates of the Castle.

Then to her surprise, after so much haste, instead of going straight up the drive, it seemed as though the Marquis changed his mind. They turned off, winding their way through the park by narrow paths, having only occasional glimpses of the turrets of the Castle above the trees.

"Where are we going?" Lady Sybil enquired.

"There is no hurry," the Marquis answered. She had the feeling that he was delaying the moment when he must approach the Castle.

They drove through an enchanted wood of silver birch trees and then, suddenly, there was a sound of voices.

A forest pool was now in view, circled by flowering shrubs and overhung with willows, the Spring green of their leaves vivid against the sunlit water.

There was again the sound of a gay voice and they saw someone standing high on a rock above the lake, a small, thin figure, ivory white in the golden sunshine, with a flame of golden-red hair hanging over her shoulders.

She was balanced on the very edge of the rock, as naked as the day she had been born, and speaking to someone down below, another child who was sitting just on the edge of the water, her bare legs splashing a cascade of silver drops high in the air.

"Shall I dive?" the voice asked from the rock.

One of the Marquis's horses shook its bridle and the sound of it traveled across the water. The naked figure stiffened, looked across to where the sound had come from, and dived.

For a moment her body was arched high in the air against the green of the trees, before it shot like an arrow into the water. It was a movement of beauty— a movement as lovely as it was unexpected.

Lady Sybil gave a gasp!

"Who is that?" she asked.

The Marquis was looking now, not at where the diver had been, but towards the child sitting beside the lake.

"I have no idea," he answered coldly and touched the horses with his whip.

Four

ARABELLA watched the Phaeton out of sight. Although she was embarrassed at having been seen and that she had been caught doing something she knew was wrong, she could not help admiring the excellence of the perfectly matched chestnuts and the manner in which their driver tooled the ribbons. It was easy to realise that, whoever he might be, he was a Corinthian when it came to controlling horseflesh.

However, as soon as she could see them no more, she swam ashore and lifted Beulah from the side of the pool.

"No, no!" Beulah screamed, "Beulah . . . paddling!"

"We have to go home now," Arabella insisted, hurrying into her clothes.

She had not meant to do anything so crazed as bathing when she was out with Beulah. She had done so on a sudden impulse which she now regretted. Miss Harrison's suggestion of the previous day that they should walk in the garden had been altered to instructions that they should go driving in the pony-carriage.

Arabella, who had been looking forward to having some exercise, felt her heart sink. But she had not argued with the governess because she had guessed that one of the reasons for the change of plan was that Miss Harrison was afraid that she might visit the stables and once again be found in a place where, as a stranger, she was apparently not acceptable.

Accordingly, as soon as luncheon was finished, Arabella was sent to put on her wide-brimmed hat, while Beulah had a bonnet tied under her chin and was given a small shoulder-cape in case she felt cold.

Miss Harrison was far too indolent to take them downstairs to where the pony carriage was waiting outside the front door. The housemaid performed this office to the top of the Grand Staircase, then George the footman took over. George chatted to Beulah as he carried her downstairs and jumped her up and down as though she was a toy rather than a real child.

Beulah screamed with delight and demanded "Again! Again!" until George said severely:

"Oi'll make ye sick and then Oi shall be in trouble!"

He winked at Arabella as he said it, as if to add there was not much fear of that, and she could not help wondering what Sir Lawrence would have said. George was not only surprisingly familiar but as usual he was walking about the front of the house in his shirt sleeves, with only his striped yellow and blue waistcoat to denote his livery.

"Enjoy yourselves," George shouted, waving his hand as they set off in the pony-cart, driven by a very old groom. He was almost completely deaf, Arabella discovered, after trying to get into conversation with him.

The pony which drew them was fat and obviously suffering from lack of exercise, but in the open carriage they at least breathed the fresh air and could feel the sunshine on their faces.

It had been cool first thing in the morning, but now that the sun was risen the day was hot. Arabella thought that the countryside had never been more beautiful. There was still the pale green of the Spring, mingling now with the blossom of the summer flowers just coming into bloom.

Beulah was happy and content to be out driving.

"Gee . . . up gee . . . gee," she kept saying in her funny, disjointed voice, which, even more than her distorted body, betrayed her affliction.

Soon, Arabella thought sadly, she might grow ugly and almost repulsive to look at, but at the moment her over-large head and moon-like face had a baby charm about them. She might look strange, but Arabella felt that anyone who saw her could feel nothing but compassion.

They drove along the dusty, uneven road which circled the park. Arabella longed to walk, to run in the grass, to move through the trees, scenting the fragrance of the pines and hearing the dead leaves of last Autumn scrunch underfoot.

Then she saw the primroses, a great golden bank of them, interspersed with purple violets in the woodland through which they were passing.

"Stop!" she cried to the old groom. "Please stop!"

She had to repeat herself several times before he realised what she wanted. Finally he drew the fat pony to a standstill and opened the door for them to scramble out.

Arabella lifted Beulah in her arms. It was quite difficult for her to carry the child, for she was heavy. But she took her from the road up into the wood, then, setting her down, told her she must walk.

She had the idea, which she was sure was right, that Beulah should walk far more than she did at present. It was so much simpler for people to pick her up and carry her from room to room than to assist her faltering steps and wait patiently for her to go at her own pace.

Beulah seemed quite content to walk and Arabella led her slowly through the wood, discovering a sudden sweep of blue-bells and giving a cry of delight as several deer scrambled ahead of them, obviously startled from their sanctuary where few people ventured.

It was then just ahead of them that Arabella saw the forest pool, encircled by willows dropping their branches into the still water, golden from the rays of the sun except in the shadows where it was green and mysterious. It seemed an enchanted place.

"Look, Beulah," Arabella cried. "Look how lovely

it is! This is where the deer come to drink. And there will be fish in the pool—little trout with brown, speckled backs."

Puffing with the exertion of walking so far, Beulah did not reply.

Impatient with her slowness, Arabella picked her up and carried down to the water's edge.

"Water! Water!" Beulah cried with satisfaction.

Arabella had a sudden idea.

"Would you like to paddle?" she asked.

Beulah looked at her uncomprehendingly.

"To put your feet in the water," Arabella explained.

Beulah stepped forward obligingly.

"No, no! You take your shoes off first!" Arabella laughed, and sitting the child down on a mossy bank. she took off Beulah's shoes and socks, then held her while she splashed her toes, first tentatively, and then energetically, in the clear water.

"Now you are paddling," Arabella said.

"Beulah paddling . . . paddling!" the child repeated, and Arabella laughed at her excitement.

The water was not cold and as she put her hand into it Arabella had an idea. She had often bathed with her father in a lake near their home. After a wild gallop, they would let their horses drink then undress themselves and jump into the cool clear water.

"You swim like a small dolphin," he had said as he watched her.

Remembering his words Arabella turned to Beulah.

"Would you like to see me swim?" she asked. "I will show you how the dolphins turn over and over in the water."

"Swim?" Beulah questioned.

Arabella easily persuaded herself that what she wanted to do could be considered part of Beulah's education, so while Beulah sat on the bank splashing her feet, Arabella slipped off her clothes. She could have worn her chemise for bathing as she had done when she had been with her father, but she was afraid, if she took a wet chemise back to the Castle, it would involve her in explanations.

She was sure that Miss Harrison, like most people, would be shocked at the thought of her swimming in a public place, even though no one should see her. Her mother had voiced the conventional attitude to this only too often.

"It is not seemly for a girl to bathe in the open as though she were a boy or a man," she said. "If anyone knew, they would be exceeding disapproving."

"No one will know," Arabella's father argued, "not unless you tell them."

"As though I should do such a thing!" her mother protested. "It shocks me far too much to want to mention it!"

But they had only laughed at her and now Arabella, knowing that she was alone except for Beulah, who was all approval, walked naked into the sunlit water. She felt the sudden shock of it against the warmth of her body, but it was one of delight. Then she swam across the pool and back again to Beulah, who sat watching her with wide eyes.

"Look, Beulah!" she cried, "now I will be a dolphin."

She turned over and over, hearing the child's gurgling laughter as she went down into the cool depths of the water and came up again to shake her hair out of her eyes.

"More . . . more!" Beulah cried.

"I will tell you what I will do," Arabella said. "Do you see that rock? I will climb to the top and then dive into the water."

"Dive?" Beulah asked curiously.

She was learning a great many new words listening to Arabella.

"Yes, dive like a bird," Arabella replied. "I will swoop down like the swallows do when they come to drink. You watch, Beulah!"

She ran to the rock, the sunlight through the trees throwing strange shadows on the whiteness of her skin.

The rock was difficult to climb because it was smooth and slippery, standing like a sentinel at the side of the lake—an age-old memento of a volcanic era. Finally, however, she reached the top and stood there, looking down at Beulah below.

"Dive . . . dive!" the child was saying.

"Watch me, Beulah! Now I am a swallow!" Arabella called, throwing out her arms wide as though they were wings. Then, almost in horror, she heard the sound of a jingling bridle and saw the horse as he shook his head the other side of the pool . . .

Now dressed again in clothes that felt clammy, she knelt down to put on Beulah's socks and shoes.

"Beulah . . . paddle!" the child demanded crossly.

"Not any more today," Arabella said. "Listen, Beulah, this is a secret. Do not tell anyone you have paddled, or that I swam. Secret!"

Beulah's small eyes lit up. Here was a word she understood.

"Beulah know a . . . secret," she cooed.

"You know two secrets," Arabella said. "Remember, Beulah, say nothing and tell nobody what we have been doing."

"Beulah know a . . . secret," the child intoned, and Arabella could only hope that she understood.

She quickly put her large-brimmed hat over her wet hair. She wished she had something to dry it with; she had wrung it out and was thankful it was not so long as it had been before her illness. Now she reckoned that when they reached the Castle she could go to her bed-chamber and rub it dry before Miss Harrison awoke from her afternoon nap.

"Please take us back!" she shouted to the deaf groom and gathered, as he had already turned the pony-carriage round, that that was what he had intended to do anyway.

The groom took them back by a route which was quicker than the one they had taken on the way out, and it was not long before the pony-carriage drew up at

69

the front door. Seeing no sign of the Phaeton Arabella heaved a sigh of relief. It must have been some neighboring Squire who was riding through Meridale Park.

Just for a moment she had been afraid that the gentleman staring at her across the water of the pool might have been the Marquis. Then she told herself such an idea was ridiculous; for had he been returning home he would have sent word and the Castle would be prepared for him.

The sense of urgency was now gone and, feeling her hair damp on her shoulders, Arabella regretted that she had not taken longer in dressing before they left the woods. However, there was nothing that could be done about it now. She thanked the groom for driving them and made Beulah do the same.

"Thank . . . you," Beulah said, almost with dignity, when Arabella prompted her.

The old man touched his forelock.

"Oi be glad ye enjoyed yerself, Milady," he said and drove the pony-carriage away to the stables.

Although the front door was open there was no one about, so Arabella picked Beulah up and carried her to the top of the steps. Stopping there she took a backward look towards the park, feeling a sudden reluctance to enter the Castle and leave the sunshine outside.

It was then she saw the Phaeton with its flashing yellow wheels and the sun shining on the silver bridles of the chestnut coming at a spanking pace down the main drive.

Hastily she picked Beulah up again and, hurrying across the hall, carried her to the top of the Grand Staircase.

"Oh, there you are, Miss," she heard Rose say as she emerged from one of the bedrooms on the first floor. "I was a'looking out for you . . . but you shouldn't carry Her Ladyship up all these stairs. Where's George, I'd like to know?"

"He does not seem to be about," Arabella replied. "Please take Lady Beulah up to Miss Harrison. I want to go to my own room."

70

"Yes, of course, Miss," Rose said. "Come along, Your Ladyship. Did you have a nice drive? Where did you go?"

A crafty look came into Beulah's eyes.

"Secret. Beulah not . . . tell . . . secret."

"Then I mustn't ask, must I?" Rose said as she carried the child up the next flight of stairs.

Arabella heard their voices receding upwards, but for a moment she made no effort to follow them. She waited, out of sheer curiosity, to see if the Phaeton came to the front door.

A moment later she heard the crunch of wheels on the gravel and the sound of horses brought to a standstill. She had a glimpse of the pink driving-coat and the elegant bonnet of the lady seated beside the driver, and then a groom, in crested top-hat and claret livery, flashed past as he ran to the horses' heads.

Arabella pulled off her hat and crouched down behind the heavily carved balustrade which ran along the landing of the first floor. She knew she should have gone upstairs, but she could not resist waiting and watching.

She saw the gentleman who had been driving come up the front steps. She had had but a brief glimpse of him across the lake; now she saw that he was extremely handsome. He wore his clothes with an elegance which made Arabella instantly dub him a dandy even while she appreciated the cut of his many-tiered riding-coat and the brilliant polish of his boots.

"I suppose I had best ring the bell," she heard him say. "They will not be expecting me, Sybil. I warned you that you would not be comfortable!"

"You know that I only wanted to be with you," the vision in pink replied as she came into the hall. She was very lovely, Arabella thought. Her slanting dark eyes and full red mouth gave her face an exotic, almost oriental look. She reached out to put her gloved hand familiarly on the gentleman's arm.

"I'm so glad to see the Castle, Julius," she said, her voice warm and ingratiating.

71

"There certainly doesn't seem to be much welcome for us at the moment," her companion answered brusquely.

He crossed to the fireplace and gave an impatient pull at the long, tasselled bell-rope.

Arabella imagined the wire traveling through the long corridor she had already traversed to the pantry, where it would clang and jingle in the hope of attracting someone's attention.

"The place looks dirty and dilapidated," she heard the gentleman said disdainfully. He walked into the centre of the hall and stood looking up at the pictures. Then he stared around him at the unpolished furniture.

"My mother always had flowers on that table," he said in a low voice, looking at a beautiful marble-topped, carved and gilt console table at the bottom of the stairs.

Arabella gave a start. So it was the Marquis!

There was no longer any doubt, and he had come home without letting anyone know that they must expect him. She must have sensed it, she thought, the moment she had seen the Phaeton across the lake and now, curious and at the same time apprehensive, she wondered what would happen.

Would Miss Harrison warn Gentleman Jack, would the highwaymen cease to stable their horses in the un-used stables? What would occur in the Castle itself?

It was almost like a story in one of the books she had read. Although she was ashamed of the curiosity which made her pry on the Marquis through the balustrade, she made no effort to go to her own bedchamber.

Impatiently the Marquis tugged at the bell-rope again.

"What the devil has happened to everybody?" he demanded, and now there was a note of anger in his voice. The lady who accompanied him sat down in one of the big armchairs beside the empty fireplace and laughed.

"You expect too much, Julius. Mice will play when the cat's away! When you go a'wandering you should leave a wife behind to see that everything is kept in order."

There was a meaning in her words which did not escape Arabella, but it appeared as though the Marquis had not heard her.

At that moment there was the sound of someone coming down the corridor from the kitchen quarters.

"All right, all right! Oi'm coming!" a cheery voice shouted, and Arabella knew it was George speaking.

He came marching into the hall, still in his shirt sleeves, his fair hair tousled on top of his head and his feet in a pair of carpet-slippers.

"What do ye want," he began, but when he saw the two people waiting in the Hall his voice died on his lips.

"Oi be sorry, Sir," he said quickly. "Oi didn't realise anyone was a'calling."

"I am not calling," the Marquis said icily. "I am your Master! And I want to know what is going on here! Where is Turner?"

For a moment George looked puzzled.

"Mister . . . Mister Turner has left, Milord," he replied. " 'Tis Mister Jacobs as be the butler now."

"Jacobs? I've never heard of him," the Marquis ejaculated. "Send him to me immediately!"

George turned to obey and as he did so Jacobs, old and unsteady, came into the Hall.

"Oi thought Oi heard th'bell," he said in almost senile tones.

The Marquis stared at him.

"Jacobs!" he repeated. "Of course, I know you! You're no butler! You were the odd job man when I was a boy."

"Why! It be His Lordship!" old Jacobs exclaimed. "Bless m'soul but 'tis good to see ye again, Milord! Yes, that be right, Oi were the odd man 'til Mister Turner left. And then they told Oi to take over th'position."

"They told you! Who told you?" the Marquis enquired. The old man looked disconcerted.

"Oi think it were Miss Fellows as gives Oi the order, Milord."

"Miss Fellows? Who is she?" the Marquis demanded. "Where's Matty . . . Miss Matherson?"

"Oi think her be in her room, Milord."

The Marquis glanced at George.

"Go and inform Miss Matherson that I am here," he said.

As if thankful to have something to do, George ran up the staircase, taking the steps three at a time. He had no eyes for Arabella, crouched down in the shadows of the balustrade, and nor had Miss Matherson when a moment later she came hurrying along the wide corridor, her black silk dress rustling as she moved.

The Marquis was talking in a low voice to Lady Sybil and for a moment he did not see Miss Matherson descend the stairs. She had almost reached the Hall when he looked up and gave a cry at the sight of her.

"Matty!" he exclaimed. "It's good to see you!"

Miss Matherson descended the last two stairs and dropped a curtsy.

"It's good to see Your Lordship after so long a time," she replied, "but we were not expecting Your Lordship to visit us unannounced."

"That is obvious," the Marquis replied. "Matty what has happened to the place? Look at the dust! No flowers! The footman in his shirt sleeves! And who in the name of Fortune appointed old Jacobs as butler? He is no more capable of being a butler than of commanding a regiment!"

"Turner wished to retire, Milord," Miss Matherson explained.

"Why the hell should he?" the Marquis asked. "He can't be much more than fifty."

"I think, Milord, that Turner had his reasons," Miss Matherson replied, and there was something she could not or would not divulge.

"Has he got a new position?" the Marquis enquired.

"No, he is living in the village in the house your

74

father, his late Lordship, gave him," Miss Matherson replied.

"Then send for him," the Marquis said authoritatively. "Dispatch a groom, tell him that I am here, and ask him to come back immediately."

"Very good Milord," Miss Matherson said.

"It must be done at once," the Marquis added sharply. "You there! What's your name?"

He was pointing at George who had returned behind Miss Matherson and was listening with his mouth open.

"Oi be George, Milord."

"Well, you heard the order. Go to the stables and send a groom to the village. Also put your coat on, and don't let me see you in that sort of footwear again!"

"No, Milord, thank ye Milord," George muttered and Arabella heard him turn and run down the corridor towards the pantry.

"And you," the Marquis said to Jacobs, "get a bottle of wine from the cellar. I expect the lady would like a glass of Madeira. I want brandy. I suppose you've managed to keep the key turned . . . or has it all been drunk?"

"No, Milord, Oi'll fetch it at once," the old man said.

He shuffled away and the Marquis turned to Miss Matherson.

"Now, Matty. What is happening?" he asked in a gentler voice.

"I'm afraid, Milord, that things are not the same as they used to be," Miss Matherson replied.

"I can see that," the Marquis said silently. "I expected to find the house in dust-sheets—that would have been understandable—but not with the door unattended, the footman half-clothed and old Jacobs dressed up like the Cheltenham Theatricals to play the part of a butler. Good God, Matty, don't you know better than that?"

"It is nothing to do with me, Milord," Miss Matherson said.

"Then who?" the Marquis asked.

"I was Her Ladyship's personal maid," Miss Matherson replied. "When she died I had no official standing in the Castle."

"But I understood that you were to be in charge," the Marquis said.

"You gave no orders to that effect," Miss Matherson answered.

"Hang it! Do I have to put everything down in black and white that concerns my own home?" the Marquis asked. "I always believed that everything would be exactly the same as I left it. When I was abroad I used to hear regularly from the Estate Office. Sheltham always assured me that everything was in good order."

"Mister Sheltham died three years ago," Miss Matherson told him. "For two years before that he was in ill health. He managed to a certain extent, but I am afraid things got out of hand and he didn't worry himself unduly."

"So everything began to rot and decay," the Marquis exclaimed. "Well, Matty, we had best set things to rights. Here and now I appoint you to run the Castle, to act as housekeeper, and to restore it as it was when my mother was alive."

Miss Matherson curtsied.

"I'll do my best, Milord, but it will not be easy."

"If you have any trouble, come to me," the Marquis said.

Miss Matherson raised her eyebrows.

"Your Lordship is staying then?"

"Of course! What did you expect?" he asked in a sharp tone. "And as you see I am not alone. This, Matty, is Lady Sybil Sheraton, a friend of mine. Her husband was killed at Waterloo."

"Good day to Your Ladyship," Miss Matherson said, dropping a respectful curtsy.

"My maid and the baggage should be here at any moment," Lady Sybil replied loftily, "and I hope you will see that the beds are aired. In a house that has not been used for some years, I am always extremely apprehensive as to the condition of the beds!"

"I will see that hot bricks are placed in the beds immediately, Milady," Miss Matherson promised.

"And what about dinner? Are we to get anything to eat?" the Marquis enquired.

"Mistress Coombe is still with us," Miss Matherson replied.

"The Gods be praised for that!" the Marquis exclaimed. "I'll go to the kitchen and see her. I expect she will want to reminisce about how I used to slip downstairs when I was a child and beg her to make me gingerbread men."

"I shouldn't go for the moment, Milord," Miss Matherson said, putting out a restraining hand as he turned to leave the Hall.

"No?" he questioned.

Miss Matherson shook her head.

"No, Milord. Give them time. They are not expecting you. The Castle needs a deal of attention before Your Lordship will feel at home."

"What has been happening, Matty?" the Marquis asked in a low voice as if he suspected there was a secret reason she had not told him.

"Everything will be put right, but Your Lordship must be patient," Miss Matherson said, soothingly. "Let me get the Salon ready first. If you and Your Ladyship would like to walk in the garden, or sit here . . . no, perhaps it would be best if you went into the Library."

"We will stay here," the Marquis said almost-aggressively. "I want to see what is going on. But first I will take a look at the Library." He turned away as he spoke.

"Very well, Milord," Miss Matherson said meekly as if she had resigned herself to the inevitable.

Miss Matherson climbed the stairs with dignity. As she reached the landing, Arabella, still crouched down in the shadow of the balustrade, saw Miss Fellows approaching from the opposite direction. The sharp-faced head housemaid was obviously surprised to see Miss Matherson as she reached the top of the staircase.

"Oh, it's you, Miss Matherson!" she exclaimed sourly.

"I was coming in search of you, Miss Fellows," Miss Matherson said. "His Lordship has just arrived and has requested me to take charge of the household. There is work to be done, as you will understand. Kindly collect your housemaids together and open up the Salon. After that, prepare the Elizabethan Suite for Lady Sybil Sheraton. His Lordship will sleep in his father's room, which having been in my charge fortunately needs little doing to it."

"His Lordship has arrived?" Miss Fellows cried. "Why wasn't I told? And what do you mean, His Lordship has put you in charge? Miss Harrison is in charge here."

"Not any more, Miss Fellows," Miss Matherson said quietly, "and perhaps you will be kind enough to inform Miss Harrison of His Lordship's decision. If you are in doubt, perhaps you will step down into the hall and query his orders."

An expression of anger came over Miss Fellows' face, but behind it there was something else.

"Do you mean to say you've told His Lordship about him?" she asked in a low voice that was only just audible to Arabella.

"Told him what?" Miss Matherson questioned clearly and distinctly. "I'm afraid, Miss Fellows, I have no idea to whom you are referring. Perhaps you will not waste time but be good enough to set about the tasks I have requested with all possible speed."

Just for a moment Miss Fellows hesitated as though she would refuse. Then with a toss of her head she turned and walked swiftly away, apparently to obey Miss Matherson's commands.

Arabella watching, wide-eyed, forgot about her own position and only when Miss Matherson walked almost on top of her did she rise up from where she had been crouching, looking slightly shame-faced.

"Oh, it's you, Miss Arabella," Miss Matherson exclaimed. "So you are back from your drive with Lady Beulah."

"Yes, we are back," Arabella replied.

"Then perhaps you had best go and see if your tea is ready, dear," Miss Matherson said gently. "I do not know if His Lordship will ask to see Lady Beulah this evening, but perhaps you will suggest to Miss Harrison that in case this happens, Her Ladyship should be ready in one of her best dresses."

"I will tell Miss Harrison what you have said," Arabella replied and ran up the stairs to the second floor.

She went first to her own room and rubbed her hair as hard as she could. It was nearly dry and now it fluffed round her face, making her look, she thought, almost as young as she pretended to be.

Her dress was soiled from having lain in the wood and she changed it for another, a childish sprigged muslin she had worn over six years ago and which had been intended as a gift for some poor child. Now, discovered on the top shelf of the Nursery cupboard by Miss Jones, it fitted her, although it was a little short.

She put on white socks and low-heeled shoes and thought that if anyone were to guess her real age, they would have to be very perceptive indeed.

Ready, she hurried upstairs to the schoolroom to find that news of His Lordship's arrival had not yet reached Miss Harrison. Yawning loudly, the governess was just emerging from her bedroom, wearing the flashy negligée that she usually affected at breakfast.

"What's the time?" she enquired. "I think I must have slept longer than I intended. Ring the bell like a good child and ask where my tea has got to. I can't understand why they haven't brought it up."

"I am afraid they are too busy," Arabella explained. "You see, His Lordship has arrived."

For a moment Arabella thought Miss Harrison was going to faint. Holding on to the back of a chair she said in a strangled voice:

"What did you say?"

79

"I said His Lordship—the Marquis—has arrived. He has Lady Sybil Sheraton with him and Miss Matherson is arranging to have the rooms opened and cleaned on his instructions."

"Miss Matherson?" The governess, steadying herself against the chair as if her legs had given way beneath her, sank down on the sofa.

"When did he arrive?" she said.

"About a quarter of an hour ago," Arabella replied.

"Is he going to stay?"

"I heard His Lordship say that he intends to do so," Arabella said.

"But he can't! 'Tis impossible! He can't stay here!" Miss Harrison muttered, almost as if she was speaking to herself.

"It is his home," Arabella reminded her. "It seems strange that he has not been back for eight years. But he was fighting against the French, and now the War is over why should he not return? I expect he intends to live here."

The governess was pale already, but she went paler still at Arabella's words.

"Live here!" Her hands went up to her eyes, almost as if she must block out the picture that Arabella had conjured up.

"Has he asked for Beulah?" Miss Harrison said at length.

"Not yet," Arabella replied.

The governess rose to her feet and walked to the window.

"Oh, my God!" Arabella heard her whisper. "What can I do? What can I do?"

"Miss Matherson suggests that Beulah should put on one of her best dresses," Arabella said after a moment, "in case His Lordship asks to see her."

The governess gave a groan and without a word went from the room back into her bedchamber. She slammed the door and Arabella was left alone wondering what she should do.

She crossed the room to find Beulah. As she expected, the child was being changed by Rose, who was singing her a little song as she did up her slippers. Arabella saw that Beulah was wearing a fresh dress of smocked linen. It was not the best gown in her wardrobe, but nevertheless it was quite attractive and she thought it was unnecessary to change the child again.

"I think Miss Fellows will be looking for you, Rose," she said to the housemaid. "His Lordship has arrived and there is a lot to do. But if you get the chance, ask one of the footmen to bring Her Ladyship's chocolate upstairs. Miss Harrison can go without her tea but I think Beulah needs something after our drive."

"Chocolate! Beulah wants . . . chocolate!" the child cried.

"You say His Lordship's arrived?" Rose asked. "That'll mean a real commotion for us all."

"I expect there will be a lot more work to be done," Arabella said. "You know as well as I do, Rose, that the Castle is very dirty."

Rose giggled and at that moment Arabella heard someone come into the Nursery. She looked round and through the open door saw Miss Fellows. The head housemaid, her face pale and drawn and her lips tight set, went straight to Miss Harrison's room, opened the door without knocking and went inside.

She did not close the door behind her and Arabella could not help overhearing what was being said.

"You've heard that he's arrived?" Miss Fellows asked.

"I've heard," Miss Harrison replied. "What am I to do? Oh, tell me what I am to do!"

"You can't do anything," Miss Fellows said. "Let's just hope he doesn't find out."

"I ought to warn Jack!"

"How could you do that?" Miss Fellows asked. "I thought you'd be taking it hard. That's why I slipped upstairs. Just keep your head. Say nothing. You can tell Mister Jack when he comes."

"But it would be dangerous for him to come here now!" Miss Harrison cried almost shrilly.

"Why should it be?" Miss Fellows tried to reassure her. "He doesn't come in by the front door, as well you know. His Lordship is right at the other end of the Castle. Just don't take on! But, I can't stop here talking. You will hardly credit it, but he has put that pie-faced old harridan Miss Matherson back in authority. Mister Jack should have had her out when he had the chance!"

"He tried when Mister Sheltham died," Miss Harrison cried, "but she wouldn't go, you know she wouldn't go! Do you think she'll say anything?"

"I doubt it," Miss Fellows said, "she knows as well as we do what Mister Jack will do to Lady Beulah if anyone squeals on him. And besides her, he's threatened the families of everyone here. Old Mister Jacobs dotes on that last granddaughter of his and Mistress Coombe walks in fear that he'll harm her younger son. He's a bit simple and Mister Jack hates him for it, but she loves him and she'll not say a word."

"Miss Fellows, you've cheered me up," Miss Harrison declared. "When Arabella came out with the news of His Lordship's arrival, I thought I would collapse. I did, really."

"Now get dressed in case His Lordship asks to see you, and say nothing," Miss Fellows advised. "As far as he's to know it's nothing to do with you how the Castle was run. If you can put the blame on Miss Matherson, you do so. Otherwise play it simple. Say nothing. You were engaged solely to look after Lady Beulah."

"That's true," Miss Harrison agreed. "But Miss Fellows, I'm frightened. Frightened to death, I am."

"You'll be all right," Miss Fellows said soothingly. "Now get dressed. You don't want His Lordship to come up here at this time of day and find you like that.

"No, of course not," Miss Harrison said automatically.

"I'll come back when I can," Miss Fellows promised and hurried across the schoolroom and out into the corridor.

Arabella could not help smiling when, about ten minutes later, Miss Harrison emerged quietly dressed in a black gown with her hair smoothed neatly to her head. By this time George had brought up Beulah's chocolate and the child was sitting at the table drinking it.

"I am afraid we are not going to get our tea today," Miss Harrison said in a cheerful tone which was obviously forced, "but you will have your supper later, Arabella. Is there anything in particular you would like, my dear?"

"No thank you, I will have anything they send up," Arabella replied, knowing that a request for any special delicacies would not be welcomed below stairs.

"It will be a great excitement having His Lordship in the house," Miss Harrison said. "Do you understand, Beulah? Your brother is here. Your brother—the Marquis."

"Mar . . . quis?" Beulah repeated.

"She does not understand," Arabella said. "Let me tell her later."

"Of course, that's a good idea," Miss Harrison approved.

Although they waited in the schoolroom until long after Beulah's bedtime, there was no summons from down below, nor did the Marquis come upstairs. George hurried in with supper on a tray, which was certainly not as plentiful or as well served as usual. Miss Harrison made no complaint.

Her first effort at appearing pleased at the Marquis's unexpected arrival had died away. She sat silent, staring ahead of her, a frown between her eyes, her fingers twisting in and out of each other. Arabella knew she was in a state of nervous tension.

She wondered if Gentleman Jack would come tonight. Did he come every night, she wondered. Or did the highwaymen have other places in which they could stable their horses?

There were so many questions she longed to ask but knew it was impossible for her to voice any of them.

It was something to have learned that Miss Fellows, and also Miss Matherson, knew what was happening.

Why had Miss Matherson suffered such an intolerable imposition? Was it really true that Gentleman Jack threatened to harm the families of those who worked at the Castle, should anyone lay information against him?

Arabella thought it over and came to the conclusion that it would be a very easy thing to terrorise the staff. Nearly everyone who worked in the Castle came from the local village. The highwayman, with his knowledge of the countryside, could easily intimidate the whole locality into agreeing to anything he suggested. He and his gang had fire-arms which they could use against anyone who questioned their authority or threatened to inform against them.

Six armed men against the defenceless inhabitants of a small village were a very formidable enemy. It would need a whole company of Dragoons to capture or exterminate them.

Arabella began to see what the people in the Castle, defenceless, without a master, and utterly at the mercy of such a man as Gentleman Jack, had been up against. And what was more, he threatened Beulah. That was obvious; for, besides what Miss Fellows had said, Arabella remembered his conversation with Miss Harrison when she had listened to them from beneath the table, not at first knowing who he was.

Now, as she considered it, she realised in what deadly danger, quite unwittingly, the Marquis had become involved. He might have returned to his own home, but it was not now the quiet, beautiful place he had left behind. It was the hiding-place of a gang of unscrupulous, cruel, ruthless men . . . men who would stick at nothing to preserve their lives and their freedom.

Five

"THE betting in the pantry is that he'll marry her afore Christmas."

"When Mister Turner walks into the room, there she was a'sitting on His Lordship's bed, as bold as brass."

"Her maid says she has a temper like the devil when roused."

"There's not a servant in London who'll stay with her for more than a month or so."

"They even says that she . . ." Here Miss Fellows lowered her voice so that Arabella could not catch the end of the sentence.

Sitting on the floor playing with Beulah, she could not help being amused by what she overheard day after day. For some extraordinary reason while employers behaved as if their servants were deaf and dumb, children were ignored by all classes on the assumption that they did not listen to grown-up conversations.

Little went on in the Castle that was not reported in the schoolroom. It was now the third day since the Marquis had returned to his home, and so far Arabella had not met him. He had not sent for Beulah, nor had he come to the schoolroom.

"You would think he'd want to see his little sister," Miss Harrison remarked plaintively at intervals.

But Arabella had a suspicion that there was a note of relief in her voice as well. Miss Harrison had no desire to encounter the Marquis, and after the first two days of being permanently dressed in her best, and waiting in the schoolroom all through the afternoon in case he should send for her, she relaxed, went back to drinking her usual amount of wine at luncheon and was ready, when the meal was finished, to retire to bed.

Now she yawned in Miss Fellows' face despite the exciting revelations that were being poured into her ears.

"I must have my rest," she said. "Come back after tea, that is if you can."

"I'll do my best," Miss Fellows replied, "but as things are at the moment, I can't call my soul my own. Miss Matherson is on at me every second of the day. Four new housemaids she's engaged from the village and Mister Turner has five new footmen!"

"He hasn't sacked George, has he?" Miss Harrison enquired.

"Oh, no, George is still with us," Miss Fellows answered. "It's only poor old Jacobs who has been sent into retirement. But I hear that His Lordship dealt quite handsomely by him."

She rose to her feet.

"Ah, well! Back to work, I suppose. Before Miss Matherson is finished, I shall have collapsed with the vapours the way things are going."

Miss Harrison, yawning again, had ceased to be interested.

"Now, Arabella," she said sharply, "tell Rose to put Beulah's bonnet on her and then you can take the child for a walk in the garden. It's fresh air you both need. I really think you have got a little more color in your cheeks since you've been here."

"Yes, Miss Harrison," Arabella said obediently.

Beulah protested loudly as the card-castles that Arabella had been building for her were put away.

It was a bright afternoon and as soon as a footman had carried Beulah downstairs to the garden door at the back of the Castle, Arabella said:

"Come on, Beulah, let us see if you can run! I will race you across the garden."

It was difficult for Beulah to do anything but waddle but somehow she managed the semblance of a run, her legs stiff, the thickened lower part of her body looking grotesque as she attempted to imitate Arabella's lithe, effortless movements across the smooth grass.

Arabella managed to encourage Beulah to reach a little arbour at the end of a long, green glade where they threw themselves down on the ground, Beulah panting and breathless, Arabella laughing a little at the child's exertions.

"You are too fat. That is what is wrong with you!" she said, taking off Beulah's bonnet and pulling off her own hat.

"Beulah . . . fat!" the child said. "Arabella . . . thin!"

"Good, that is the right answer," Arabella approved.

She had taught Beulah a lot of new words already, and she realised Doctor Simpson had been right in his supposition that although Beulah would never be normal, her understanding and her intelligence could be improved if someone took trouble with her.

"Now, Beulah, how many butterflies do you see?" Arabella asked her.

Beulah put up her fingers.

"One, two . . . four, five . . ."

"You have forgotten "three," Arabella corrected.

"Three, three, three . . ." Beulah cried.

"That makes nine," Arabella said. "Never mind! You are getting to be a very clever girl."

"Beulah clever!" the child said with self-satisfaction.

"I am clever!" Arabella corrected. "Say it, Beulah— 'I am clever'."

"I . . . am . . . clever!" Beulah repeated.

They spent some time on the grass by the arbour. Then, drawing Beulah to her feet, Arabella took her by the hand and they walked further on into the garden.

There was endless delight for Arabella in exploring the Castle and its surroundings. She knew, by now, her way around and she was leading Beulah towards a statue which stood in a pool filled with goldfish, when she saw a familiar figure approaching.

Although she had not met the Marquis, she had peeped at him continually over the banisters, watched him from the window and listened, interminably it seemed to her, to the speculations about his love-affair with Lady Sybil.

She had told herself, whenever she thought of him, that she despised him utterly. Here was a real social waster! A man who neglected his estates, his castle, his whole heritage for the immorality and looseness of the social life of London.

She was not shocked, nor indeed surprised, by the fact that his "amoretta", Lady Sybil, should have accompanied him to the Castle unchaperoned, and that they were openly living there together.

It was what she expected of dissipated noblemen and comparing the Marquis with her stepfather, Sir Lawrence Deane, she proved to herself, once again, that all men were despicable and hateful.

The fact that the servants spoke of him as being kind and generous, and that Miss Matherson obviously adored him, did not impress her. It was easy to be pleasant to those you could patronise!

Arabella told herself that the example the Marquis set by coming back to the Castle with a mistress in tow was the type of behaviour one might well expect from someone who was dead to all decency.

But watching him coming towards them now she could not help being struck by the Marquis's appearance. His broad shoulders, his air of health and well-being, did not fit into her picture of a *débauché*.

Two dogs were gambolling behide him and she guessed that he had taken them for a walk, an activity which, she fancied, Lady Sybil would not welcome.

The Marquis, apparently preoccupied with his own thoughts, did not perceive Arabella and Beulah until he was almost upon them. They were standing on the grass walk but were half concealed by a huge azalea bush in full flower. Then, as she came to within a few feet of them, some movement caused him to turn his head and he saw them.

He stopped and looked full at Beulah. To Arabella's surprise, he seemed to stiffen and there was an expression on his face she could not fathom.

For a few seconds none of them moved until almost, it appeared, with an effort the Marquis turned his eyes from Beulah to Arabella. He stared at her with a sudden recognition in his expression before he said:

"But I thought . . . Why, you are only a child!"

Arabella dropped a curtsy.

"I am Arabella, my Lord, and this is Beulah."

She did not know why she took it upon herself to make the introduction. Somehow it seemed important that she should say something.

"Yes, I know it's Beulah," the Marquis replied in a deep voice.

"Say, 'How do you do,' Beulah," Arabella said to the child.

"Doggies!" Beulah cried. "Doggies!", pointing a fat finger at the spaniels.

The Marquis looked at her and again there was that strange expression on his face. It was not disgust or horror; it was almost one of relief—as if he had anticipated she might look worse, Arabella thought. Then she told herself she was imagining things.

And yet she had the idea that on his first glance at Beulah, he had gone pale beneath the sun-tan on his face. Now his eyes went from Beulah again to Arabella, noting the red-gold of her hair falling over her shoulders. Quite unexpectedly a smile twitched at the corners of his mouth.

"You were bathing, I think, when I arrived."

Arabella blushed. She had hoped that he would have forgotten what he had seen, or at least not recognise her. She had felt embarrassed when she first learnt who he was but until now so many other things had happened that the memory had almost ceased to trouble her.

"It was on an . . . impulse," she said in a low voice. "It was a . . . hot afternoon . . ."

"You don't have to explain yourself to me," the

89

Marquis interrupted. "I often bathed in that very spot when I was a boy—and got punished for it."

Quite suddenly Arabella found herself laughing.

"Why is one always stopped from doing the things one wants to do?" she asked.

"That is the boredom of being a child," the Marquis said, "and yet one has no idea how happy one is until one has grown up."

"It depends where you live, does it not?" Arabella asked, "and . . . with whom."

He saw a shadow pass over her face as she thought of how her happiness at home had been ruined by her stepfather.

"I can guess," the Marquis said gently, "that you have not been happy. Is that why you have come to live here?"

"He is quite perceptive," Arabella thought in surprise.

"Yes, it is," she replied, "and I like being with Beulah. I am teaching her a lot of things no one else has bothered to teach her before."

The Marquis frowned.

"Why haven't they?" he asked. "I have ordered that proper wages should be paid to nurses and governesses and that she should have everything that was necessary for her comfort."

"She is content," Arabella said, and indeed at the moment Beulah looked happy enough, patting and caressing the dogs who, with the irrepressible sentimentality of spaniels, were gratefully licking her face.

The Marquis seemed anxious not to look at Beulah but at Arabella.

"You are very thin," he said. "I hope my staff are feeding you properly."

"I have been ill," Arabella explained, "and the food is very good."

"Mistress Coombe has been here ever since I can remember," the Marquis said. "She came as a scullery-maid when she was little more than a child, and she worked her way up. Her mother had been at the Castle before her and her grandmother before that. I expect you realize that we are very feudal."

He was talking to her as if she were a grown-up, Arabella noted, and thought he found it pleasant to speak to someone of such personal aspects of his home. Lady Sybil was unlikely to be interested in the domestic arrangements at the Castle so long as she personally was comfortable.

Arabella remembered Miss Fellows saying:

"Mister Turner says as how Her Ladyship makes him laugh when they are having their meals together, but she has a tongue like an asp's when it comes to talking about their friends."

Instinctively Arabella said the right thing:

"The Castle is very beautiful and so are the gardens."

"I'm glad you think so," the Marquis smiled, his face lighting up. "My mother laid out the gardens herself. They had been sadly neglected before my father inherited. In a week or so the roses will be in bloom and the Rose Garden is one of the most beautiful in the whole length and breadth of the land. Have you seen the Herb Garden?"

Arabella shook her head.

"Let me show it to you," he suggested.

Arabella took Beulah by the hand. She was about to propose that the Marquis take the child's other hand so that between them they could lead her more quickly but somehow she knew instinctively that he did not want to touch his sister. He was repulsed by the child. Arabella thought she could understand it.

She calculated that the Marquis must have been twenty when Beulah was born. The fact that she was deformed would have shocked him. Could that be the reason why, when the War ended, he had not returned home?"

They walked very slowly because of Beulah, while the Marquis talked of the Herb Garden.

"My mother made a study of herbs. She replanted the garden exactly as it was in the days of Henry VIII.

91

She found plans in the Library and books which gave the name of every herb that had grown there."

They reached an iron gate in the centre of a yew hedge. The Marquis opened it and they stepped into a small square garden laid out in a pattern with its symmetrical beds edged with dwarf privet.

It was obvious from the first glance that the place had been neglected. The shrubs and plants were still there and their fragrance scented the air. But the beds needed weeding, there were many gaps where a plant had died, and some had become overgrown. Nevertheless, those in flower gave the garden a gay and colorful appearance.

"Dammit!" the Marquis exclaimed furiously. "Here's another place that has gone to rack and ruin!"

"You have been away," Arabella said softly. "People grow disheartened when there is no one to approve or disapprove their work."

Some of the anger faded from his face.

"You are right of course."

"My father always used to say," Arabella went on, "that a gardener is an artist. If you do not consult with him, he cannot create the picture you desire. Then if you do not praise him for what he has created he will not try so hard another time."

"That is true," the Marquis agreed. "I was a fool to stay away so long."

His eyes went to Beulah and quite suddenly he crouched down beside her, so that his face was level with hers.

"Beulah!" he said, "I am your brother. Do you know that?"

"Bro . . . ther," Beulah repeated.

"No, say Julius," the Marquis commanded, "say Julius!"

"Ju . . . lius," Beulah managed with difficulty.

The Marquis stood up.

"There you are! Now we are properly introduced," he said, and Arabella felt as if she had watched a man ride his horse at a five-bar gate and jump it."

"I must speak to the gardeners about this place," the Marquis said, looking round him.

"Tell them to make it beautiful in memory of your mother," Arabella said. "I understand everyone in the Castle loved her."

"I will do that," the Marquis promised. "She was a very lovely, very wonderful person."

He gave a sigh and looked back at the great Castle standing behind them as though he almost expected to see his mother waving to him from one of the windows or coming out onto the lawn to greet him.

"You miss her, do you not?" Arabella asked.

"Of course," he said in a non-committal voice, and she realised that he still mourned his mother so poignantly that he could not speak of his feeling where she was concerned.

"What a funny little thing you are," he said suddenly, as if making an effort to change the subject. "I can't imagine myself talking like this to most children. How old are you?"

"Not too old to be thought a suitable companion for Beulah," Arabella replied, and they both laughed at the absurdity of it.

"She is lucky to have you," the Marquis said. "Whose idea was it?"

"The new doctor's," Arabella answered. "He looked round locally for a child to be with Beulah and picked on me."

"The new doctor, whoever he may be, has obviously a lot of good sense," the Marquis approved. "I tell you what, I will take you driving in my Phaeton. I am sure you would like that!"

"Beulah would love it," Arabella said, and she knew by the quick glance the Marquis gave his sister that he had not for a moment remembered that Beulah must be included in the invitation.

They walked slowly back towards the Castle.

"I must come up to the schoolrom and see you," the Marquis said, as if making a decision for himself rather than a promise to Arabella. "It used to be my nursery —let me see, the name of your governess is . . ."

". . . Miss Harrison," Arabella supplied.

"Yes, Matty told me. It was stupid of me, but when I saw you at the lake, I thought you must be the governess!"

"No, no," Arabella said. "We were playing truant. Miss Harrison would not have approved at all!"

"It was just bad luck that I should surprise you," the Marquis said. "I bathed there a hundred times and nobody has ever seen me. The only give-away used to be that my hair was wet when I got back to the Castle, and my nurses or tutors were frightened lest I should catch cold."

"And did you?" Arabella asked.

He shook his head.

"I was as strong as a bull!"

"Bull . . . bull!" Beulah cried suddenly, having caught one word of the conversation. They laughed at that.

"Which way do you go into the Castle?" the Marquis asked.

"By the garden door," Arabella replied.

"I think I will take the dogs round to the front," the Marquis said.

Arabella had a feeling that now they had returned home he was anxious to be rid of them, and thought it likely that he did not wish Lady Sybil to see Beulah.

"Goodbye," Arabella said as they reached the garden door.

He stood looking down into her small, pointed face. The sunshine playing on her hair seemed to turn it to shimmering fire and her large eyes, raised to his, had deep purple depths which reminded him of violets.

"I will not forget our drive," he said, almost as if it was a promise.

"We will wait eagerly for the invitation," Arabella answered.

There was something in his face which made it almost an effort for her to look away from him.

"Say 'Goodbye' to your brother, Beulah," she instructed.

Beulah had her arms round the spaniels.

" 'Bye, doggy," she was murmuring. "Good . . . bye, doggy. Beulah see you . . . 'gain . . . soon."

George appeared in the doorway.

"Want a piggy-back upstairs?" he asked Beulah cheerily—then saw the Marquis. "Beg pardon, Milord," he apologised.

"I'm glad to see you are so attentive to Her Ladyship's needs," the Marquis said. "Good afternoon, Arabella!"

He raised his hat and walked away, the dogs at his heels. Arabella and George, for no obvious reason, stood watching him out of sight.

"Well, he's seed Her Ladyship at last," George said familiarly. "Where did ye meet him, Miss Arabella?"

"In the garden," Arabella replied.

"We were laying the odd on how long it would be before he asked to see her," George said as they walked up the stairs.

Arabella did not reply. She knew she should not encourage familiarity in servants or allow them to discuss their master in her presence. But in their eyes she was only a child, and an unimportant child at that. She was well aware that they thought there must be something odd about her circumstances if she had come to the Castle to companion Beulah.

"He be a well-breeched swell, bain't he?" George asked, with the enthusiasm of a schoolboy speaking about his hero. "Ye should see him astride a horse! M'uncle's the Chief groom and he says there's never been a High-Flyer with a better seat. Some don't agree. They say he's only as good as his father. But from all I hears, the old Marquis had a way with horseflesh as was well-nigh miraculous!"

George picked up Beulah and carried her up the stairs to the schoolroom. He joked with her as they went, and when he had set her down on the schoolroom floor, he walked across to the window, flexing his muscles as he did so.

"There's them as understands horses . . . and them as don't," he said, obviously continuing his train of thought about the Marquis. "That Lady Sybil, for instance. M'uncle says that, if he had his way, he wouldn't let her touch an animal that weren't made o'wood. Ah! Here she be now!"

Arabella crossed the room to stand beside George at the window.

"Has Her Ladyship gone riding alone?" she asked.

George grinned at her.

"In a proper tantrum her was, after lunch, when His Lordship insisted on taking the dogs for a walk. "They must have exercise," he says. "What about me?" Her Ladyship snaps. "I won't be long," he replies. "I may not be here when you return!" her answers. But 'e takes no notice. If you ask me, His Lordship can have any woman he wants a'running to him if he so much as lifts his little finger!"

Arabella looked out the window. She could see Lady Sybil, exquisitely dressed in a habit of emerald-green velvet, come riding onto the gravel sweep in front of the Castle. She was having difficulty with her horse, which was prancing, moving sideways, trying to rear, and altogether showing a contempt for its rider.

"Our horses want exercising," George exclaimed. "Uncle's a'getting old and they have cut down on his stable-boys. Now that His Lordship's back he'll school 'em . . . they need a man's hand."

Lady Sybil's horse reared again and then lashed out with its hind legs.

Arabella, who loved horses, knew that it was just playing and being mischievous. She could see at a glance that Lady Sybil had no control over her mount. She was sitting stiff and nervous, holding the reins too tight, her expression cross and disdainful.

A groom came running to hold the bridle while she dismounted. The horse shied at the last moment and Lady Sybil was nearly thrown from the saddle but managed to save herself by holding onto the pommel. Then the groom helped her to dismount, while speaking soothingly to the horse.

"Whoa, boy," Arabella heard him say through the open window. "Whoa, now!"

"Whoa, indeed!" Lady Sybil said sharply. "The animal is a fiend. It should be taught a lesson!"

She was carrying a small, silver-handled riding-whip and now, safely on the ground, she turned towards the horse and lashed it.

She hit it several times about the head, while the groom, clinging to the bridle, had the greatest difficulty in keeping the frightened, rearing animal from bolting.

"See to it I am not given such a mount again!" Lady Sybil snapped and walked furiously up the stone steps and in through the front door.

"That was cruel!" Arabella exclaimed, aghast. "The horse was only fresh!"

"Oi told ye what m'uncle said about her," George said in disgust. "That be one of the best 'orses in the Stables."

"It was a beastly action," Arabella said hotly, "His Lordship should be told of her behaviour!"

George turned from the window to grin at her. "And who'll be doing the telling?" he asked. "Not Oi! It'ld be more than m'place is worth. Besides, when Her Ladyship be mistress here, she'd not forget the insult."

"No, indeed, none of us can say anything," Arabella agreed, but she felt furious that anyone should treat an animal in such a way, especially such a fine piece of horseflesh.

Rose took Beulah away to her bedchamber and Arabella went to her own. Instead of tidying herself she sat in front of the dressing-table, staring at her reflection in the mirror with unseeing eyes. She might despise the Marquis, but she would not wish the worst man on earth to be married to someone like Lady Sybil Sheraton.

Now she began to remember things Miss Fellows had repeated about her, information apparently culled from

Miss Archer—lady's-maid to Lady Sybil, a garrulous soul ready to confide in anyone who would listen . . . "deeply in debt" . . . "determined to marry before the Summer is out" . . . "has thrown her bonnet over the windmill as far as the Marquis is concerned" . . . "her tantrums are terrible" . . . "no servant will stay with her".

That would mean, Arabella calculated, that Matty, Rose and George would leave the Castle when Lady Sybil became its mistress, or maybe they would be sacked.

She felt a sudden hatred for this spoilt, promiscuous beauty, who, born into the nobility, was behaving no better than "a soiled dove"—one of those unfortunate creatures of whom her mother had once spoken in a shocked and lowered voice.

Arabella realized that if she were as innocent as she should have been, she would not understand such matters; but in fact her reading had taught her far more than any parent would have been willing to impart to a young girl. She had found the history of the Borgias amongst the books in her father's library. She had discovered the writings of Juvenal—the Roman satirist— who described the excesses of the dissolute Roman society of the Empire with a frankness which would have appalled Lady Deane if she had known what her daughter was reading.

It is not difficult for a student of history to find that the behavior of human beings varies little down the centuries. Arabella could find a counterpart for Lady Sybil through every era and she merely despised the Marquis the more for being deceived into thinking she was desirable.

And yet she wondered if he did know the truth about Lady Sybil. To him she would be all honey and sweetness. He might never learn of her cruelty, her meanness, her temper, until it was too late and they were married.

Arabella made up her mind that for the good of the Castle and those living in it she must get rid of Lady

Sybil Sheraton. It was not only the horses that would suffer if she stayed.

The whole place had altered in the last few days. Now the sunshine poured in through clean windows, there were flowers everywhere, scenting the air, and added to their fragrance was the wholesome smell of lavender and beeswax. The floors were now so clean that Arabella was almost afraid to tread on them, lest she should make a mark with her tiny feet, and she could literally see her face in the newly polished furniture.

Miss Matherson was everywhere, admonishing the young housemaids for not laying a fire properly, making them lift carpets so that they could be beaten and the brightness of their colors seen again, turning out room after room until the girls who obeyed her were, in Rose's words, "limp as a corpse" before she was satisfied.

The return of Mister Turner, the Butler, had also transformed that part of the household directed from the pantry. Now there were tall, young footmen with freshly powdered hair, clean livery, their polished buttons dazzling bright, in attendance in the front hall at every hour of the day.

Arabella learned from George that they had polished the silver until they had almost rubbed the hallmarks off it, and in the back premises, in Mistress Coombe's kingdom, there were clean flagstones, new kitchenmaids and a hustle and bustle which started, correctly, at five in the morning.

But underneath all the improvements Arabella knew there was still a deep, terrifying undercurrent of fear. The Marquis might be back in his house, but he was ignorant of what had been taking place during his absence and no one seemed ready to report what Gentleman Jack thought of it all.

Arabella did not wish to know. At night, when she went to her bedchamber, she locked herself in and pulled the bedclothes high about her ears, so that if there were footsteps outside in the passage, going towards Miss Harrison's room, she would not hear them. But she had the feeling that Gentleman Jack had not come. There was a watchfulness about Miss Harrison, and lines of strain on her face. As again and again she went to the cupboard for a nip of brandy, Arabella knew she was on edge.

Someone, sooner or later, Arabella thought, would have to tell the Marquis. But who? She was well aware that the terror under which Gentleman Jack held the whole village was a very real thing. And even if the Marquis knew—unless he fetched a company of Dragoons—what could he, one man, do against these dangerous and desperate cut-throats?

Yet somehow, some time, he would have to be warned, Arabella thought. But it would be best to be rid of Lady Sybil first.

She sat wondering how this could be accomplished until, at the very back of her mind, she heard Miss Fellows say:

"Keep those cats in the nursery, Miss Harrison. Don't let them go wandering all over the place. Not only do they make messes and I'll not stand having any more clearing up to do, but Miss Archer tells me that Her Ladyship cannot abide cats."

"Her Ladyship cannot abide cats." How could she best turn that to advantage? Arabella wondered.

Almost without thinking she went from her room along the passage and down the stairs to the first floor. Lady Sybil's suite of rooms was almost directly at the top of the stairs.

As Arabella approached, she heard voices in the hall below and looking down saw Her Ladyship coming from the Salon, her arm linked through the Marquis's.

"As you neglected me," she was saying, in a pretty, pouting voice, "I went riding all by myself. I felt very lonely and miserable Julius, and thought it best if I posted back to London, where at least there would be someone to appreciate me!"

"Only this morning you said you did not wish to ride," the Marquis said.

"I changed my mind," Lady Sybil retorted. "A woman's privilege, my dear, but I will be honest and admit I did not enjoy myself without you. Things are only amusing, Julius, when we are together, surely you realise that by now?"

"I think you flatter me, Sybil" the Marquis replied.

"When I have felt incensed with you," Lady Sybil answered in a low voice, "it always makes me love you . . . or should I say desire you . . . the more."

She threw back her head and looked up into his eyes, both her hands still linked through his arms.

Arabella could see very clearly how beautiful she was, with eyebrows black as a raven's wing in flight over her strangely upturned eyes, while her dark hair showed up the perfection of her skin.

"I am sorry if you were upset," the Marquis said, seemingly impervious to the invitation in Lady's Sybil's eyes, "but you know that I must have exercise. You prevented me from riding this morning and this afternoon I must have walked at least three miles. I went as far as the forest on the other side of the cornfields I showed you yesterday."

"Yes, I am sure you did," Lady Sybil said impatiently, obviously disinterested as to where he had been, "but what I want to know Julius, is if you missed me? Were you thinking of me as you walked that long distance? On your return, did you hurry a little quicker because you knew I should be in the Castle waiting for you?"

"If I did, it was a wasted effort," the Marquis said with a smile. "When I arrived back, I was told you were out riding, and what was more, had insisted on taking Pegasus. That's not the horse for you, Sybil."

"I soon discovered that," Lady Sybil replied, "a more tiresome, unbroken beast I have seldom mounted!"

"Now, Sybil, that isn't fair," the Marquis expostulated. "You know as well as I do that you like a very quiet, well-mannered horse. I wouldn't mind betting that you took Pegasus just to annoy me, because I told you on the way here that there were several horses at

101

the Castle that needed schooling and I intended to set myself the task of doing it."

"Really, Julius! How you try to misunderstand me!" Lady Sybil said sharply, taking her arm away.

They were on the verge of quarrelling, Arabella thought with satisfaction, and then as she watched and listened from the top of the stairs, she felt something soft brush her leg. She looked down. It was one of Beulah's kittens which had escaped once again.

She picked it up in her arms, stroking the softness of its fur and, as she did so, knew what she could do.

Carrying the kitten, she slipped into Lady Sybil's bedroom. It was an enormous, impressive room, one of the grandest in the whole of the Castle, with a huge four-poster, carved and gilt, which had been slept in by the Virgin Queen herself.

But Arabella looked only towards the dressing-table, which, as she expected, was littered with creams and lotions of every sort. She had always heard that the ladies of fashion spent a fortune on aids to their complexions: eye-shadow, lip-salve and potions which varied from those made of goose-grease to drops of dew collected from the blossoms of flowers under a full moon.

Lady Sybil's dressing-table might well have groaned under all it carried on its polished surface. Still holding the kitten, Arabella deliberately undid the stoppers on the *flacons* and tipped them over, until there were at least half a dozen different substances mixing together in a little pool on the dressing-table. Then she removed the tops from the pots and laid them sideways. Some creams oozed slowly out, others merely rolled as it were drunkenly from side to side.

Then in the centre of the mess she had created Arabella put down the kitten. She was only just in time for as she did so she could hear someone coming up the stairs. Swiftly she ran across the room, to stand just inside the door as Lady Sybil appeared.

"What are you doing here, little girl?" she asked sharply.

Arabella dropped a curtsy.

"I was looking for Beulah's kitten, My Lady," she answered, thinking as she spoke that it was the second time she had used this excuse.

"Well I am quite certain it isn't in here," Lady Sybil said positively. "If there is one animal I detest, it's a ca . . ."

Before she had finished the word she saw the kitten on her dressing-table and the confusion of pots and bottles all around it. For a moment she opened her mouth and no sound came. Then she screamed in a long, high-pitched note.

As Lady Sybil screamed again and yet again, someone could be heard running up the stairs and Arabella knew it must be the Marquis.

"There's the kitty!" Arabella cried loudly and snatched it from the dressing-table just as Lady Sybil raised her hand to strike the tiny creature to the ground.

Clutching the kitten tightly against her chest Arabella turned to face a harridan with flashing eyes and furiously contorted lips.

"Get that cat out of here!" Lady Sybil screamed. "Look what it has done to my cosmetics! All my precious lotions! It should be destroyed . . . give it to me and I'll twist its neck!"

"What is happening?" a calm voice asked from the doorway.

"Look what this filthy creature has done!" she said, pointing to the dressing-table. "Everyone knows that I will not have cats in my room and yet it finds its way here. I know it belongs to your sister . . . that deformed idiot that you keep in hiding from me. Well, let me tell you that I am going to punish her. I'll beat her for not controlling her cursed pets and permitting them to plague me!"

Arabella was watching the Marquis.

She saw his face pale at Lady Sibil's reference to Beulah, and then a sudden anger made his face grim and stern.

"Be silent!" His voice was low and yet it checked

Lady Sybil's screaming rage more effectively than anything else could have done. Quite suddenly she was silent, staring at him with her mouth open, her beauty seeming to shrivel, her whole appearance becoming coarsened and unattractive.

"I deeply regret," the Marquis said slowly and icily, "the damage that has been done to Your Ladyship's property. You must, of course, allow me to reimburse you for any expenditure you will incur in replacing what has been upset. This, I am certain, you will wish to do immediately. A carriage will be waiting within an hour to carry Your Ladyship to London."

He turned on his heel as he finished speaking and went from the room. Only as he disappeared did Lady Sybil realise what had happened.

"Julius!" she called, "Julius!"

She ran to the door after him but he was already half way down the stairs. She hurried to the top of the staircase.

"Julius, forgive me," she pleaded. "I lost my temper. I should not have spoken of your sister like that. You must believe me!"

Still holding the kitten in her arms Arabella followed Lady Sybil out of the bedroom and onto the landing. The Marquis went on down the stairs at an unhurried pace.

In the Hall he snapped his fingers at the spaniels lying on the hearthrug. In an instant they were at his heels. A footman, seeing his action, handed him his high-crowned hat.

"Julius!" Lady Sybil called once again. "Julius, pray hear me!"

The Marquis did not look back but walked through the front door and Arabella knew that he turned in the direction of the stables. She saw Lady Sybil clench her hands and make a little sound that was half a sob and half a mutter of fury.

Arabella thought it was time for herself also to disappear, and slipping away before Lady Sybil could turn round she ran up the second flight of stairs and returned

Beulah's kitten to the schoolroom. It had done what she had required of it.

With a feeling of satisfaction Arabella knew that in an hour's time Lady Sybil would leave the Castle and the Marquis's life for ever.

Six

THE High-Perch Phaeton moved swiftly down the narrow lanes which rounded the wide acres of the park and led to the farms and outlying fields and forests of the Estate.

The sun was warm and golden. Arabella put her arm round Beulah and thought it was a long time since she had known such happiness.

"Faster . . . faster!" Beulah kept crying and after a while the Marquis looked down with a smile and said:

"If I urge my team to travel much faster, they will grow wings and fly over a hedge."

He was in good humour and Arabella noticed that he was more at ease with Beulah. He no longer looked at his sister with the strange expression on his face that she had observed previously.

The Marquis also did not appear to repine at the loss of Lady Sybil's company. In fact, Arabella was convinced he was relieved that the tempestuous society beauty had left and he could now be alone. She felt he was exploring his home anew and finding it provided him with a fresh interest.

Certainly the Castle had never seen such a use of elbow-grease. The furniture and the floors shone like mirrors. The windows were cleaned and re-cleaned until, when Arabella turned her head and looked back at the great stone building, it appeared as if it were set with sparkling gems.

And yet Arabella knew that although outwardly life at the Castle had been revived with a new zest, there was still a dark and sinister secret lurking beneath the smiling surface, which sooner or later would have to be challenged.

"It is not my problem," she tried to tell herself; but she knew that she was deeply involved and nothing she could do, except to go away, could extricate her from it.

She had thought, not once but a dozen times, that she would tell the Marquis the truth. Then she remembered the expression on Gentleman Jack's face when he had found her in the stable-yard, and she knew the threats he had made to punish the families of the servants, and perhaps even to kill Beulah, were not idle words. He meant them. And unless there were some way of capturing him and all his gang together before any who escaped could revenge themselves, someone was bound to suffer.

"Where are you driving us?" Arabella asked aloud, thinking how handsome the Marquis looked. He handled his horses with a skill that she knew exceeded that of any man she had ever seen before tooling a tandem. He must, she thought, be a Non-pareil.

"We are on our way to visit one of my farms," he replied. "I must admit, Arabella, I had no idea that country life could be so strenuous. These last few days I have done nothing but work. I have interviewed farmers, agents, managers, herdsmen and grooms until my head whirls on my neck. Yet still there is the devil of a lot to be done."

"But you are enjoying it!" Arabella smiled.

"Am I?" he asked. "Why do you think that?"

"Because I am convinced that everyone should have enough to do," Arabella explained. "Gentlemen like to be occupied, and ladies too. When their hands are not engaged they become bored and querulous."

"You are very perceptive for one so young," the Marquis answered, "but you're right. The happiest time of my life was when I was with my Regiment. We were

107

continually on the push and therefore we had no time to worry about anything but keeping ourselves alive!"

"I would like to hear about your adventures in the Army," Arabella said. "If I were a man I would be a soldier, but unfortunately I was born a woman."

She spoke bitterly. The Marquis laughed.

"You won't be regretting that you are a female in two or three years' time," he said. "You will be a beauty, little Arabella. Has anyone told you that before? That white skin, that golden-red hair, will set all the local swells a-twitter."

Arabella was just going to reply hotly that she had no desire to attract any man's interest, when the Marquis's words made her realise that he had no idea of her social status.

"Of course," she told herself, "he was just told that a local girl had come to the Castle to play with Beulah."

He must realise, she thought, that she was educated and that she had the manners and carriage of someone gentle born, but he obviously did not suppose that her parents were of consequence. And that, she reflected, was the best thing that could have happened.

She had been half afraid when the Marquis took her driving that they would encounter someone she knew, perhaps a foxhunting Squire who was acquainted with Sir Lawrence, or some old friend of mother; for her real home, the house where she had lived when her father was alive, was less than twenty-five miles from the Castle.

But as they traversed the park they had met no one. So with a feeling of relief, Arabella bit back the answer she had been about to make and said with a hint of laughter in her voice:

"I am not likely to meet many beaux if I stay at the Castle."

"I suppose it must be lonely here for a child," the Marquis said. When I was young, the Castle was always full of people. Then my mother was alive and she enjoyed entertaining. There were dinner parties, balls, meets of the hounds and, of course, during the Winter parties for the shoots."

"It all sounds very formal," Arabella remarked.

"My mother made everything amusing!" the Marquis went on. "Naturally I did not take part in all the festivities, but there was always something of import for me to do."

"I think there are never less than a dozen tasks waiting for attention in one's own home," Arabella said.

"Indeed, I am beginning to see the truth of that," the Marquis smiled. "But what about my house in London? Who's going to look after that if I stay here too long?"

Do you enjoy London?" Arabella asked.

"I thought I did," the Marquis replied. "It is very gay and there is always something new to engage one's attention."

"What sort of things?" Arabella enquired.

The Marquis laughed.

"You are curious," he said. "I suppose if I were to say racing, gambling, cock-fighting and mills, you would be shocked."

"Indeed I would not," Arabella replied. "I think those are all proper sports for gentlemen."

"And what about balls and theatres, routs and masques, with a lovely lady as a companion?" the Marquis enquired in a teasing voice.

"Do you enjoy that?" Arabella asked scornfully.

"Of course," he answered. "The ladies of St. James's are very attractive, Arabella."

"Like Lady Sybil?" Arabella asked. It was a slightly spiteful question but she could not help it.

"Yes, like Lady Sybil," the Marquis replied. "Did you admire her?"

"She hit her horse over the head with her riding-whip," Arabella declared. "I only wish I could have hit her!"

The Marquis glanced down.

"You are obviously dangerous when you are

109

aroused," he chuckled. Then a thought struck him. "Arabella, tell me the truth! Did you deliberately put that cat in Lady Sybil's room?"

The question was unexpected and Arabella felt the blood rising in her cheeks. She did not answer.

"Answer me, Arabella!" It was a command.

Still Arabella did not reply. The Marquis took one hand from the reins and reaching across Beulah, took hold of Arabella's shoulder to turn her round to face him.

"Do not touch me!" She spoke sharply but instinctively, forgetting for a moment that it was not the kind of remark a child would make, and saw the surprise on his face.

The Marquis drew the horses to a standstill. He turned in his seat to look at Arabella. She had taken off her hat and her hair half fell over her face. He could see her small, straight nose etched against the sky, and her mouth set in a hard line.

For a moment the Marquis said nothing. He was thinking how lovely this strange child was. At the same time, he was determined to know the truth.

"I am waiting, Arabella," he said sternly.

"Go on . . ." Beulah cried. "Horses go . . . on! Fast again . . . fast!"

"No, the horses have to wait," the Marquis said, "until Arabella gives me an answer."

"We cannot sit here all night," Arabella said defiantly, breaking the silence.

"I am quite prepared to do that," the Marquis replied. "I always get my own way. I want to know the truth, Arabella!"

She turned her face round to look into his eyes.

"Very well," she said angrily, "you shall know the truth. She hit your horse. I saw her do it from the window. She had ridden him deliberately to annoy you, and, because she was no rider and the animal knew it, he played her up. When she dismounted she hit him cruelly and unnecessarily. He was just fresh—mostly,

110

I imagine, owning to lack of exercise because you were not here."

The Marquis watched Arabella's flashing eyes and animated little face.

"That is certainly a straight left," he said quietly when she finished. "Thank you, Arabella, for answering me frankly. But could you contrive in future to allow me to rid myself of my own guests, without resorting to such drastic methods?"

"Would you have told her to go?" Arabella asked shrewdly. "I think Her Ladyship was determined to stay."

"You are the most unusual and precocious child I have ever met in my whole life," the Marquis exclaimed. "I don't know whether to laugh at you or to spank you."

"Go on . . . go on!" Beulah said.

"I think perhaps the question has been decided," the Marquis said. "Very well, Beulah, we will proceed. But your friend Arabella has certainly given me something to think about!"

Arabella did not answer and they drove for some way in silence. Then she realised they were passing the little lake where she had bathed the day the Marquis had arrived. He looked towards it and said with a hint of laughter in his voice.

"Do you feel like a swim?"

Beulah caught the word.

'Ara-bella, swim," she cried with glee. "Beulah . . . paddle."

"Would you like to stop?" the Marquis enquired of Arabella. A blush suffused her pale skin as she shook her head.

"No . . . no . . ." she murmured and heard him chuckle.

Already her anger was evaporating and she was feeling shy and embarrassed. Perhaps it would have been wiser to lie, as she had lied to her stepfather.

She had the feeling that, if she had denied that she had placed the kitten in Lady Sybil's bedroom, the

Marquis would have believed her. But somehow it had been impossible not to tell him the truth.

They drove on and shortly they saw a big, straggling farmstead with its barns and byres, and in the fields around it a herd of golden-skinned cattle.

"This is Eastcote's Farm," the Marquis said. "I always believed he was one of the best farmers on the Estate, but now he has told me that he wishes to hand in his notice. I can't understand it."

He drove with a flourish into the farm-yard, and the farmer, a big, burly man, came hurrying out.

"Good afternoon, Milord. I wasn't expecting you to come to me, I thought you would want me up at the Castle."

"I have to see for myself what is wrong," the Marquis replied.

"If you'll come into the house, Milord," the farmer suggested, "the Missus would be glad to offer you a glass of cool ale."

"Just what I would like!" the Marquis approved. "Come along, children!"

He jumped down from the Phaeton as the groom, who had been sitting at the back, ran to the head of the leading horse. The Marquis took Beulah in his arms, lifted her down and put her safely on the ground. Then he turned towards Arabella. For a moment she hesitated, standing on the box looking down at him.

"I know you have a dislike of being touched," the Marquis said with a smile, "but if you slip you'll ruin that pretty dress in the mud."

Without speaking Arabella moved forward and he lifted her very gently from the Phaeton. Just for a moment she was close against him, but instead of the revulsion she expected, something she had always felt in close proximity with her stepfather, she felt instead a sense of security and safety. It was almost as if she need no longer go on feeling afraid. Then he set her on the ground, and she felt she must have imagined it.

They walked into the big farmhouse. Beulah and Arabella were provided with glasses of milk, fresh

112

from the cow; the Marquis was proffered a long glass of cooled home-brewed ale

The ceilings were low and rested on rafters of dark, mellow oak, beams from ancient ships. There was a delightful smell of fresh baked bread. Mrs. Eastcote, a fat, bustling woman with rosy cheeks and a smile which embraced them all in a motherly fashion, welcomed them to her parlour.

" 'Tis a real pleasure to see you again, Milord," she said. "It seems a long time since you used to come here as a small boy."

"When I had been riding hard, you would give me a slice from one of your big pork pies," the Marquis said. "Do you still bake them?"

"Indeed I do, Milord. There's one I cooked but yesterday. Would you care for a bite?"

"I couldn't refuse such a generous offer," the Marquis replied.

"And I've something nice for the young ladies, as well," Mrs. Eastcote said, hurrying towards the kitchen.

The Marquis sat down in one of the high-winged chairs which stood in front of the open hearth.

"Now, Eastcote," he said to the farmer, "what's wrong?"

The elder man's eyes shifted a little.

"I be wanting a change, Milord."

"That's nonsense, and you know it," the Marquis retorted. "Your family has lived in this farmhouse for three generations. I remember your father, and my father often used to talk of your grandfather and say what a splendid farmer he was."

"I'm sorry, Milord, but I've made my decision," Eastcote said.

There was a sound outside the window. Arabella, who was sitting on the low, wooden window-seat, glanced through the diamond-shaped panes. She saw three children, or rather, one who was almost fully grown, a pretty girl of about sixteen, buxom and well built, holding by the hand a child of about seven. Following them at a distance was a small boy, perhaps

113

a year or two years younger. There was no mistaking his resemblance to his father.

"Listen, Eastcote," the Marquis said. "I know you've been through a bad time. I have already gathered that Sheltham was not a good agent, or rather that when he grew ill he grew lax. If you have grievances, I will put them right. I shall be at the Castle a great deal in the future. I ought to have come home before but I had reasons for not doing so."

"You've been frank with me, Milord," Eastcote said, "I'd like to be frank with you. But I can't and that's a fact. So I've got to go."

The Marquis stared at him in perplexity. At that moment Mrs. Eastcote came back into the room, her tray laden with food. There was a large pork pie, its crust golden-brown, crip and inviting, a rich fruit-cake, and a freshly baked loaf of bread whose fragrance seemed to scent the room. Besides these the tray contained golden butter and a pot of home-made strawberry jam, labelled in an uneducated hand.

A snowy cloth was spread on the table and then the plates and cutlery were laid swiftly.

"Jam!" Beulah exclaimed. "Beulah wants . . . jam!"

"Say 'please'," Arabella corrected almost automatically.

"Please . . ." Beulah said, "Jam, lots . . . of . . . jam."

Mrs. Eastcote smiled.

"And you shall have it, my pet. It's just what my own little ones like—bread fresh from the oven and strawberries from our own garden last summer. Although I says it myself, the jam has kept beautiful. 'Twill soon be time for me to start again. Perhaps Her Ladyship'ld like a jar to take back to the Castle?"

"I am sure she would," Arabella replied.

"And what about you, my dear?" Mrs. Eastcote asked. "What will you have?"

"Might I have a small piece of bread and butter?" Arabella asked. "It is not long since I had luncheon."

"You look as though you could put away another

114

meal and not notice it," Mrs Eastcote smiled. "It's too thin you are, Miss."

As she busied herself buttering the bread, the Marquis rose from beside the fireplace and came to sit at the table.

"Now Mrs. Eastcote," he said. Perhaps I can talk sense to you. Why should you want to leave this farm?"

"We don't, Milord, and that's the Gospel truth," Mrs. Eastcote said hastily, "but we've got to go. There's nothing else we can do! Not with the children . . . and Marlene growing up and all."

"I don't understand," the Marquis protested.

"No, Milord, I don't think you do," Mrs. Eastcote said, "and we're not the ones to tell you. Not isolated here, as we are."

"Now, Mother," the farmer interposed, "guard your words, woman! For the love of Jesus, guard your words!"

"I am guarding them! You know I am!" Mrs. Eastcote replied passionately, "but 'is Lordship is right, it'll break my heart to leave what has always been our home, and a good home at that! But what else can we do?"

The farmer's wife burst into tears as she spoke, and picking up her apron mopped her eyes and went from the room.

"What is going on?" the Marquis demanded.

"You will forgive me, Milord, for what may seem an impertinence," Eastcote said heavily, "but we can say no more, either of us. Indeed, we have said too much. My notice stands, Milord, for next quarter-day. You'll find everything in order . . ."

It seemed as though there were a catch in the gruff voice, and then, without saying more, the man left the room as his wife had done.

The Marquis stared after him.

"What in God's Name does this mean?" he asked.

This was the moment, Arabella thought, when she should tell him the truth, and yet the voices of the children outside seemed to stifle the words as they came to her lips. How could she speak? Perhaps Gentleman Jack would find out that it was the Eastcotes who made the Marquis suspicious and he would take his terrible revenge on Marlene and her little brother and sister.

Perhaps there was more to it than just fear of the children being killed. Marlene was growing up, she was a pretty girl and highwaymen were notorious for their behaviour towards local women. Arabella had over-heard unpleasant stories whispered by the servants when she had lived at home.

"I've got to discover what is at the bottom of this," the Marquis muttered as if he were speaking to him-self. "I'll make them tell me!"

"Do not press them," Arabella said quickly, without thinking.

The Marquis looked at her in astonishment.

"What do you know about it?" he asked.

"Nothing," Arabella said. "But you can see they are frightened. They are frightened of something or some-body and the mere fact of telling you what frightens them might bring some terrible retribution upon them."

"I cannot imagine what you are trying to say," the Marquis expostulated.

"It is difficult for me to put into words what I feel," Arabella said slowly, choosing her words with care, "but I do know that you might do immeasurable harm if you force that man to speak to you on a matter about which he is convinced he must keep silent."

"But it's incomprehensible!" the Marquis protested. "They like the farm, they have always been happy here. You saw that Mrs. Eastcote was in tears at the idea of leaving, and I want them to stay! It's not the rent! I've already sent a letter to everyone on the Estate to tell them that they needn't pay any rent for a year while they make repairs that should have been done long ago. I have also offered to help with any heavy expen-diture, new ploughs, cattle or horses. What more can I do?"

"That is indeed generous of you," Arabella said. "I

116

know most of the farmers round here are sadly in need of help. They did well during the War, but now Parliament is making it hard for them to sell their grain."

"I remember my father saying that it's always the same," the Marquis interrupted. "Governments pet and cosset the farmers during a war and starve them in time of peace. But that doesn't explain the Eastcotes' attitude. Why can't they tell me what is wrong?"

"Do not press them," Arabella begged again.

The Marquis pushed back his chair, his pork pie untouched.

"You may be right," he said, "but I am determined to find out what this mystery is."

He spoke with a determination which made Arabella suddenly afraid. What could one man do against this horror which was gripping the whole neighbourhood? She could see all too clearly how Gentleman Jack and his gang had gained a grip over the whole countryside. It was quite easy to do if they were sufficiently unscrupulous. They must often need shelter in the outlying farms, a place to hide in when the pace got too hot. And what farmer was likely to refuse a party of armed and determined men who would threaten to kill his children, were the request for concealment refused?

"There must be a way out," Arabella thought desperately to herself. She could not see what she could do, although it seemed to her as they drove back to the Castle that she explored every avenue of escape from this terrible tangle.

The Marquis was silent too, deep in his own thoughts, and only Beulah, quite indefatigable, went on calling for greater speed, till finally she became sleepy and, leaning against Arabella, closed her eyes.

"Who would be likely to enlighten me?" the Marquis asked. "You come from this part of the world; you must have an idea what is at the back of all this flapdoodle!"

"I cannot think of anyone," Arabella replied. "Perhaps it would be best for you to return to London."

"Why should I do that?" the Marquis demanded.

Arabella picked her words.

"I conjecture," she said, "that people are frightened to speak out because somebody is threatening them. Maybe, if you were away, and the information could not be traced to them, they could send you word of what was afoot."

It was hard to formulate the idea that had only just occurred to her, and the Marquis pounced on one word.

"People!" he demanded. "What do you mean by people? Do you mean to imply that the Eastcotes are not the only family involved in this?"

"I do not know," Arabella said hastily.

"I am persuaded that you know more than you are telling me," the Marquis said.

Arabella shook her head, but she thought to herself, "He's not easily deceived! I must be more careful!"

They reached the Castle. Beulah woke and the Marquis lifted her down. Then he looked up at Arabella, waiting on the high box.

"Still want to do it all yourself?" he asked, in the teasing tone that a man would use to a child.

"No, you may assist me," Arabella consented, almost as though she were conferring a favour upon him.

"I am honoured!" he said sarcastically, then took her in his arms.

She had expected him to put her down on the ground, but instead he held her and looked down at her tiny, pointed face and her red hair against his shoulder.

"Is this so bad?" he enquired. "Why, you are as light as a piece of thistledown. I could carry you to the highest turret and not take an extra breath on the way."

"Put me down," Arabella commanded in a low voice.

"Why do you hate being touched?" the Marquis asked.

"Put me down," Arabella persisted.

"Has somebody hurt you?" he asked. "You're such a little thing. A man who would be cruel to you would be the type that would want to pull the wings from a butterfly."

Still holding her in his arms, the Marquis walked up the steps and into the Great Hall. Beulah was already being carried up the stairs in the arms of George. She was trying to tell him how fast they had driven.

The Marquis glanced up at them and then looked down again at Arabella.

"Shall I carry you," he said, "or are you old enough to walk?"

He was teasing, but Arabella became suddenly speechless. She had the strange, unaccountable feeling that she would not mind him carrying her up the stairs, that once again in his arms she was safe from all the troubled fears which lay in and around the Castle.

Then, almost against her conscious volition, she struggled as he held her. It was not against him personally that she fought but against men in general—men whom she both hated and feared.

She was like a song bird struggling in a net, the Marquis thought, and instantly he set her down on the lowest step of the Grand Staircase.

"You're a little monkey!" he said. "I don't know what to make of you. I should, indeed, be extremely angry at your behaviour towards Lady Sybil and I am convinced that you know more about the Eastcotes and their determination to leave than you are willing to tell me. But, though I'll wait now, remember, Arabella, I am very persistent when I want to know something—and I am determined to solve this mystery!"

As his voice rang out, with a sudden sense of shock Arabella remembered they were back in the Castle and someone might be listening. Someone who might report to Gentleman Jack what the Marquis was saying. And then who would be blamed?

With a little incoherent exclamation she turned and ran up the stairs, leaving the Marquis looking after her with an expression of surprise on his handsome face.

When Arabella reached her own room, she put her hands to her temples. Supposing, just supposing there was someone in the Castle who reported what had been said to Gentleman Jack. It would not be Miss Harrison, who was too lazy to leave her room, but it might be one of the footmen or perhaps a housemaid. There were so many of them, and not only those who had been there before the Marquis's return could be in Gentleman Jack's power, but also those who had recently been engaged from the village.

If the Eastcotes, whose farm was some miles away, were afraid of the highwayman, what about those who lived at the very gates of the Castle? This was a tangle to which Arabella could see no solution; yet she knew that, sooner or later, as the Marquis had assumed, something would have to be done.

Arabella washed her face and hands, tidied her hair and went to the schoolroom. Miss Harrison was just coming from the bedroom after her afternoon nap.

"Did you have a nice drive, children?" she asked.

"Fast . . . drive very . . . fast!" Beulah said.

Miss Harrison yawned. She was obviously not interested in what they had done.

"Ring the bell for tea," she commanded Arabella, who did as she was told.

The bell had hardly rung before Miss Fellows came bustling in.

"Oh, you're awake, Miss Harrison," she exclaimed. "I've some news that I know will interest you."

"What's that?" Miss Harrison enquired.

"A groom arrived an hour ago with a message from His Lordship," Miss Fellows replied. "We're to have the Lord Chief Justice as a guest tonight. He is on his way back to London from Wiltshire, and he sent one of his outriders ahead to ask permission to stay at the Castle."

"Good gracious! We seem to be in a continual bustle of hospitality," Miss Harrison exclaimed and she did not seem pleased at the prospect. "First the Marquis and his paramour, now this new gentleman!"

"The Lord Chief Justice always came here in the old days," Miss Fellows said, "though he hasn't, of course, been these last few years. 'Tis strange he should know His Lordship was here!"

"I suppose news gets around," Miss Harrison said laconically.

"Well, Mister Turner's delighted, at any rate," Miss Fellows snapped. "It gives him a chance to show off his silver. I've prepared the West Room—Miss Matherson's orders of course! Trust her to interfere! Without even waiting for His Lordship to return from his drive, she sent the outrider back immediately to say there was a welcome for the Lord Chief Justice at any time."

"The things she takes upon herself!" Miss Harrison cried. "I only hope the Marquis will be annoyed at her presumption."

"He won't be," Miss Fellows said in a disappointed tone. "He thinks that everything 'dear Matty' does is perfect."

"Oh, well. I hope other people are going to be as pleased," Miss Harrison said. There was a meaning in her voice that Arabella could not help understanding.

"You'll have to tell him, won't you?" Miss Fellows said almost in a whisper.

"I'll tell him all right!" Miss Harrison promised. "I've a feeling that he might be here tonight."

They were speaking so quietly that Arabella could only just hear what was said. She was sitting on the floor, looking in the toy-cupboard for some bricks that Beulah liked to build, one on top of another.

"Well, I must get back. I thought you'd want to know," she heard Miss Fellows say.

"Thank you," Miss Harrison replied and the head housemaid hustled out of the room.

So, Gentleman Jack was likely to come tonight, Arabella thought. Could this be the moment when she should tell the Marquis what was going on? But supposing she did so, what would the Marquis do?

She had a feeling that he would challenge the highwayman. She could almost see the two men meet, both of them holding pistols in their hands.

Then she remembered all the things that had been said about the highwaymen: that they were deadly

121

shots, that they killed anyone who was foolish enough to fire at them when they were holding up a coach.

She had known one of the men who had died in such a manner. He had been a friend of her father's, a man who rode hard to hounds, a strong man, a man who, doubtless, knew how to handle a gun. But he had received a bullet in the throat and the highwaymen had got away with everything he carried with him. His wife, stripped of her jewellery, had collapsed by the roadside, crying bitterly, until someone passing had taken her back to her home.

Arabella remembered all the talk there had been about it. There had even been a search for the highwaymen, but they had not been found. Was it likely, she thought now, that they would think to search the Castle for these cut-throats?

And yet she thought too how stupid the County Justices had been not to realise that Gentleman Jack would wish to lie in comfort. He had received his nickname because he was always so elegantly dressed and and because those who had heard him speak had vowed that he was, indeed, a gentleman, or at least that he spoke like one.

"They swear he hasn't the trace of an accent. He's handsome, elegant, with the most polished manners," she could remember her father saying to her mother. "He might even be one of our friends, darling. It could be a convenient way of paying one's debts."

"You would never be ruthless enough," Arabella's mother had laughed. "You know as well as I do that if anyone tells you a hard luck story, or a woman has even the suspicion of a tear in her eye, you empty your pockets for them. No, my Love, I don't believe you would make a good highwayman."

"The only thing I have ever wanted to steal," Arabella's father answered, "was you, my darling, and that I succeeded in doing very effectively. You could have married someone much richer and more important than me!"

"I married the man I loved!" his wife answered. "What woman could ask more?"

Arabella gave a little shiver. She could hardly bear these memories of the past when she remembered that her father was dead and her mother had put Sir Lawrence in his place.

If Gentleman Jack had shot down Sir Lawrence, she might even have been pleased. But Sir Lawrence had been too crafty, he had handed over everything that was asked of him without making even the pretence of a fight. He knew, only too well, how deadly Gentleman Jack could be with his pistol.

And now the Lord Chief Justice was coming to the Castle. Was this the moment when she could speak? After all, His Lordship was the one person who could bring real pressure to bear on the authorities, so that the scourge of the highwaymen could be swept away from the countryside and people like the Eastcotes could live in peace.

"I must think what to do," Arabella told herself. "I must do something."

Without realising it, she had built the bricks she had taken from the cupboard for Beulah into a high castle in front of her.

"Arabella, put away those toys and come and have your tea," Miss Harrison said sharply. "You're too old to be playing about. You should know what you have to do by now without being told."

The sentence seemed almost prophetic as Arabella rose from the corner of the room and walked towards the tea-table.

Seven

LATER that evening Arabella went to her bedchamber. A footman had brought a note from her mother while she was at supper in the schoolroom. She had not opened it in front of Miss Harrison but waited until she was alone.

Now she was impatient to see what her mother had to relate, and she tore it open eagerly. At a first glance the letter was disappointingly short. Her mother's neat, elegant handwriting was easy to decipher, and Arabella read it quickly:

My Dearest—It seems very Empty and Quiet here without you, but I am Praying that you are Happy at the Castle, and not desirous of returning. Your Stepfather was exceedingly incensed that you had left without his Permission, and it would be most unwise to encounter him before his Anger is Abated. Even so I am afraid he will insist on Punishing you most Severely. I have heard that your Father's Sister is in ill health so I cannot request her to Accommodate you. Make every effort, my Love, to be content with your present Environment. At the moment I can suggest no other Place where you could Sojourn. That God may bless you, Dearest Arabella, is the Sincerest hope of your most distracted but loving

Mother.

Arabella read the letter through twice, then she shut her eyes to stop the tears. So she dare not return home, and there appeared to be no other haven where she could escape from her stepfather.

She knew what Sir Lawrence's anger entailed, she knew how she would be forced to cringe beneath the lash of his whip, and he would continue to beat her until she pleaded for mercy. Once she had defied him and stifled her cries, until she fell unconscious at his feet. Afterwards she knew that with his superior strength it was only a question of time before she must capitulate and humble herself as he wished her to do.

But even while she pleaded with him, he knew she was still undefeated. She would defy him again as soon as she was strong enough to do so. She would go on fighting him so long as she lived and breathed.

With a little sob Arabella brushed aside her tears. Sir Lawrence might exclude her from her home, his brutality might separate her from her mother, but she would still carry her head high and continue to hate him.

"He will never break me!" she swore beneath her breath.

Resolutely she put her mother's letter away in a drawer of the dressing-table, and set about changing her gown.

She had made up her mind that when the Marquis and the Lord Chief Justice had finished dinner, she would go downstairs and tell them the truth. She felt that the present situation could continue no longer. The Marquis must be informed of what was happening in the Castle; and, once he knew, who better to advise him than the Lord Chief Justice?

Among the clothes her mother's lady's-maid had packed was a dress that Arabella had worn for parties when she was eleven, nearly seven years ago. Yet seeing it hanging in the wardrobe, she thought how pretty it was and hoped it would still fit her.

She remembered it being made, and how the expres-

125

sions of admiration she had received when she wore it had been repeated to her father.

"Everyone said Arabella looked lovely!" she could hear her mother saying proudly.

"So I am going to have an "Incomparable" for a daughter, am I?" her father had asked with a smile. "Well, the ladies of St. James's will have to look to their laurels in a few years' time!"

Arabella wondered what her father would say if he could see her now and know that, far from winning compliments from the *beau ton,* she was now embroiled in the machinations of a murderous gang of highwaymen.

She gave a little sigh. At times she missed her father unbearably, and she could not help feeling that in some ways the Marquis resembled him. They both had fine-cut features, both carried themselves with an easy elegance which prevented their appearing foppish while they were obviously dressed in the Tulip of Fashion. There was also a kindliness about them both which she had known, from the first moment she had set eyes on him, was not a characteristic of Sir Lawrence Deane.

Then she remembered that she hated all men, and the Marquis was very much a man. Yet Arabella conceded, with a little twist of her lips, that she had no desire to spend the whole of her life with women if they were the type either of Lady Sybil or of Miss Harrison.

"Perhaps I should have chosen to be a nun," she thought nonsensically. Then regarding her reflection in the mirror she knew she had no real desire to renounce the world or to dedicate herself to a life of poverty.

She felt a sudden surge of excitement, a thrill of adventure! There might be difficulties, dangers and even terror which must be faced, but there must be a way for brains and intelligence to defeat brute force. If there was, she would find it!

The dress she had chosen, with its inset lace and blue ribbon sash, was very tight; but she managed to button it at the back and knew that it made her look exactly the age she pretended to be.

She parted her hair in the centre, brushed it until it shone and fell over her shoulders in soft waves of fiery gold. Attached to the dress she found the hair-ribbon with which her mother, when she was eleven, had tied back her unruly locks. As a last concession to vanity, she tied a bow now at the back of her head and thought the contrast of the blue ribbon against her hair was extremely becoming.

When she was dressed she still had a long time to wait; for she knew the gentlemen would linger in the dining-room over their port. Finally, when she was certain they must have repaired to the Library, Arabella picked up one of the books she had been reading and tiptoed down the corridor to the Grand Staircase.

The tapers were alight in the silver sconces and the big cut-crystal chandeliers. There was a bowl of lilac on the console table at the bottom of the stairs and the fireplace, not in use because it was almost Summer, was filled with a fragrant display of carnations, lilies and azaleas from the hothouses.

The whole place looked very different from when Arabella had first arrived.

She stood at the top of the staircase and listened. The doors were thick but she was convinced that she could hear voices from the Library, and she was sure of it as she descended the stairs.

George was on duty in the hall and he gave her a cheerful grin, but being on his best behaviour these days he did not joke with her as he would certainly have done a week ago.

Demurely Arabella walked to the Library door. Now she could hear the Marquis. He was talking exceptionally loudly and she guessed that the Lord Chief Justice was deaf. She opened the door and walked into the room, closing it behind her.

As always, she felt a little thrill of delight at the beauty of the Library with its enormous wealth of books. Then she walked forward towards the two men who were sitting by the hearth.

It was a second or so before the Marquis saw her. When he did, his eyes seemed to light up, and she knew from his expression that her interruption had relieved him from what was obviously an evening of boredom.

"Arabella!" he exclaimed. "I was not expecting to see you at this hour."

"I must apologise, My Lord, for my intrusion," Arabella said softly as she curtsied. "I thought you would be in the Salon. I came to exchange a book for another."

"Let me introduce you to His Lordship," the Marquis suggested, and rising he took Arabella by the hand and led her forward to where, on the other side of the fireplace, the Lord Chief Justice was sitting.

Arabella, taking one look at him, felt all the plans she had made fall to pieces and lie in shattered fragments around her feet.

"It would be impossible," she told herself, "to explain to this very old man the intricate, tangled situation that exists in the Castle."

She had imagined the Lord Chief Justice would be tall and distinguished. Old, perhaps, but full of the wisdom engendered by his profession.

The man she saw sitting in the wing-backed chair was small and wizened; his hands resting on an ivory-handled walking-stick were almost those of a skeleton. His eyes-sight was failing; for he peered at Arabella as the Marquis introduced her, lowering his wrinkled old eye-lids as if it were difficult for him to focus his sight.

"This is Arabella, My Lord," the Marquis said in a loud voice, which seemed to echo round the room. "She is my guest."

"Annabella, did you say?" the Lord Chief Justice asked in a wheezy voice.

"No, Arabella, My Lord."

"A pretty child, a very pretty child," the Lord Chief Justice approved. "Is this your sister?"

"No, My Lord," the Marquis explained. "My sister
128

is er . . . younger and it is too late for her to come downstairs."

"Younger, you say . . . and this little girl . . .?"

"Is Arabella, My Lord."

"A very pretty child."

His Lordship was obviously not very interested. Arabella gave a little sigh.

"May I change my book?" she enquired of the Marquis.

"Of course," he answered. "Let me see what has interested you."

He took the book from her and she realised that, without thinking, she had brought with her a book in Latin. Just for a moment she felt anxious lest he should suspect from her reading that she was older than she seemed. But the Marquis merely looked at the book and laughed.

"You must have chosen this in a hurry," he said, "for it will certainly be of little use to you!"

"No, of course not, My Lord," Arabella agreed. "That is why I have brought it back."

"You will find the books I used to enjoy on the third shelf in the corner by the window," he said.

Arabella dropped a little curtsy.

"Thank you, My Lord."

"I will show you where it is," he said and she felt he was making an excuse to get away from the Lord Chief Justice.

They walked the length of the Library together.

"This is the shelf," the Marquis showed her. "I doubt if anyone has removed a book from it since I was last here."

He started to run his fingers along the titles.

"This I enjoyed enormously," he said with relish, taking down one volume, then taking out another and turning over the pages to find an illustration.

"This used to make me laugh!"

"It is well drawn," Arabella commented.

"What do you best enjoy reading?" the Marquis asked.

"I enjoy anything and everything!" Arabella exclaimed. "When one has been starved of reading, this Library seems the most wonderful place in the world."

Gently she touched the books in front of her, her eyes alight with the joy of knowing that no one would forbid her to read them.

Suddenly she was aware that the Marquis was no longer looking at the books but at her. She felt his eyes taking in her appearance, and candlelight on her hair, her eyes wide and full of happiness, her mouth curved in a happy smile.

"What a strange child you are," he said, almost as if he spoke to himself. "Somehow I find myself continually wondering what you are thinking. What do you think about, Arabella, in that little head of yours?"

Just for a moment Arabella hesitated. Should she tell him now? she thought. Then she bit back the words as they came to her lips.

She was not sure of him. How would he behave when he knew the truth? She had a feeling he would be ridiculously and unnecessarily brave. He would want to attack the highwaymen, perhaps to capture Gentleman Jack single-handed. In which case, Arabella knew all too clearly, he would be shot down and killed without mercy.

What good would that do? How would that help anyone in the Castle, the tenants on the Estate like the Eastcotes who trembled beneath the power of Gentleman Jack?

"You were about to say something," the Marquis prompted.

"Not now," Arabella answered. "Your Lordship should return to your guest."

The Marquis gave her almost a boyish grin.

"It's as hard as riding over newly ploughed land," he complained, and Arabella laughed.

"I did not think he would be so old," she whispered.

"You need not whisper," the Marquis replied in his ordinary tone, his eyes twinkling, "His Lordship was

130

unable to hear a word of my most interesting discourse across the dining-room table!"

"But is he not too aged to be Lord Chief Justice?" Arabella enquired.

"He retires at the end of the year," the Marquis replied. "Old men always cling on to office. They enjoy power and hate to relinquish it to a younger chap who, in this case, will be at least sixty years old!"

The way he spoke made Arabella laugh again.

"You haven't yet chosen a book," the Marquis reminded her. "Take this one!"

He held it out to her. She glanced at it and shook her head.

"I have already read it."

"Have you really?" he enquired. "I read that in my last half at Eton. You must be very precocious, or are you that terrifying thing . . . a female with a brain-box?"

"Is it so terrifying?" Arabella asked. "Do you really prefer women who simper behind their fans, or cast sheep's eyes at you because you are a man?"

She spoke without thinking, and only as the Marquis threw back his head and roared with laughter did she realise that her words must seem curiously out of character coming from a young child.

"I must go now," she said quickly, and taking another book without even looking at its title she dropped the Marquis a hasty little curtsy and turned towards the door.

"No, wait, Arabella!" he said. "Please do not leave yet. Stay here and make me laugh. I am insatiably curious to know more of your opinions."

"I should be in bed by now," Arabella replied. "Miss Harrison would be extremely vexed if she knew I were downstairs."

"Do not fret over Miss Harrison, I will placate her," the Marquis promised. "Besides, I have a suspicion that you did not trouble to inform her where you were going."

Arabella smiled at him, she could not help it. She

131

liked the way his eyes creased at the corners when he was amused. He might be dissolute and careless with his possessions, but it had to be admitted that he was, at the same time, a very prepossessing young gentleman.

"So you are playing truant," the Marquis said with mock severity. "However, instead of admonishing you, as I feel I should do, I will tomorrow show you a secret passage of which nobody is aware of but myself."

"A secret passage!" Arabella cried. She could not help being intrigued.

"Yes, indeed," the Marquis replied, "there are, as it happens, two or three in the Castle. But one which excited me most was that which leads from the nursery down to the first floor. It isn't a particularly important secret staircase. There is a far better one in the East Wing which leads from one of the turrets down to the cellar. But everyone has knowledge of that one. The nursery passage concerned me so intimately because it meant that I could escape from the surveillance of my nanny, and later of my tutors, when they thought I was fast asleep in bed."

"In which room is it concealed?" Arabella wanted to know.

"I am not going to tell you that now!" the Marquis demurred. "I will show it to you and then you must promise me not to tell anyone else! I discovered it quite by chance when I had been shut in my room as a punishment. After that, I used to hope that any bad behaviour on my part would receive the same penalty."

"So the punishment was no punishment!" Arabella smiled.

"Exactly!" the Marquis admitted. "With the result, you see, that having never been properly punished, I have grown up into an inveterate and unrepentant sinner."

He was joking, but Arabella longed to say that without meaning to he had spoken the truth. Yet she could not despise this gay, smiling young man as she felt she should.

"I can see myself now," the Marquis went on, following his own train of thought, "creeping down the narrow stairs and finding my way to the first floor, and from there down the back stairs to the garden. I must have escaped in such a manner dozens and dozens of times, yet I was never caught."

"And now you will reveal your secret to me," Arabella said softly.

"Tomorrow!" the Marquis promised.

"That is very gracious of you. Good night, My Lord."

Arabella would have left, but to her consternation the Marquis reached out his arms and picked her up, so that her face was level with his.

"Aren't you going to kiss me goodnight?" he enquired.

"No! Of course not!" Arabella said sharply and added in a sudden panic:

"Put me down, please put me down!"

There was an urgency in her voice that surprised the Marquis, and for a moment he stared at her, his deep blue eyes looking into hers. She felt as though she could not look away.

"You are frightened!" he exclaimed. "Why, you funny little thing! Why are you afraid?"

He put her down very gently and stood looking down at her, a troubled expression on his handsome face.

"Something or someone has hurt you, Arabella," he said quietly. "No child should look as you looked then! Tell me, what is wrong?"

"I hate being touched," Arabella replied defensively.

"By me?" the Marquis enquired, "or by anyone?"

"By any man!" Arabella replied. "They are all beasts! Ruthless and cruel . . . and I hate them! Yes, I hate men!"

She spoke wildly, feeling Sir Lawrence's whip lashing her again and again until she was half unconscious, and then feeling him draw her to him, kissing her, fondling her . . . as she writhed and squirmed to be free while knowing herself utterly in his power!

133

"Arabella!"

The darkness of her memories seemed to vanish at the sound of the Marquis's voice. Quite suddenly she realised that she had spat out her feelings without really considering her words.

He was staring at her in utter astonishment, his eyes perturbed and anxious. He sat down in a chair so that he no longer towered above her. His hands were by his side, but she felt as though he reached out to pull her towards him.

She wanted to turn and run; yet somehow she could not leave.

"Arabella! Who can have done this to you?" he asked again. "What man can have hurt you so that you see each one you meet as a potential enemy? I am a man, but I am also your friend, Arabella. I want to help you."

For a moment, Arabella shut her eyes as though she would shut out the persuasion and the kindness on his face.

"I am sorry, My Lord," she said in a very different tone. "I should not have spoken like that."

"You have every right to speak as you wish," he answered. "I only detest whatever has made it necessary. What has occurred to make you speak in such a manner? Hear me, Arabella, some men are beasts but not all. Most men believe that a woman stands for everything that is beautiful and noble in their lives."

Arabella wondered at the tenderness in his voice.

"I wish my mother were alive to talk to you," the Marquis continued. "She would have understood what was wrong. Perhaps I, as a man, cannot solve your problems. But let me promise you one thing. If anyone should hurt you in word or deed, I will deal with them. I would kill any man, rather than see that expression of fear on your face again! Do you believe me, Arabella?"

Almost against her conscious volition, Arabella found herself looking once again into his eyes. It was as if something magnetic passed between them, something that seemed to awaken a little flicker within her heart, something which made her catch her breath.

For a moment everything was very still. They neither of them moved. And then with a little sound that was almost a sob, Arabella turned and ran.

She crossed the Library on flying feet, opened the door and ran across the hall and up the stairs, without looking back. She half fancied she heard the Marquis call her name, but she could not be sure. She knew she must escape. Only when she was in her own bed-chamber, with the door shut, did she realise that her cheeks were burning and her heart thumping in the most unaccountable manner.

She threw herself down on the bed and tried to think; but all she could remember was the gentleness of the Marquis's voice and the expression in his eyes. Then, after a long time, Arabella recalled she had not done what she had set out to do.

And yet, what good would it have done to have spoken to the Marquis of the highwaymen, and what protection could that deaf old man, even though he be Lord Chief Justice, offer against six armed and desperate men who would fight like cornered rats for their freedom?

They would have to get help from London, Arabella thought; but she knew that to try to make explanations to the Lord Chief Justice would be hopeless. He was too deaf and too old.

She rose from her bed and undressed slowly. She must have taken a long time about it; for when she climbed into bed and blew out the candle she heard the clock in the stable yard strike midnight.

"How can I sleep!" Arabella asked herself. "There is so much to ponder over, so much to be decided."

It was then she heard footsteps in the passage outside and she knew whose steps they were. Yet she had to make sure.

She slipped out of bed, went to the door and very, very softly opened it. The footsteps had passed and she knew they had entered the schoolroom. She heard a door close . . . the door to Miss Harrison's bedroom.

Without thinking of any danger to herself, Arabella slipped a wrapper over her nightgown and crept out into the darkened passage. There was a faint light from the tapers burning low along the corridor. Silently, her feet bare, Arabella slipped through the open door of the schoolroom.

She could hear Gentleman Jack's harsh voice quite clearly and she could see a light beneath Miss Harrison's door. Without making the slightest sound, Arabella stole across the carpeted floor towards the light.

"Thank God you've come!" she could hear Miss Harrison cry. "I've been out of my mind!" Where have you been?"

"I've been in Bedfordshire," the highwayman replied. "An excellent haul, my Love-bird. I've a present for you which will make your eyes glitter like a sparkler when you see it."

"Jack! Haven't you heard what has happened? His Lordship has returned!"

"Yes, I know," Gentleman Jack replied in a quite cheerful tone. "Do you suppose there were not a dozen fearful faces and gloomy tongues to tell me the news as soon as I crossed the county border."

"But you should not venture here," Miss Harrison said anxiously. " 'Tis dangerous!"

Gentleman Jack laughed.

"Dangerous for whom?" he enquired. "Now, don't push yourself into a pucker, Olive. Leave such matters to me. It may turn out to be an ace that the young cock should have come swaggering home to his dunghill. You'll hear him soon crow on a different note, you'll see!"

"But His Lordship is staying here!" Miss Harrison cried.

"What if he is?" Gentleman Jack demanded. "He'll not be visiting you this evening, I presume?"

He laughed coarsely.

"Jack! Why should you say such things? Miss Matherson has been put in charge and, indeed, I have no notion now of what is happening in the household."

"Miss Matherson will not be in charge for long," Gentleman Jack said ominously. "You shall be mistress —and not from the second floor."

"But how? What do you mean?" Miss Harrison questioned.

"I have my plans," the highwayman replied.

"The Lord Chief Justice is here tonight!"

"Yes, I know," Gentleman Jack answered. "And I know something else, my dear, which will interest you. He carries in his coach a thousand golden sovereigns! Money that the City of Bedford wishes to bank in London. They thought it would be safe in the old man's hands. By God, they will learn their mistake!"

"Surely you'll not be taking it from him?" Miss Harrison protested.

"What do you expect?" Gentleman Jack asked. "That I'd let it slip through my hands?"

"Jack! If you do it here, they will guess!"

"Don't be so cork-brained, my dove," Gentleman Jack replied. "Give me credit for a bit of horse sense. Nothing will take place within the neighborhood of the Castle. This is our fortress, our place of safety, as you well know. No, His Majesty's Justice will be apprehended on the road."

He paused and chuckled.

"And shall I tell you something else? Someone else will be with him . . . someone of whom I intend to rid myself as speedily as possible."

"Whoever do you mean?" Miss Harrison asked.

"Who else but the most noble Marquis himself?" Gentleman Jack said in a jeering, ugly voice.

"But how? He will not wish to leave the Castle," Miss Harrison objected.

"He will receive a message that his presence is required immediately in London," Gentleman Jack replied. "He will call for his Phaeton. The wheel is unaccountably buckled."

"What then will he do?"

"It is obvious, my plump little partridge! He will accept a seat in His Lordship's coach and that will be my opportunity."

"You would not kill him!" Miss Harrison cried in tones of horror.

"Not in cold blood, my dear," Gentleman Jack replied. "Damn these boots!"

There was a sudden crash on the floor which made Arabella jump.

"No," he continued. "I never kill a man in cold blood —not if anyone sees me do it. That would ruin my reputation. Do not forget that I'm called Gentleman Jack . . . not only because I am in fact a gentleman, but because I also behave like one and shoot only in self-defence. Yet as you know full well, there's not a swell alive who does not desire to blow a hole through me. If my lead travels quicker than theirs, who am I to complain?"

"So, the Marquis will die!" Miss Harrison said nervously. "And what then, Jack? What will happen to us?"

"I have my plans," Gentleman Jack replied grandiosely. "I have great plans, Olive. Plans for you and plans for me. Plans for the future. I am not a common gentleman of the road, my love. I have brains, intelligence. This is something that has occupied my mind for a long time."

"What will occur?" Miss Harrison enquired apprehensively.

"You will see when the time comes," Gentleman Jack replied soothingly. "Do you want me to go on gabbing all night? I thought when I arrived that you were pleased to see me."

"I am, you know I am, Jack! I have missed you more than I can say. Oh, my dear one! I am afraid. Afraid for you and feared for myself. If things should go wrong, if they should catch you, what would I do then?"

"They will not catch me!" Gentleman Jack boasted. "Come on, Olive! Kiss me as though you were warm

138

to my touch, instead of fidgeting about things that should never concern your pretty, stupid head."

"Oh, Jack!" Miss Harrison sighed ecstatically.

Arabella slipped away from the door. She had heard enough. She knew now that she must warn the Marquis.

She crept across the schoolroom floor, slipped through the door and turned along the passage which led to the staircase. Then suddenly she stopped dead and drew back into the shadows.

Someone was standing there!

The candles were spluttering low in their grease. But there was no mistaking the figure of a man with his hat drawn low over his forehead and wearing high riding-boots and a pistol in his belt. Arabella, after one quick glance, crept back down the passage in the opposite direction.

She passed her own bedroom door and crept a few paces further on. The passage turned and there, at the far end of it, in the direction of the back staircase, she saw another man!

Gentleman Jack was taking no chances tonight! He had posted sentinels to guard him, and Arabella knew there was no possibility of her eluding them.

Eight

TOSSING and turning in the darkness Arabella went over what had happened during the evening, step by step and word by word. Finally she came to the conclusion that she had been wrong in wishing to warn the Marquis after she had overheard Gentleman Jack's conversation with Miss Harrison.

It was obvious, now that she thought it over, that the Marquis was safe, so long as he remained at the Castle. He was also comparatively safe so long as he did not challenge Gentleman Jack.

It was difficult to believe that the highwayman had any code of decency or honor; but he had said that he would not kill a man in cold blood when anyone was there to see him do so. Arabella could only pray that he would keep his word.

The difficulty now lay in planning how she could prevent the Marquis from traveling to London with the Lord Chief Justice.

She was convinced that, if he knew the truth, and if she pleaded with him to stay, it would be the one thing he would refuse. He would feel it was a challenge to face Gentleman Jack and he might even believe, optimistically, that many of the people on the Estate who served him, and his father before him, would support him against the highwaymen.

Unfortunately, Arabella thought sadly, he had been away too long and while those who served the Castle might wish to be loyal, the ties of family and their affection for their own flesh and blood must come first.

It was obvious that Gentleman Jack was astute in that he had found a vulnerable spot in everyone he wished to terrorise: Farmer Eastcote's family, Mistress Coombe's idiot son, old Jacob's granddaughter. These she knew about and there must be dozens more whom Gentleman Jack had subdued by sheer, undiluted fear.

Yet think, wonder and ponder as she might, it was hard to find an immediate excuse to prevent the Marquis from leaving the Castle. Here again there was treachery. The groom who would bring him the message commanding his attendance in London, and the stable-hand who would say the wheel of the Phaeton was buckled, were also in the plot.

It was a tangle which seemed to have endless knots, and a multitudinous number of complications which became more and more terrifying the deeper one delved into them.

It was daylight before Arabella decided what she must do. Then she rose and dressed herself. Leaving her bedroom she met George coming along the passage, carrying a tray on which were the china and cutlery for the schoolroom breakfast.

"Mornin", Miss Arabella," he said cheerfully.

"Good morning, George," she replied. "Do you know at what hour the Lord Chief Justice is leaving for London?"

"Do y'want t'kiss him goodbye?" the footman asked cheekily. "Well, he's having his breakfast at half-after-eight and his carriage has been ordered round for nine-thirty."

"Thank you, George," Arabella said. She hurried into the schoolroom to find that Beulah had not yet been called but the child was awake, sitting up in her bed, playing as usual with her kittens.

"I am going to start dressing you," Arabella said. "We have got something very exciting to do this morning!"

"Exciting?" Beulah asked, with round eyes.

141

"Yes," Arabella nodded, "and it's a secret too!"

This was a magic word as far as Beulah was concerned.

"Secret . . . secret," she cooed. " 'nother . . . secret. Beulah like . . . secrets."

"*I* like secrets," Arabella corrected automatically.

Beulah was up by the time Rose came to awake her.

"I have dressed Her Ladyship," Arabella explained, "because we are going out early this morning."

"That'll be nice. Are you going to say "goodbye" to His Lordship?" Rose asked. "We've just been told that he's a'going to London."

"That is unexpected, is it not? Arabella asked deliberately. "He did not speak of it yesterday."

"No, a groom brought a note for him early this morning."

"A groom from London?" Arabella enquired.

"I expect so," Rose replied uninterestedly. "Anyway, His Lordship is a'leaving. I hope he'll come back. He's that handsome, he makes my heart go bump-bump every time I sees him! A slap-up blade, the footmen call him."

Arabella wondered what Rose would say if she told her there was every likelihood of the Marquis being dead before the day was out! Would she be distressed and try to help? Or, like the others, would she be too afraid to do anything but keep the silence Gentleman Jack had imposed?

Schoolroom breakfast was at eight o'clock. Miss Harrison did not apear until nearly twenty minutes past, and by that time Beulah, despite the fact that she ate with maddening slowness, had nearly finished.

"I promised Beulah that she should see the Lord Chief Justice's carriage and outriders drive off to London," Arabella said, when Miss Harrison complained of their having started breakfast before her.

The governess was tired and therefore in a bad temper this morning. Without even glancing at the breakfast-table, she went straight to her special cupboard and drew out the bottle of brandy.

A wineglass seemed to sweep away some of her lassitude. She came to the table, still looking heavy-eyed but prepared now to toy with some of the delicacies in the crested, silver dishes.

"What time is the Lord Chief Justice leaving?" she asked at length.

"At half-after-nine," Arabella replied. "I thought Beulah would get a better view of the *entourage* if I took her a short way down the drive."

"You don't want to make nuisances of yourselves," Miss Harrison said. "Just wave and curtsy."

She seemed to speak automatically, her thoughts elsewhere.

With her dark hair falling over her shoulders she looked unusually voluptuous, Arabella thought, and wondered how any woman, however coarse, could tolerate Gentleman Jack as a lover!

"I intend to rest this morning," Miss Harrison announced without any preliminaries. "If you are taking Beulah outside you may keep her out. I want no noise in the schoolroom when I am trying to sleep."

"No, of course not," Arabella said. "May we please go now? It is difficult to make Beulah hurry."

"Get someone to carry her," Miss Harrison replied. She got up from the table, yawning loudly, and went once again to the cupboard in search of her brandy bottle.

Arabella hurried Beulah from the table, snatched up her bonnet, and lifting her in her arms carried her to the top of the stairs. She was just wondering whether she dare try to carry the child down when George appeared.

"Here! Where are you a'going?" he asked. "You're off bright and early this morning! I suspect it's in search of some mischief."

"Gee-gees. Going . . . see . . . gee-gees," Beulah answered, before Arabella could speak.

"Real fond o' animals, ain't she," the footman remarked to Arabella.

"She loves them," Arabella replied. "That is why I

143

thought she would like to see the Lord Chief Justice leaving for London."

"His Lordship's a'going with him," George said confidentially. "You can wave to him as well."

"Oh, is he?" Arabella asked innocently. "Why is he not traveling in his own Phaeton?"

She knew the answer before George replied.

"I hears there be somat wrong with one of the wheels. His Lordship sweared like a trooper when Mister Turner brings him the message from the stables. I suspicion he don't relish a journey a'shouting at the old'un!"

"No, indeed," Arabella said. "Deaf people are very difficult."

"Well, he'll have to put up with somat this time," George grinned. "The old gentleman says, 'You come with me, m'boy. My coach is big enough for two.' You should have seen 'is Lordship's face! There was naught he could do but agree."

"When did all this happen?" Arabella enquired.

"Just as the two gentlemen came down for breakfast," George replied. "I was in the hall when Mister Turner tells 'is Lordship that he can't travel in his Phaeton. It looked right and tight to me when I was having a peep at it, yesternoon."

"What can have happened?" Arabella asked.

"Stap me if I knows the answer," George grinned, "but as my uncle always says, if a wheel's out of true, not even a Nonsuch can tool it through a turnpike!"

How cleverly it had all been contrived, Arabella thought. Could Gentleman Jack have really planned every detail with such accuracy, or had he been helped by Turner?

Surely the butler too was not in the plot, as well as the others?

She felt in a kind of despair, as if she and the Marquis were encircled by hostile tribesmen, every one of them carrying poisoned spears. Not wishing to hear any more from George she bustled Beulah away by a side door down towards the bridge.

She wanted to be well away from the Castle. This

144

meant covering a quite considerable distance, and it was soon obvious that Beulah waddling slowly would never manage it on foot.

Arabella picked her up in her arms. The child was heavy and had no wish to be carried.

"Beulah . . . walk!" she stormed.

"I have something to say to you," Arabella tried to placate her. "A secret! A very important secret! I want you to help me."

"Secret! Beulah like . . . secrets," the child answered.

"Yes, I know. And mine is a very big one," Arabella said. "Now listen, Beulah. This is very, very important."

It was difficult to talk carrying such a heavy weight but somehow Arabella managed it. She crossed the bridge and reached the shelter of the great oak trees, which formed an avenue over a mile long leading to the entrance gates.

The trees partly concealed the Castle, Arabella knew, but after a little while she turned off the drive, plunging into the grassland of the park. Finally she set Beulah down and once again told her what she wanted her to do.

"Do not forget, Beulah!" she urged. "Shut your eyes and lie very still when you hear me coming. It is a secret, do not forget. A secret between you and me."

Beulah nodded her head.

"Secret . . . secret!" she said. "Beulah . . . shut . . . eyes."

Arabella glanced towards the Castle. Now she could see that a coach standing in front of it was moving off.

"Do not forget, Beulah," she reminded her, "shut your eyes."

Then she ran as fast as the thick grass would let her back to the drive. She heard the coach rattle over the bridge before she stepped onto the centre of the gravel track, waving her arms. Just for a moment she was afraid the coachman would not stop. However she stood her ground until the horses were nearly on top of her, when, reined in violently and champing at their bits, they came to a standstill.

145

The Marquis put his head out of the coach window.

"What's the matter? Why are we stopping?" he demanded before he saw Arabella.

"It's the little girl, Milord," the coachman answered unnecessarily.

Arabella ran to the coach door.

"It is Beulah, My Lord," she said breathlessly. "She has fallen! I think she is unconscious! Please come and see for yourself."

"Of course!" the Marquis promised instantly.

The footman sprang down from the box and opened the door for him.

"What's the matter? What's happening?" a querulous old voice asked from inside the coach.

The Marquis, half out of the door, turned towards him. "I'm afraid there has been an accident to my sister, My Lord."

"Do you want us to wait?"

The Marquis hesitated.

"Beulah is some way from here," Arabella said agitatedly. The Marquis made up his mind.

"No, I can't keep the horses waiting," he said. "Goodbye, My Lord. I am indeed distressed I cannot accompany you to London.

He stepped out of the coach.

"Drive on!" he said to the coachman and stood aside as the horses started off again, the wheels raising the dust.

Two outriders, their white wigs under peaked caps, spurred their horses forward to get ahead of the coach, and as the cavalcade moved away, the Marquis reached out to take Arabella's hand in his.

"What has happened?" he asked quietly. "Is Beulah hurt?"

"I do not know," Arabella replied.

"Why are you both out here alone?" the Marquis asked irritably.

Arabella decided that the fewer questions asked and answered, the better. Pulling childishly at the Marquis's hand she said:

146

"We had best hurry. She is over here in the park."

They started to move quickly between the trees and Arabella began to talk in a loud voice, which she knew Beulah could hear.

"It was such a lovely day," she said, "and Beulah wanted to see the horses. She loves animals!"

Arabella's voice had the effect she had hoped for. When they reached Beulah, she was lying on the grass, her eyes closed.

"Here she is!" Arabella exclaimed.

"Did she fall?" the Marquis asked.

"Yes, I think she must have tripped over a tree stump," Arabella replied. She saw Beulah's lips twitch and realised she must do something quickly.

"Perhaps . . . if you wet your handkerchief . . ." she said to the Marquis, pointing to the lake a little way below them.

"I'll do that," he agreed.

Throwing his beaver hat down on the ground he hurried across the grass.

He was very elegant, Arabella thought, in his coat of dark blue whipcord, which fitted without a wrinkle, while the tassels on his hessian boots swung from side to side as he moved.

Beulah opened her eyes and giggled.

"Beulah . . . knows . . . secret."

"You are very clever," Arabella whispered.

"Beulah . . . paddle . . . in . . . lake," the child cried excitedly.

"No, not yet," Arabella answered. "Wait until His Lordship comes back."

"Beulah knows . . . one . . . two . . . three . . . secrets," Beulah crowed.

"Yes, but you must not talk about them," Arabella admonished, "or they will not be secrets!"

The Marquis was returning with his dampened handkerchief.

"She seems better," he observed.

"I think falling down must have rendered her un-

147

conscious," Arabella said. "But if she sits quietly for a short while, I am sure she will be all right."

"I think we should take her back to the Castle and send for the doctor," the Marquis suggested.

"Beulah . . . want to . . . paddle!" the child said insistently.

"I honestly do not think now that anything serious is wrong," Arabella said. "I was afraid, but she seems to have recovered."

"Re . . . covered," Beulah echoed.

The Marquis laughed.

"I believe you were shamming," he said.

Beulah looked at him with round eyes.

"Shamm . . . ing?" she questioned.

"It is a word she does not know," Arabella said quickly. "Let us take her down to the lake. The sooner she forgets what has happened, the better!"

"Beulah . . . paddle!"

The Marquis picked her up in his arms.

"Come along then," he said.

Carrying her over the grass to the lake the Marquis set Beulah down among the daisies beside the water, and finding some stones he taught her to throw them so that they splashed. Then he stretched himself full length on the ground beneath an oak tree.

"I must admit, it is pleasant here in the sunshine, in spite of the fact that you have undoubtedly ruined me socially."

"How can I have done that?" Arabella enquired.

"I had a message this morning to say that the Prince Regent and Lady Hertford wished to honour me by their presence at Meridale House this afternoon. It is exceeding difficult to explain to Royalty that one had better things to do!"

"Will His Royal Highness be incensed with you?" Arabella asked.

"Hurt and piqued, more likely," the Marquis replied lazily. "Prinny is always jealous of anything that occupies the minds of his subjects to the exclusion of himself."

"He sounds very selfish," Arabella remarked.

The Marquis laughed.

"That is *lèse-Majesté*," he said. "If you talk like that, you will be put in the Tower and have your head cut off!"

Arabella gave a little gurgle of amusement. The Marquis said quickly:

"I forgot! You are a serious-minded, well-read young woman and wouldn't believe such fustian."

"There are enough hazards today," Arabella remarked, "without being afraid of being beheaded! Have you heard of the highwaymen who control the Hertfordshire roads? Do you think the Lord Chief Justice will reach London in safety?"

The Marquis, lying with his hands behind his head, looked up at her as she sat demurely beside him, her head silhouetted against the blue of the sky.

"Of course His Lordship will be safe," he asserted confidently. "Who has been frightening you with such moonshine?"

"It is true, unfortunately," Arabella replied.

"I have heard of these men," the Marquis admitted, "but I always think such stories are grossly exaggerated. People say they have been held up by footpads on the London streets, but I have never been subjected to their attentions."

"Perhaps you do not walk abroad alone," Arabella said. "But I assure you the Hertfordshire highwaymen are dangerous. There has been talk of their crimes for a long time."

"Well, a highwayman had best not ask me to 'stand and deliver'," the Marquis said. "I should blow a hole through him without the least compunction!"

Arabella sighed. It was exactly the answer she expected from him, and Gentleman Jack, with the same expectation, would undoubtedly fire—to kill.

"You have your pistol with you?" she asked curiously.

The Marquis laughed.

"Now you mention it, I have left it in His Lordship's coach. Ah, well! Perhaps he will find it a protection."

"His hand is too old and too shaky," Arabella retorted scornfully.

"You're a bloodthirsty little chit," the Marquis said. "I believe you are half hoping that he will be held up by your highwaymen. If you want a bet, I'll lay you a monkey to the daisy-chain you are making that he will reach London in safety."

"An easy way to make five hundred pounds!" Arabella thought, but shook her head.

"The daisy-chain is for Beulah," she explained, "and I do not approve of ladies gambling."

"My society friends certainly would not agree with you on that," the Marquis said. "They enjoy their flutter at Faro."

"All gambling is senseless," Arabella declared with an edge to her voice, remembering how her father's debts had resulted in her mother being left penniless when he died.

"A Puritan!" the Marquis teased. "Would you take all the pleasure out of life?"

"Is that the only pleasure you can find?" Arabella reproached him. "To throw on the tables money which could be well spent in helping other people or improving your property? There is always the fear that if you lose someone may suffer because of it."

The Marquis was silent for a moment.

"Out of the mouths of babes and sucklings . . ." he quoted. "You are right, of course you are right. But dammit! I didn't expect to be preached at in my own park!"

"I am sorry," Arabella said quickly.

"Don't be sorry," he told her, "it is as refreshing as it is unexpected. You are full of surprises, Arabella! I swear there has never been anyone quite like you."

She turned her head to look down at him. How easy it was to talk to him, she thought.

"You are very beautiful, Arabella," he said slowly,

150

in a voice so low that she could hardly hear it. "I wonder what will become of you? At the moment you look like a small angel that has fallen out of the sky. How soon, I wonder, as you grow up will you lose your purity and your innocence?"

There was something in his words that made Arabella flush a little. As the colour rose in her cheeks, she turned her head away.

As if he felt that he had said too much, the Marquis continued in a different tone: —

"I tell you what we'll do. I'll walk back to the Castle and see if I can find a vehicle to take us for a drive. They might even have repaired the Phaeton by now. If not, there must be a gig of some sort in the stables. My father had a wealth of carriages . . . Lord knows what has happened to them all!"

"Beulah would enjoy a drive," Arabella agreed.

"I won't be long," the Marquis promised, getting to his feet. "I must also pen a note to the Regent, and explain that only the most unforseen family circumstances would have prevented me from receiving him at Meridale House."

"Will he understand?" Arabella asked.

"He'll have to, will he not?" the Marquis replied with a twinkle in his eye. "If I am here, I cannot be in London. It is as simple as that. Even Beulah could understand it."

"Beulah . . . want . . . stones," the child cried, hearing her name.

"I will find some for you," Arabella promised.

"Start moving slowly towards the drive," the Marquis suggested.

"We will," Arabella replied.

He walked briskly. She watched him cross the bridge, a prayer of thankfulness in her heart.

The highwaymen would be waiting for him, but for the time being he had eluded them. She would have to explain to Miss Harrison, Arabella thought, carefully what had happened, for she must allay any suspicions

151

in Gentleman Jack's mind that the Marquis's action had been prompted by anything but genuine concern for his sister.

As she watched the Marquis walking away from them, the Castle, towering beyond him, looked so magnificent and so impregnable that it was hard to credit the hidden terror lurking beneath it like a stinking sewer. It was small wonder that the Marquis was unperturbed by tales of the highwaymen. No one in their wildest dreams would guess what was happening unless, Arabella thought, they had overheard, as she had done, Gentleman Jack speaking in those harsh, pitiless words of his murderous intentions.

For a moment the buttercups and the cuckoo-flowers in the grass, the water lilies and the king-cups on the lake, and even the Castle itself, seemed to swim before her eyes and disappear into a dark mist.

She wanted to cry out at the fear within herself, which felt like a tight band round her heart, pressing and squeezing the very breath from her body. This she knew was but cowardice, which her father would have despised. She had to fight . . . even if it meant fighting alone . . . to save the Marquis and to save everyone else who lay beneath Gentleman Jack's spell.

With the sunshine blinding her eyes Arabella looked up at the sky.

"Help me, God! Please, help me!" she prayed and she felt that in some still unpredictable way her prayer would be heard.

She and Beulah reached the drive long before there was any sign of the Marquis. Beulah began to get bored, and only the promise of a drive behind the 'gee-gees" kept her from being cross and querulous. Finally, when Arabella had begun to fear that something untoward had occurred, she heard the sound of horses hooves and saw him come driving from the direction of the stables, tooling his own High-Perch Phaeton with his chestnuts between the shafts.

Beulah was instantly all smiles and excitement.

"Gee-gees . . . horses!" she said. "Beulah drive . . . horses!"

The groom sprang down from behind the Phaeton to assist first Beulah and then Arabella up beside the driver. Arabella glanced at the Marquis. He looked a trifle grim, she thought, as though something had upset him, but he smiled at her and said quietly:

"You must have thought I was taking an unconscionable time."

"I was indeed a little anxious you had forgotten us," Arabella answered.

"No, I hadn't done that," he said quite seriously.

"And the Phaeton has been repaired!"

"So they tell me," the Marquis replied drily. "I am going to have my head coachman in London look at it when I return. I have an uneasy feeling there was nothing wrong in the first place."

He drove magnificently, Arabella thought. The horses were fresh and for the moment it was difficult to have further conversation. She had never seen a man take his corners so deftly and keep his horseflesh so well in hand.

They drove some miles at a very swift pace, Beulah quiet with excitement, the Marquis obviously not disposed towards conversation. It was enough for Arabella to look at the hedgerows; the dog-roses, pink and white, covering them with a mantle of color; the yellow irises growing in the ditches; the chestnut-blossom like tallow candles pointing towards the sky.

When they returned homewards Arabella felt a pang of regret that they must return to reality. The drive had been an enchantment and she had felt that somehow there had been no need to talk; that instead they were all close to one another and at one with the horses and the swiftness of their passage.

The Castle loomed ahead and the Marquis drew up at the front door with a flourish. The footman hurried forward to assist Arabella to alight and to carry Beulah inside. Arabella waited a moment to look up at the Marquis.

153

"Thank you," she said softly. "It was a wonderful drive!"

"I will see you in a short while at luncheon," he said and touching the horses with his whip drove off.

The groom had been ready to take the Phaeton to the stables, but now he had to run and scramble on behind as the Marquis drove the horses across the front of the Castle to where the stables lay beyond the West Wing.

"So we are to lunch together!" Arabella thought. This was an unexpected innovation! She wondered what Miss Harrison would think of it.

Beulah had already been carried up the steps by the footman. Arabella followed them into the hall, only to stand astonished—for down the Grand Staircase, wearing a traveling-cape, came Miss Harrison!

She was followed by Rose, a carpet-bag in her hand, a shawl over her arm. The governess was talking in an angry voice to Miss Matherson, who was standing in the middle of the hall, her hands folded over her black, silk apron.

"If you think I'm leaving from the back door like a dismissed servant, you're much mistaken!" Miss Harrison was saying in a high, angry voice. "You may think you are rid of me; but I shall be back and then you will all suffer . . . every one of you!"

The stairs ended and Miss Harrison stood facing Miss Matherson, her features contorted with anger.

"You scheming old devil!" she went on in a violent tone. "I believe you've contrived this. Mark my words, you'll get your deserts sooner than you think!"

"In the meantime, the wagon is at the side door, Miss Harrison," Miss Matherson said slowly with complete composure.

Miss Harrison hesitated a moment as though she intended to hold her ground. Then she tossed her head and with an oath which Arabella had never expected to hear spoken by any woman, swept across the hall and down the passage which led to the pantry, followed by Rose.

Miss Matherson stared after her, her face very pale. Then she turned to the footman holding Beulah.

"What are you waiting for, James?" she asked sharply. "Take Her Ladyship upstairs to the schoolroom. And Miss Arabella, please come with me."

Quickly Arabella followed Miss Matherson up the staircase and along the corridor to her sitting-room. They entered and Miss Matherson shut the door behind them.

"I am afaid, Miss Arabella," she said slowly, "that there has been trouble. His Lordship has dismissed Miss Harrison."

"Dismissed her for good?" Arabella questioned.

Miss Matherson looked perturbed.

"Yes, indeed. He came back a short while ago and found Miss Harrison in the schoolroom. She was not dressed and . . ." Miss Matherson paused, obviously to find the right words:

". . . . and she had drunk too much brandy," Arabella supplied.

"I was afraid you might have noticed her . . . weakness," Miss Matherson said primly.

"So His Lordship told her to leave," Arabella said.

Miss Matherson nodded.

"I am afraid it is going to make things difficult for us all," she said with an effort. "His Lordship has asked me to find another governess. There might be someone locally, or I may have to send to London. I can only ask, Miss, that you will do your best for Her Ladyship, until we can find somebody."

Arabella took a deep breath.

"You know, Miss Matherson," she said quietly, "that we cannot have a stranger here at the moment."

Miss Matherson started and looked at her with fear in her eyes.

"I must tell you the truth," Arabella said. "I am not what I appear. I am nearly eighteen. It is because I have been ill that I have grown so thin and can pass for a child. But I am not a child, and I know full well what is happening here!"

155

"You know about . . . *him?*" Miss Matherson could hardly breathe the word.

"I have heard him and seen him," Arabella replied, "and you must know as well as I do that the Marquis is in deadly danger."

"Oh, no!" Miss Matherson cried and put her hands up to her face.

"We have got to obtain help, but it will not be easy," Arabella said. "Gentleman Jack has planned to hold up the Lord Chief Justice's coach. He may be doing so at this very moment!"

"Oh, no!" Miss Matherson moaned again.

"I know of the hold this terrible man has over you all," Arabella told her.

"I should have tried to inform His Lordship a long time ago what was taking place," Miss Matherson confessed in broken tones. "But I had not seen him for so many years that I was not certain what he would do."

"It is not your fault," Arabella comforted her, "but we have to be very careful. Gentleman Jack means to destroy His Lordship!"

Miss Matherson seemed incapable of even crying out at what Arabella told her. She could only droop her head in utter despair while her hands trembled.

"At least there is no reason for you to obtain a new governess for Beulah," Arabella said. "The only difficulty is my appearance. Can you find me a dress befitting my real age?"

As if the request roused Miss Matherson from her misery, she stoped trembling and said in a different tone:

"Yes, of course I can, Miss Arabella. There are all Her Ladyship's gowns. They will be a trifle long, but I can easily alter them for you. Fortunately she was very slim."

Miss Matherson led the way through the bathroom to what had been the Marchioness's bedchamber. She crossed the lovely sunlit room and opened the door on the other side. Arabella, following her, found herself in

156

a complete wardrobe-room. There were cupboards, every one with a mirrored door, along each of the four walls.

Miss Matherson opened one and revealed a positive kaleidoscope of color. There were gowns of every hue; pink, blue, yellow, green, white. They were as gay as the flowers in the garden outside.

Arabella was aware of the delicate, sweet fragrance of lavender together with a more exotic perfume, which she did not recognize.

"Her Ladyship was always ahead of fashion," Miss Matherson said proudly. "She had the new Empire line long before any of the country folk in this neighborhood had heard of it. In London she set the trend for colored muslins. Look, Miss! This is what she wore at the last ball she ever attended."

Miss Matherson held up a dress of pale pink gauze, embroidered with diamonds and pearls. It was exquisite, a robe fit for a queen.

"It is lovely," Arabella said softly. "And I would greatly appreciate it if some day you would show me all these glorious gowns. But now, if you can find something very plain, something befitting a governess . . ."

It was an hour later that the Marquis, drawing his gold watch from his waistcoat pocket, glanced at it impatiently.

"Tell Miss Arabella I am waiting for lunch!"

"I think the young lady will be down in a moment or two," the butler replied apologeticaly. "I understand she has been helping to put Her Ladyship to bed."

"Her Ladyship is not lunching with us?" the Marquis asked.

"No, My Lord," Turner explained. "I've learnt from Miss Matherson that Her Ladyship is a trifle fatigued after the excitements of her drive this morning. She, therefore, had a light lunch in the schoolroom and has retired to rest."

"Most sensible!" the Marquis approved. "But it's late, Turner, and I'm hungry!"

"Yes, My Lord. Here come Miss Arabella now!"

There was a note of surprise in Turner's voice which did not escape the Marquis, and when Arabella stepped into the Salon he stared at her for a moment in utter astonishment.

She was wearing a gown of pale green muslin with a crisp white fichu draped round her shoulders. The dress clung to her figure, revealing the sweet curves of her body—curves that had never been apparent when she was dressed as a child.

Her hair was arranged high on her head in the latest fashion which, although the Marquis did not know it, was a copy of the coiffure Lady Deane had adopted since she last visited London.

Just inside the door Arabella stopped. She stood looking at the Marquis and for what seemed a long time neither of them spoke. Finally the Marquis said quietly:

"Then I was not mistaken that first day when you stood on the rock on the other side of the pool!"

There were many things that Arabella might have expected him to say when he saw her changed appearance—but not this! The color rose in her cheeks, creeping up to her eyes. It made her look very young, very vulnerable, but at the same time very much a woman.

"The doctor thought me young enough to be a companion for Beulah, for . . . personal reasons I wished to accept." She spoke simply.

Still without moving the Marquis said:

"It bewildered and surprised me that you could be a child . . . you seemed so intelligent—so interesting. Now I understand! But why have you ceased to pretend?"

"Because I wish to ask a favour of you," Arabella replied.

"A favour?" he asked.

Now she approached him, moving across the room towards him so that he could see that her big eyes were anxious and there was a questioning expression on her face.

"I want you to allow me to become Beulah's governess in place of Miss Harrison."

"Why did you endure that blousy, drunken female?" he asked angrily. "Why didn't you tell me!"

"It was not my place to do so," Arabella replied. "I was a child, remember, sent here to play with Beulah."

"Matty knew! All the servants must have known!" the Marquis expostulated. "How could they have allowed such an intolerable woman to stay in my employment? I cannot understand it. In the old days no one in the Castle would have permitted such a creature even to cross the threshold!"

"You have been away," Arabella reminded him.

"For far too long, I can see that now!" the Marquis said sharply. "But I imagined that in deference to my father and mother, through their regard, if not gratitude, for the manner in which they have been treated since they have worked here, the staff would not have permitted anyone so unpleasant to come into close proximity with a member of the family."

"They did not engage Miss Harrison," Arabella said. "It would be interesting to know who did appoint her."

"I have learned it was Sheltham," the Marquis replied. "He must have been to let in his attic to do such a thing! Drunk or sober, she was not the type that any respectable household would countenance!"

"There may have been . . . reasons for his decision," Arabella faltered.

The Marquis rounded on her.

"Reasons? What reasons?" he demanded. "That is the way Matty talks. What is all this mystery? What is going on behind my back that no one will tell me? Perhaps you know the truth."

Arabella did not answer and he continued:

"But no! You are as intent on deceiving me as all the others. I believed you to be a child; now I find you are a woman. What is your age?"

"I . . . I am nearly . . . eighteen," Arabella replied.

"A woman!" the Marquis exclaimed. "At least old

enough to know the difference between right and wrong."

"But I was not in a position to do anything about it," Arabella protested.

The Marquis glared at her for a moment; then his face softened.

"You are right," he allowed. "It was not your contrivance. And you still want to stay here?"

"I have no desire to leave the Castle," Arabella said. "Please let me remain and look after Beulah. She trusts me. Already I think she has an affection for me. I could help her as no one else has been able to do."

"Very well, if that is your wish," the Marquis answered.

"Thank you," Arabella said, "thank you very much. I was afraid you might think me too young."

There was a moment before the Marquis's lips twitched. Then suddenly he was laughing.

"Arabella, you're incorrigible!" he said. "You would twist any man round your little finger. Who taught you such tricks?"

"No one," Arabella replied demurely. "I must have been born with a natural aptitude for deception."

"I don't know what to think," the Marquis said. "One moment you seem to be an angel, the next a very provocative little devil. But now, whatever you may be, I know that I am exceedingly hungry. I could eat an ox! And I only hope they have killed one for us."

He turned towards the door and Arabella hesitated.

"A governess does not eat in the dining-room, My Lord. Do you not think it would be best if I went back to the schoolroom?"

"And whom would that impress?" the Marquis asked. "Arabella, I can see you are a very strange and very unusual type of governess. But, unusual or not, you will eat with me at this moment in the dining-room. That is an order!"

He spoke with a note of amusement in his voice.

160

There was also something in his expression as he looked at her which made Arabella drop her eyes. Her long, dark eyelashes fluttered on her cheeks.

"Very well, My Lord," she said meekly.

Nine

PERHAPS because she felt free from subterfuge and pretence after such a long time, luncheon seemed an exhilarating meal.

Arabella could not remember what she ate from the innumerable crested silver dishes which were proffered to her, one after another, by the footmen with their powdered hair and smart livery.

She was a little dazzled by the wealth of gold ornaments which decorated the great table in the Baronial Hall, where the Normans had once dispensed justice and dined with their enormous households.

Yet strangely it seemed to Arabella, despite the numerous flunkeys and Turner, the butler, hovering round their chairs, as though she and the Marquis were alone. For the first time she felt she could speak to him as an equal, without remembering that he must believe her to be a child, and they talked and laughed while the time sped by on winged feet.

It was with a sense of guilt that Arabella heard the clock chime softly on the mantelshelf.

"I must go upstairs," she said," and see if Beulah is awake."

The Marquis rose reluctantly to his feet.

"I have promised to inspect some horseflesh this afternoon," he said. "It is an appointment I made before I arranged to go to London; so perhaps I had better keep it and see if there is any piece of blood worth adding to my stable."

"What is the dealer's name?" Arabella asked.

"Hanson," the Marquis replied. "Do you know of him?"

"Yes, indeed," Arabella answered, "he is honest and trustworthy. If he tells you an animal is a high-stepper, you need not fear that on closer acquaintance you will find it short in the wind."

"Your local knowledge is invaluable," the Marquis smiled, but Arabella quickly changed the subject. She had no desire for him to probe too deeply as to who she was or where she came from. At the back of her mind there was always the fear that Sir Lawrence might make enquiries about her, and if he found that the Marquis was residing at the Castle, she had no doubt that she would be commanded to return home.

They walked together out of the dining-room, into the passage and towards the Hall.

"Thank you for inviting me to luncheon," Arabella said a little shyly.

"You will dine with me tonight?" the Marquis asked.

She hesitated.

"You could not condemn me to a lonely meal," he insisted.

"It is not conventional for the governess to dine downstairs," Arabella said with a little smile.

"It is not conventional for governesses to look like you!" the Marquis replied. "Besides, after dinner I thought we might turn over some of the books in the Library. I have a suspicion that the book in Latin was not such a mistake after all."

"I can read a little Latin," Arabella admitted.

"You have so many qualifications," he teased, "I think you had best start tutoring me."

"I dare say there is quite a lot Your Lordship could still learn," Arabella said daringly.

She ran a little way up the stairs as she spoke, when she was arrested by his voice calling her name.

"Arabella!" he said and somehow it was a command,

163

so that she stopped and looked down at him over the banisters.

"Yes, My Lord?" she replied.

His face was turned up to hers and, as he looked at her, she could see something in his eyes that made her feel unaccountably shy.

"You will dine with me?" he asked.

"Is it a request from Your Lordship, or a command?" she enquired.

"Both," he replied. "In all humbleness I am requesting you to do so. But, if you refuse, I shall doubtless issue a command!"

"Then I would rather acquiesce gracefully," Arabella replied. "Yes, My Lord, I will dine with you."

She ran on up the staircase and told herself that her whole reason for consenting to dine with him was that it was important that he should remain at the Castle, and not be so bored that he must post to London in search of amusement.

At the same time she knew that she was excited at the thought. She had never before dined alone with a man and she wondered what her mother would say.

She could imagine that Lady Deane would disapprove most heartily. But then her mother would not be aware of the circumstances in which she found herself. How could anyone be a disinterested party to the dangers which beset the Castle and the Marquis himself in particular?

"He must stay here," Arabella thought, wondering what excuse she could contrive to stop him the next time he wished to leave for London.

She reached the schoolroom to find Miss Matherson and two housemaids piling Beulah's toys into a heap on the floor and carrying her clothes from the wardrobe in her bedroom.

"I'm moving you downstairs, Miss Arabella," Miss Matherson explained. "I thought that the schoolroom and the bedrooms here needed a proper Spring-clean, and it would be best for you and Her Ladyship to move while we turn them out."

Arabella met the older woman's eyes and a look of understanding passed between them. Arabella was grateful for Miss Matherson's perception. She knew that she would have been afraid to sleep alone with Beulah in that part of the Castle to which Gentleman Jack had an easy access.

"Thank you," she said quietly.

The two housemaids, carrying their heavy loads, left the room, and when they were alone Miss Matherson said:

"I have put you on the first floor, Miss Arabella, not far from His Lordship. If you should be frightened in any way and scream, I am persuaded he would hear you. Anyway, his dogs will not be far away and they would bark if anyone approached His Lordship's bedroom."

Arabella felt that in Miss Matherson's confident assertion there was also an underlying anxiety for the Marquis.

"His Lordship is safe so long as he stays in the Castle and does not take to the highway," she assured her.

"I suspect that that is why you somehow persuaded him not to leave with the Lord Chief Justice," Miss Matherson said.

"I told him Her Ladyship had hurt herself," Arabella explained. "We must contrive to get word to London and ask them to send us protection."

Miss Matherson looked frightened.

"If Gentleman Jack should hear of it . . ." she began.

"That is the whole point," Arabella emphasised. "He must not hear of it from anyone until it is too late."

"We daren't send a groom," Miss Matherson whispered. "He holds them all in his power."

"I felt that must be the position," Arabella replied.

She walk across to the window to look out with unseeing eyes towards the lake. Then a movement below made her look down to see the Marquis emerge from the front door and mount a prancing black stallion, which the groom was having difficulty in holding.

He swung himself into the saddle, quietened the restless horse, and set off towards the drive. He looked magnificent on the stallion and Arabella wished that she could ride beside him. She had a sudden longing to have a horse beneath her and the wind blowing her cheeks as she galloped over the soft turf.

"I have an idea," she said excitedly, turning back to Miss Matherson. "Is there a riding-habit among Her Ladyship's clothes?"

"Indeed there is," Miss Matherson replied.

"And could you have it altered to fit me?" Arabella asked. "I am sorry to ask so much of you, but perhaps, if I can persuade His Lordship to take me riding, I might somehow escape the highwaymen's net and get through to London."

"You must take no risks," said Miss Matherson quickly.

"We all risk our lives as it is," Arabella replied. "I am persuaded Gentleman Jack would not hesitate to murder any of us if it served his purpose. But it is the Marquis who is our immediate problem because, for some reason I cannot yet fathom, Gentleman Jack intends to kill him."

Miss Matherson's hands trembled but her voice was steady.

"I will have the habit altered for you, Miss. I have already started the under-housemaids stitching at a number of dresses which I though you would find useful."

"I am sorry that I have to make use of her late Ladyship's possessions in this way," Arabella said, "but you do understand that I cannot send home for my own belongings."

"Even if it were possible, it would be unnecessary," Miss Matherson declared. "I hold many gowns which will suit you admirably, and I know that Her Ladyship, were she here, would wish you to have them."

"I will come and see them later, if I may," Arabella said. "It may be unseemly, in the midst of so much trouble, but I cannot help feeling excited at the thought of having such beautiful clothes to wear. Those children's dresses I have grown out of were becoming uncomfortably tight!"

"You were a pretty child," Miss Matherson said with a smile, "but now you are a very beautiful young lady."

"You are flattering me!" Arabella laughed, but she could not help feeling pleased as she went from the schoolroom into Beulah's room.

The child was awake and was dressing up a struggling kitten in a bonnet that belonged to one of her dolls.

"Careful!" Arabella admonished. "You will hurt him!"

She took the kitten from the bed and, when Beulah started to protest, said quickly:

"Hurry and get up! There are all sorts of excitements this afternoon. You are going to leave this room and sleep downstairs in a big bed in one of the guest rooms near your brother."

"Go . . . away?" Beulah queried.

"Well, we are going downstairs," Arabella said. "They are going to clean and tidy this room and perhaps one day you will come back. In the meantime you will have a new schoolroom and a new bedroom. Isn't that fun?"

To her surprise, Beulah merely looked sulky.

"Beulah stay . . . with . . . secret!" she announced at length.

"Is your secret here?" Arabella asked, fetching the child's dress from the chair to slip it over her head. "Perhaps we can take it with us."

"Beulah tell . . . no one . . . secret!"

"No, if it is a secret you must not talk about it," Arabella agreed. "But if you want to bring it downstairs perhaps you could carry it in your arms while I shut my eyes so as not to see it."

She buttoned Beulah's dress at the back and the child walked to the other side of the room.

"Beulah's . . . secret . . . here," she announced, pointing at a white panel.

167

The schoolroom was in the oldest part of the Castle, where the walls were very thick and mostly covered with antique panelling, dating back to the reign of Henry VIII. To lighten the schoolroom and Beulah's bedroom the panelling had been painted white, but where the paint had cracked it was easy to see that the original woodwork was oak.

"In the wall?" Arabella questioned. "A secret cannot be inside the wall!"

"Secret . . . here!" Beulah insisted.

Arabella walked across to look and an idea suddenly struck her. Perhaps this was where the secret staircase lay which the Marquis had used as a child. He had promised to show her where it was, she remembered. It would be amusing if she found it first!

"Where is the secret?" she asked.

"There . . . there!" Beulah pointed.

Arabella bent down and looked closely at the carving. There was a secret passage, she thought, the doorway would be concealed somewhere amongst the ornamentation, and the catch could be hidden by one of the carved flowers with which the panels were decorated.

She felt first in one place and then another in the ornamental design.

"Beulah's . . . secret . . . there!" the child said, pointing again.

Now Arabella touched another scroll a little higher up. There was a sudden click and, as she had half anticipated, a narrow portion of the paneling swung inwards.

"Beulah's . . . secret!" the child exclaimed, jumping about and clapping her hands. "Pretty . . . pretty! Beulah tell . . . no one!"

Arabella gave a gasp. The door did not give immediately onto a flight of narrow stairs as she has expected. There was first a small landing at the top of a staircase, piled high with fantastic profusion of treasure: diamonds, rubies, emeralds, pearls, in dazzling heaps, and

168

beside the jewels innumerable purses of velvet, leather and satin.

There were canvas bags, too, out of which sprawled golden sovereigns, glittering in the light which came from the bedroom window.

"No wonder," Arabella thought, "Miss Harrison has been afraid! For here lie the spoils of hundreds of hold-ups, robberies, thefts and, perhaps, murder!"

She could only suppose that Beulah had revealed to Miss Harrison that she had seen Gentleman Jack hiding his spoils. The governess, aware of the danger of such a disclosure to Beulah's life, made the child promise to keep such knowledge secret. It had been a terrible risk, but Gentleman Jack had not been likely to hold any conversation with Beulah. It would, however, have been disastrous if he had learnt that the child he despised and hated knew of his hiding-place.

Swiftly, not daring to look any longer, Arabella shut the secret panel.

"Listen, Beulah!" she said to the child. "It is a splendid secret! But it is a secret, and we must not speak of it. Tell no one! Do you understand? You must tell no one."

"Beulah tell . . . no one," Beulah said. "Beulah . . . promised."

"It will be quite safe there," Arabella said quickly, knowing that the child did not want to leave her secret behind, "and in a day or two we will come back, you and I, and take all the secret downstairs."

It was the only way, she thought, that she could ensure that the child would not speak of what she was leaving behind.

"Come . . . back," Beulah said happily.

"Yes, of course," Arabella agreed. "Now you will tell nobody. Do you understand? Secret, Beulah!"

The child nodded and Arabella picked up a doll of which Beulah was very fond.

"We will leave Caroline here to guard the secret," she said. "Is that not a good idea?"

"Caroline . . . guard secret," the child repeated.

"That is right," Arabella agreed. "And now let us go downstairs."

She took Beulah by the hand and led her through the schoolroom. Rose, who was coming along the passage, picked up Beulah in her arms.

"Come and see Your Ladyship's new room," she said. "You're a'going to be very smart, like a princess, with a big, big bed all to yourself."

"Beulah . . . princess," Beulah repeated happily.

For a moment Arabella felt as though everything swam dizzily around her. Was there no end, she wondered, to the surprises and shocks which occurred almost every moment in the Castle?

It had been clever of Gentleman Jack, she thought, first to find the secret staircase or learn of its existence from some old retainer, and then to use it as a hiding-place for the fortune he was amassing night after night.

She had often wondered what happened to the spoils the highwaymen collected. She remembered, after her mother had been robbed, that Sir Lawrence had speculated about the jewelers who were brave enough to buy from highwaymen, knowing that many of the gems they wished to dispose of were known in the trade.

Here was the answer! The more distinctive jewelry Gentleman Jack would keep, perhaps until he had pressing need of it, or maybe until he found it wise to leave the country. She had often heard that there was a link-up between the highwaymen and the smugglers. While the smugglers brought brandy, tea and other heavily taxed goods into England from France, they also carried back across the Channel golden sovereigns and jewels that were freely negotiable on the Continent.

"Perhaps I should look for my mother's rubies," Arabella thought. Then she shuddered at the thought of touching the highwaymen's spoils, all of which had been extorted by fear, often from those who could ill afford to lose their most precious possessions.

One thing Beulah's secret had revealed all too clearly: that Gentleman Jack would return whenever he was in need of money. For, as he had said himself, the

Castle was his sanctuary, a place of hiding he could ill afford to relinquish. He would therefore keep it inviolate as long as possible.

The new room that Miss Matherson had chosen as a schoolroom was delightful and after Arabella had been shown the bedchambers, she took Beulah into the garden.

They walked to the goldfish pool and on to the Herb Garden, but this time there was no sign of the Marquis. The Herb Garden, however, was very different from when Arabella had last seen it. Now there were three gardeners at work, clearing the weeds and planting out flowers in the places where the herbs had died.

"It be only for this year we be a'planning these," an old gardener explained to Arabella when he saw her looking at what he was doing. "Next year we'll have the right shrubs and herbs that 'er Ladyship planned."

"It will look lovely then," Arabella smiled, "and it should be useful, too. Herbs cure many ailments. My mother always used them when any of us were ill."

"Aye, they be good for th'colic and th'quinsy," the old man said. "But wait till next year, Missy. You'll see every herb that any lady could want in her still-room, a'growing in this 'ere garden."

"I wonder if I shall be here to see it," Arabella thought with a little contraction of her heart.

She knew suddenly that in a very short space of time she had grown to love the Castle. Despite the intrigue, the mystery, the terror encompassed within its massive walls, there was something about it which made her feel as no house had ever made her feel before.

It was not only that she admired its grandeur but she could understand why those who had once lived here would never wish to live elsewhere. One had a feeling of belonging, it was almost as if by being in the Castle one became a part of its history.

"Our castle's strength will laugh a siege to scorn," Arabella quoted aloud, then shivered as she remembered that where Meridale Castle was concerned the enemy was often within the walls.

Beulah was tired and Arabella carried her back to the Castle. She played games with her in their new schoolroom until it was time for Beulah to go to bed.

When Rose came to bath the child, Arabella slipped away down the corridor.

"Come in, Miss Arabella," Miss Matherson smiled when Arabella, having knocked, opened the door of her room. She was sitting at a table in the window, stitching the hem of a gown. Now she cut the thread with her scissors and held it up for Arabella to see.

"Is that for me?" Arabella gasped.

"It is for you to wear tonight," Miss Matherson answered.

It was a gown of very soft gauze, the colour of the palest periwinkle that ever lifted its face to the sun, and it was embroidered on the bodice with tiny diamante dewdrops. The high bodice was encircled by ribbons of the same color, woven of a peerless satin.

"It is beautiful!" Arabella exclaimed.

"The material was smuggled from France during the War," Miss Matherson replied. "Oh, no one admitted anything so unpatriotic, but there it was in a shop in Bond Street and Her Ladyship could not resist it.

" 'I feel it is sadly reprehensible of me, Matty,' she said to me, 'but if I had not purchased it someone else would have done so and I wish for His Lordship's sake to be in good looks. He has enough worries at the moment without being depressed by the dreariness of a drab wife!' "

"I am sure she could never have been that," Arabella declared.

"No, indeed," Miss Matherson replied, "Her Ladyship was like the sunlight, gay, beautiful, elegantly dressed, and the late Marquis adored her. We all did."

Miss Matherson spoke with such warmth in her voice that Arabella was touched.

"Are you quite certain," she asked softly, "that you do not mind my wearing Her Ladyship's gowns? You

172

have kept them so carefully that I would not like you to feel it was sacrilege for anyone else to put them on."

"You are lovely enough to be worthy of them," Miss Matherson said simply, and Arabella bent forward and kissed the older woman's cheek.

"You are so kind to me," she said.

"Now, Miss, you'll have me crying if you talk like that," Miss Matherson admonished. " 'Tis you who are kind to us. You have made everything seem different since you came to the Castle. You've given me new heart and there's her little Ladyship advanced out of all knowledge. Why, she talks quite sensibly now! And His Lordship saved, for the moment at any rate, from those terrible villains."

"Why did you not do something in the beginning when Gentleman Jack first came here?" Arabella enquired.

To her surprise, the expression on Miss Matherson's face changed completely. It was suddenly as though a shutter were closed so that Arabella should see no more.

"We'll not talk about it any more, Miss, if you please," she said primly. "Come and see which of Her Ladyship's gowns I've chosen for you. I've laid them out on the bed."

She led the way to the great bedroom.

"I've chosen all the youngest styles," Miss Matherson went on. "We must not forget Her Ladyship was thirty-nine when she . . . when she died."

"As young as that?" Arabella exclaimed.

"Yes, indeed. She was married when she was not quite eighteen."

"My age," Arabella smiled.

"His Lordship was born the following year."

"Then there was a big gap of years between His Lordship and Beulah," Arabella said.

"Yes, indeed," Miss Matherson agreed. "And now, Miss, if you will look at these gowns and tell me if they are to your liking . . ."

"But of course they are." Arabella said, realising

173

that the lady's-maid had no wish to speak further of her late mistress.

Each gown was lovelier than the last; of crêpe, gauze and muslin they were like the blossoms on the shrubs in the garden. Fashion had changed very little since their owner had ordered them. The only alteration, as far as Arabella was concerned, was that the waist had to be made smaller and several inches taken off the length of each skirt.

The riding-habit made her cry out in delight. In deep-blue velvet, frogged with braid across the front, it was a habit that any woman would dream might some day be hers.

"I will ask the Marquis if I can ride with him to-morrow," Arabella said. "Oh, Miss Matherson, how can I ever thank you for all this?"

"Perhaps you will call me 'Matty'," the old maid suggested.

"I shall be honoured to do so, Matty," Arabella replied. "And now I must go back to Her Ladyship."

"I'll put the gown in your bedchamber," Matty promised, "and I will come later to arrange your hair. You must look your best for dinner with His Lordship."

"I certainly would not want you to be ashamed of me," Arabella smiled.

She knew as she went down to dinner and saw the expression in the Marquis's eyes that no one need be ashamed of her. She felt a little embarrassed in the blue gown; for it clung to her figure and she could not help feeling that while it made her sylph-like, it also emphasized the exquisite curves of her body just coming to maturity.

Now that she was free of her stepfather and much of the tension had been released, her thiness was not so pronounced; and because she felt better and held herself proudly without effort, she appeared taller.

But her face was still tiny, her little chin pointed, and her eyes were very large against the whiteness of her skin.

It was, indeed, her skin which the Marquis noticed most. It was as delicate as the petals of a magnolia, he thought, and breath-takingly lovely against the blue of her gown and the dancing fire of her hair.

Arabella dropped him a conventional curtsy, without speaking. Bowing in the best Court fashion, he bent forward to take her hand. She stiffened as she felt his lips against her skin. Then he released her, and when Turner announced dinner he offered her his arm with due ceremony.

Dinner was, perhaps, not such a gay meal as luncheon had been. There were sudden silences when Arabella's eyes were held by the Marquis's and it seemed as if there were no need for words, because they were speaking to each other without them. When finally they repaired to the Library, alone, Arabella felt ill at ease.

"Perhaps I had best go upstairs to Beulah," she said uncertainly.

"Have you left a maid with her?" the Marquis enquired.

"Yes, Rose is in the sitting-room and Beulah always has her bedroom door a little ajar," Arabella replied.

"Then I think we can assume that were there any urgent need for your presence, you would be informed," the Marquis said.

He watched Arabella move restlessly across the room towards one of the bookshelves.

"Are you shy of me, Arabella?" he asked.

She stood with her back to him and did not answer. After a moment he said:

"I want an answer to my question!"

It seemed as though now she must reply, and she turned her head so that he could see her face and the sweet curve of her lips as she spoke uncertainly.

"I think . . . perhaps . . . I feel strange because I am alone . . . with Your Lordship."

"You have never before dined alone with a man? the Marquis asked.

Arabella shook her head.

"I'm indeed honoured that I should be the first," the

Marquis said in a deep voice. "It is strange to find someone so beautiful and so unspoilt. In fact, I did not believe that a woman such as you still existed in the world today!"

"Not in London, perhaps!" Arabella flashed.

"Why do you hate the social world so much?" the Marquis asked in an amused voice. "Can it be that you are jealous of it? I assure you, Arabella, there is no need. Amongst all the belles of Almacks and the *haut ton*, there is no one who can hold a candle to you!"

"I think, My Lord, that you are mocking me," Arabella replied.

"Good Lord! Don't you believe me?" the Marquis asked. "Have you never looked in your mirror? You're a beauty, Arabella! Exquisite! Glorious! If you appeared at Carlton House, the Prince would go wild about you. It's a crime against nature that you should remain here, unappreciated except by a lot of local yokels and of course—myself."

Arabella did not reply. She turned once again to the bookshelves.

"Come here, Arabella," the Marquis commanded. "I am tired of talking to the back of your head. Come to me!"

Arabella hesitated and then somehow felt that she must obey him. She walked slowly, the candlelight glinting on her hair, the clinging folds of her dress revealing the grace of her body.

She moved a little way towards the Marquis and then stood looking at him, with a troubled expression in her big eyes.

He stood staring at her, and then suddenly, almost roughly, it was he who turned away to stand with his back to her, his hands on the marble mantelshelf.

"You must go away, Arabella."

"Go away?" She echoed the words in bewilderment.

"Yes," he said, and his voice was harsh. "You must return home, or wherever you came from. You cannot stay here any longer!"

"Why? Why are you sending me away?" Arabella asked. "What have I done? I cannot leave!"

"You will do as you are told," the Marquis said, still without looking at her. "I will arrange for a carriage to be at your disposal tomorrow morning."

"But why? Why are you saying this?" Arabella pleaded. "How have I offended you? What have I done that was wrong?"

The Marquis did not speak, and after a moment Arabella said:

"I cannot go home! I cannot! You do not understand!"

"You must," the Marquis insisted.

"But why? Please explain!" Arabella begged. "What can I have done?"

There was a break in her voice on the last words, and now at last the Marquis turned round to face her.

"Can you not understand, Arabella," he said, "that I cannot keep you here and not make love to you? But you are young, innocent and utterly unsophisticated. I'll play a tune with a woman who is up to snuff and knows what she is about, but I will not defile you with my love-making! I'm man enough to want you . . . and gentleman enough to know you are not for me!"

Arabella stared at him, her eyes very wide, and then, seeing the expression in his face, the smouldering fire in his eyes, she knew why this strange shyness had beset her and why there was a feeling of constriction in her throat, while her heart was fluttering against her breast.

Her eyes met his and they stood loking at each other —spellbound.

"Don't look at me like that," the Marquis begged, in a voice hoarse with passion. "You have no idea how lovely you are, or what you do to me. I want to touch you, Arabella, I want to kiss you. And then you will hate me! Perhaps that would be best, for then you would be willing to go!

He took a step nearer to her and now she could feel the very closeness of him. She felt that he already touched her and, strangely, she was not afraid.

"Arabella!" he said hoarsely, and suddenly, as though he broke under the strain of it, he swept her into his arms.

His mouth found hers and he held her so close that she felt she could hardly breathe. She meant to struggle against him. Then his lips awakened something live and insistent within her. It was like a flame that flickered deep inside, so that she could not move or resist him. Indeed, she had no desire to do so!

"If this is being in love," she thought to herself, "I am his. I belong to him. We are one! One!

She felt his kiss grow deeper and more passionate, and still she could not move . . .

Then, as suddenly as he had taken her, he released her, so that she almost fell and had to steady herself against the back of a chair.

"Now you understand," he said, "so go! Go whilst I can still let you!"

Very slowly Arabella put her fingers up to her mouth. She could feel herself tingling, the strange excitement still rising within her, almost as though a fire ran through her whole body.

The Marquis walked away the length of the Library.

"Go, Arabella," he said with his back to her. "What are you waiting for?"

She did not move. She was, indeed, incapable of doing so. And now he walked back again and she saw an expression on his face which made her tremble, though not from fear.

"I love you, Arabella!" he said. "Do you understand? I love you! I don't care who you are or what you are. I think I fell in love with you that first moment when I saw you standing on the rock on the other side of the pool. You were so exquisitely beautiful! The most beautiful thing I had ever seen in my life! And when you dived, it was like some nymph or goddess from another world flighting through the air into the silver of the water."

He took a deep breath before he continued.

"I knew then that I had seen what few men are

178

privileged to see . . . perfect beauty. And when I found you were a child, I was bewildered and perplexed. I couldn't believe that I had been mistaken in what I had seen. And yet you convinced me, except that I could think of nothing but that moment of exquisite beauty!"

The Marquis put his hand in front of his eyes, as if he would shut out everything else but his memory. Then drawing nearer to Arabella, he said:

"Then I met you in the garden. And after that I found myself thinking of nothing but you—the little girl upstairs. I told myself that you amused me, that you were different from other children. I know now that I was drawn to you irresistibly."

Again he paused, and his voice deepened as he went on:

"And when you walked into the Salon before luncheon today, I knew that I had been waiting for you all my life."

The Marquis's voice ceased for a moment and now Arabella put out her hands. They were trembling but she held them out with a smile on her lips.

"Why are you so upset?" she whispered.

He gave a little cry that was half a sound of pain and half of triumph.

"I've not frightened you?" he asked. "Oh, Arabella, was there ever anyone like you?"

He swept her once again into his arms and now he kissed her like a man who has been starved of love. He kissed her mouth, her eyes, her cheeks, her forehead, the little pulse that was beating in the whiteness of her neck, and the tips of her shoulders beside the soft blue of her gown.

"I love you! I love you!" he repeated. "Oh, my darling, my sweet, my little love, whom I believed I would never find!"

Then holding her very close, so close that she felt him squeeze the very breath from her body, he said in a voice raw with pain:

"But you understand, Arabella, that I must send you away because—I can never marry you!"

Ten

ARABELLA sat at the secretaire in her bed-chamber, composing a letter. She threw away half-a-dozen sheets of crested writing-paper before finally it was written to her satisfaction.

Then she addressed it to "The Home Secretary", at the Houses of Parliament, Westminster, sanded and wafered it. Rising from the desk, she picked up the pieces of paper she had discarded and tore them into minute fragments before placing them behind the coal in the unlit fire. Whatever happened, no one in the Castle must know to whom she had written.

Lying awake, long after she had left the Marquis, she had come to the conclusion the right person to inform about the highwaymen and the need of the Military to apprehend them was the Home Secretary.

There was always a chance, she thought, that someone might call at the Castle through whom she could dispatch the letter secretly to London. Miss Matherson had said that sometimes servants were required for Meridale House. That would mean that the baggage-wagon would come from London to collect them, perhaps driven by someone who had no family connections with the Castle or the Estate.

Arabella's plans were vague, but she knew that it was wise to have the letter ready against any contingency so that she should not have to write it in haste and without choosing every word carefully.

Now that her task was finished, she wondered where she should hide the letter and decided that the best place was in a reticule that Miss Matherson had given her as an accessory to a day-gown which had once belonged to the Marchioness. It was made of green velvet, threaded with a satin ribbon of the same color.

Arabella slipped the letter inside and prayed that it would not be long before it was on its way to London.

Now that was done she glanced out of the window and saw the pale fingers of the dawn that were only just creeping up into the sky. It was still very early. She slipped off the shawl that she had put on over her nightgown and crept back into bed. She left the curtains drawn back and the casement open. The freshness of the morning breeze coming in touched her cheeks and soothed the skin which had burned the night before with the ardour and the passion of the Marquis's lips.

She shut her eyes and could hear him saying harshly:

"I can never marry you!"

For a moment she had felt almost as though he struck her. Then, in a voice she hardly recognised as her own, she had asked:

"Is it because I am not of sufficient consequence, My Lord?"

He had turned at that to face her, his eyes burning.

"How can you think such a thing? Of course it is nothing of the sort. I have no knowledge of who you are or who your parents may be; but I do know that, if you would bestow your hand upon me, I should be deeply honoured. Indeed, I should not be worthy of you."

"Then I do not understand," Arabella had said in a voice that was hardly audible.

He moved towards her.

"My darling little love, I have hurt you!" he said in a contrite voice. "I said once that to do so would be like pulling the wings from a butterfly—you are so small, so fragile and so utterly beautiful."

His voice had lost its roughness and had become deep and caressing. Then, abruptly, his mood changed.

181

"You're tempting me again, Arabella! Indeed, I find it hard to think of anything but you when I look into your eyes and see your lips trembling a little, and know how greatly I want to kiss you. Can you not understand that you are torturing me? If you will not leave, then I must go!"

"No! No!" Arabella said quickly, thinking of the danger if he should leave the protection of the Castle. "You must not do that, not on my behalf. But if you would only explain so that I could comprehend how you feel."

"Why I can never marry?" the Marquis asked. "Is it not very obvious?"

"No," Arabella answered, her eyes, bewildered and questioning, turned towards his.

"Not when you look at Beulah?" he asked in a low voice.

"Beulah!" Arabella ejaculated.

"Yes, Beulah!" he replied. "Do you think that I wish to father a child that would be like that? Think if it should be my son . . . the heir to my title and to all I possess."

"It is very unlikely . . ." Arabella began.

"Why should you say that?" he interrupted sharply. "It is there, in the blood, is it not? The blood of the Belmonts, of which I was so proud! I have studied all the history of my family. The first of our line to gain any prominence was Treasurer to Henry VIII. The General who commanded the armies of Charles II was my ancestor. It was my great-great-grandfather who fought with Marlborough. They were all fine, strong men of whom any family might be proud."

"Beulah is surely an exception," Arabella said.

"Is she?" the Marquis asked. "How do we know what secrets were hidden from the historians? How do I know there is not a long line of deformity and lunacy, handed down from father to son?

There was so much agony in his voice that Arabella put her hand on to his arm.

"Oh, My Lord, do not suffer so!" she pleaded. "I cannot believe that is the truth."

"You cannot prove it a lie," the Marquis retorted.

He put his hands to his face and turned away from her.

"Now you understand," he said, "why I would not come home."

"Because you were afraid to look at her?" Arabella asked.

"Yes, afraid!" he said, bitterly. "I who was commended for my bravery in battle, who would face a thousand of Napoleon's soldiers without fear, was a coward, yes, an abject coward, Arabella, when it came to facing that poor, pathetic creature upstairs!"

"Had you seen her before?" Arabella asked.

"I owe it to you to tell you the whole story," the Marquis said with a sigh. "I had sworn never to speak of it, but you must understand why our love can never be anything but a dream—which you must forget."

"I shall never do that!" Arabella vowed.

"I adore you for those words," the Marquis said, "but listen to what I have to tell. Perhaps then you will condemn me as I condemn myself!"

"Come and sit down," Arabella suggested gently. She drew him to the sofa which was set on one side of the fireplace and the Marquis seated himself beside her, his face suddenly haggard. He seemed to Arabella to have aged tragically since they had first come into the room.

"I was at Oxford," he began, "when I learned that my father had been injured in an accident. I came home when my mother told me of it and found him desperately ill. I offered to remain here but my mother refused, being anxious that I should continue with my studies. I was twenty at the time and it seemed important to us both that I should get my degree.

"I went back for the next term and returned in the vacation to find that my father was worse and my mother seemed to be suffering from strain. She was on edge, which was unlike her, and easily inclined to tears,

183

clinging to me when it was time for me to return to the University. Naturally I attributed it to her anxiety over my father's ill health."

The Marquis paused and then continued as if with an effort.

"The doctors did not seem to hold out much hope of his getting better; but even so it was a terrible shock when I received the message that he had died. I hurried from Oxford to the Castle to help my mother with the arrangements for the funeral."

He stopped speaking, then in a deep voice he said:

"I had not been in the house many hours before I suspicioned that my mother was with child. I did not like to question her and instead went to Matty, who told me it was indeed the truth. I wondered why my mother had not told me herself and felt wounded that she had not confided in me."

There was such pain in his tone that once again Arabella put out her hand to touch his arm.

"Perhaps I was imagining it," he went on, "but there seemed, for the first time, to be a barrier between us. We had always been so very close . . . perhaps there is always a link between mother and son which is different from any other relationship. Anyway, I felt shut out and I resented it.

"The funeral took place the following day and it was at the grave-side that my mother suddenly collapsed. We carried her back to the Castle and that night the baby was born! Prematurely, I was told."

Now the Marquis ceased speaking and put his hands up to his face. Arabella felt her whole being reach out to him but there was nothing she could say.

"I think I ought to tell you," the Marquis continued after a moment, obviously struggling for self-control, "that when I was small, about five or six, a shepherd on the Estate thinking, I suppose, it would amuse me, showed me a lamb that had been born with two heads. It would have been a nauseating object, even for a grown-up person. To a small child it was terrifying!

"I remember being violently sick, and then I ran

back to the Castle and hid myself in my bedroom. I wouldn't tell anyone what had upset me, not even my mother, but I had nightmares for months afterwards, nightmares in which I saw revolting, grotesque objects and could not escape from them."

"Oh, you poor little boy," Arabella murmured.

"I suppose everyone has a secret fear," the Marquis said harshly. "Because of my subsequent, utter revulsion against deformities of any sort, it is always my fate to encounter them. I have seen men crushed by cannon-ball into a bleeding mess and felt only a deep compassion. But if I see a travelling circus, if I go to the races, if I am part of any crowd, there is always someone deformed or deranged to remind me of my own heritage—of Beulah, who is now my closest relation!"

"But you must not think of her like that!" Arabella pleaded. "Poor little thing, she is harmless and pathetic."

"I have studied the history of these unfortunate creatures," the Marquis replied. "They can be harmless for years and then suddenly become a danger to those for whom they have an affection. They can also become completely and absolutely insane, so that there is nothing for them but to be kept confined. The best hope is that usually they do not live to be old but die before they are twenty."

Arabella gave a little cry.

"Believe me, I have gone to great pains to find out if anything could be done for Beulah," he went on. "I did not come home because I could not bear to encounter her, but I gave instructions that she should be well looked after, and two years ago, when I returned from France, I discussed her case with the most eminent physicians in London. They all told me nothing could be done!"

"But you must not let this spoil your life," Arabella pleaded.

"Spoil my life!" the Marquis repeated with a bitter twist to his lips. "Do you really imagine that I can think of myself as normal when my blood is thus tainted? If you could have seen my father! He was so handsome, strong and manly. I admired him more than any man I have ever known in my life. And yet he could sire that wretched, brainless little creature, with a distorted, grotesque body."

"How can God allow such things?" Arabella questioned.

"God?" the Marquis asked. "I wonder if He knows or cares? I have prayed, Arabella, yes, I'll admit to you that I have prayed on my knees that there was some mistake, that what I saw that day, when the midwife showed me Beulah after she was born, was just a figment of my imagination. I prayed that I was bemused, the victim of an hallucination! But Beulah was no horror of my own imagining, but a human being."

Arabella took one of the Marquis's hands in hers.

"This fear of yours," she whispered, "could we not fight it together?"

The Marquis raised her hand to his lips.

"I love you," he said. "I love everything about you. You are so gentle, sweet and understanding. But no one can help me, Arabella, no one. I knew that when I fled from the Castle the day that Beulah was born!"

"You did not say goodbye to your mother? Arabella asked.

The Marquis shook his head, and now she saw an expression of pain in his eyes that almost made her cry out at the intensity of it.

"I could not speak to her at that moment," the Marquis confessed, "and when, a little while later, I heard that she had died, I knew that I could never forgive myself!"

"How terrible for you!"

"I had not meant to treat her cruelly," the Marquis said, "but I know now I must have hurt her intolerably. I was possessed by the same blind fear that I had known when I was a little boy . . . and so I ran away."

"Perhaps she understood," Arabella tried to comfort him.

"How could she have thought that I was anything

but a callous brute?" the Marquis asked. "I was her son, her only child until that moment, and instead of helping her I thought selfishly only of myself!"

"It was understandable," Arabella said soothingly.

"It was a damnable thing to do, and I know it," the Marquis retorted, his voice raw. "I didn't go back to Oxford, I travelled to London and joined my Regiment. My father had already arranged for me to take up a commission after I had gained my degree. I went to see the Colonel and he told me that the Regiment was leaving for Portugal within two days. I went with them."

"Without saying goodbye to your mother?" Arabella asked.

"I felt there was nothing I could say," the Marquis answered. "It was only later, when I learned that she was dead, that I not only blamed myself for my cowardice and my unkindness, but I also knew that I had failed her when she needed me most." He drew a deep breath. "Now you see what type of man I am! A man not worthy of your love, Arabella. So forget me."

"Look at me," Arabella said softly.

He did as she asked, looking into the violet eyes which were raised to his, and saw in them understanding, sympathy and a love which reached out towards him, almost as though he was enveloped in an aura of healing.

"I love you because you have told me the truth," Arabella murmured. "I love you, more than I had deemed it possible to love anyone in the whole world."

At her words the Marquis pulled her closely towards him, holding her tightly in his arms and hiding his face against the softness of her neck, and she knew that he was near to tears.

She could now fill in so many gaps that he had left unsaid. The nights when he must have lain awake, hating himself for his desertion, agonised at the thought of what his mother had suffered, knowing he was powerless to do anything to put right the past.

"It is all right," she heard herself say softly, "it is all right now. I am sure your mother understands. She loved you as you loved her, and therefore she would have understood what you felt and, indeed, what she must have felt at the sight of the new baby."

"I failed her," the Marquis muttered again. "Perhaps I shall fail every woman that entangles her life with mine! That is why, my little love, you must leave me alone. I can mean nothing to you."

"I will not leave you," Arabella said quietly.

"You must!" he answered with something of the old mastery coming back into his voice, and released her. "You must find some decent, clean-living man who will marry you and who can give you strong, healthy children, which I cannot."

Arabella moved a little closer to him.

"You must put this misery behind you," she urged. "You cannot ruin your life with thoughts and fears such as this."

"Do you imagine I haven't tried to dispel them?" the Marquis asked. "I used to forget it for a little while when I was fighting, and since I returned from France I have thrown myself into the gaieties of the social life. People talk of me as the 'Merry Marquis'. Did you know that?"

"I have heard it said," Arabella admitted.

"My friends will tell you that I am very gay when I have imbibed a lot of wine," the Marquis said. There was a cynical twist to his lips as he added, "But when the door is closed upon them and I am alone, I remember who and what I am."

"You cannot throw yourself into a depression for the rest of your life," Arabella declared.

The Marquis rose to his feet.

"I shall not do that!" he replied in a harsh voice. "There will always be charmers like Lady Sybil to help me pass the time! There will always be French brandy, green baize tables and my friends! You must not pity me, Arabella. I shall deal comparatively well . . . but alone."

"And so you do not . . . want me," Arabella faltered.

"Want you!" The Marquis repeated the word as

sharply as the crack of a pistol-shot. "You know that I want you. You know that you are the one beautiful, unspoiled, perfect thing that I have ever known in the whole of my life. You are the woman that every man hopes is waiting somewhere for him. And it is because you are so perfect that I would not spoil you with anything that is ugly or vile. The only thing that I could not endure to see is you turning from me in repugnance!"

"I should never do that," Arabella replied simply.

"My darling, you are so young," he said, "you do not know what you would feel if you brought a child . . . my child . . . into the world and it looked like Beulah."

Arabella was silent, for this was something she could not deny. The Marquis gave a little harsh laugh, in which there was no touch of humour.

"You see, there is no answer, is there, to that? Go to bed, Arabella. It is very late and I intend to sit here, drinking, with my memories. Tomorrow we will try to come to some sensible decision as to what you should do."

"I will not leave you," Arabella protested.

"You cannot stay," the Marquis replied, "for if you did I might forget to be noble and self-sacrificing. I might forget that you are perfect and unspoiled and remember only that you are also a woman. A woman whom I want, Arabella! With every breath that I draw!"

"I cannot leave you," Arabella whispered.

She, too, had risen to her feet and her face was very pale, her eyes dark pools of suffering.

The Marquis looked at her, and their eyes held each other as though they were united by some magnetic bond which could not be broken.

"I love you," he murmured, almost beneath his breath, "and I want to kiss you, Arabella, from that flaming, wonderful, fiery head of yours down to your little feet. I want to kiss you, and if you do not leave me now, I might forget that I am a gentleman and your

189

host. So go! Go to bed! And forget about a man who is not worthy of you!"

There was something in the way he spoke that told Arabella he was near to breaking-point. And because she loved him, she understood that a man must not be driven too far.

"I will go," she answered softly, "because you command me to do so. But do not believe that I have surrendered or lost the battle! I will go on fighting for you and against you, and perhaps you are right and this is not the time or the place."

She walked towards him and raised her face to his in a trusting, childlike gesture which tugged at his heart.

He took her in his arms very gently. His lips searched for her mouth but with tenderness, and not the wild passion he had shown earlier. Only as he kissed her did she feel a sudden fire rise within him, and knew it was echoed in herself. Then she moved away, walking across the room to the door, knowing that his eyes were upon her, that he was standing watching her go with his hands clenched at his sides until the knuckles showed white.

At the doorway Arabella turned and said softly:

"Goodnight, and please, for tonight at any rate, think and dream of nothing but our love."

She was gone before the Marquis could answer, and only when she reached her room did she realise that she was crying, the tears running down her face at the thought of all he had gone through.

She was weeping also for herself, because she could see there was no solution to their problem.

At last, she thought, the Marquis had not to worry, as she had, about the highwaymen and the safety of everyone in the Castle.

Perhaps by now Miss Harrison had found Gentleman Jack and told him that she had been dismissed. Would that urge him on to a revenge they had not yet anticipated? Arabella wondered uneasily. Suppose he came and shot them all? Suppose he entered the Castle and murdered the Marquis?

Arabella felt, however, that this was too public an act for Gentleman Jack to attempt, knowing that there would be retribution to pay sooner or later. A man of the Marquis's status could not be destroyed without there being a hue and cry which must inevitably end in Gentleman Jack's being brought to justice.

No, he would try more subtle methods, she thought, and her only hope was that she would have time to get word to London. It was then that she thought of the letter and rising drew back the curtains so that she could see enough to pen the words in the light of the dawn. . . .

She must have dozed a little from sheer weariness; for she was awakened by the housemaid coming to call her.

Arabella rose, dressed and went to the schoolroom to find Beulah was nearly ready.

The breakfast was on the table, and after the child had been fed Arabella was seized with an ardent desire to see the Marquis. She must know what he was doing today, what plans he had made! Always in the back of her mind was the fear that he might decide to go to London and that Gentleman Jack would waylay him on the highway!

Taking Beulah away from the kittens, which were being given milk and pieces of fish from the breakfast-table, she took her downstairs. In the hall James the footman was on duty.

"Has His Lordship finished breakfast?" she asked.

"He is still in the dining-room, Miss," James replied.

Arabella guided Beulah's unsteady footsteps towards the dining-room. When she reached the door, she paused for a moment, knowing that it was unconventional and almost an intrusion. At the same time she felt such formalities were of little consequence where she and the Marquis were concerned. She opened the door.

The Marquis sprang to his feet. He was looking tired

and drawn and there were deep lines under his eyes but his whole face seemed to light up at the sight of her.

"Arabella!" he exclaimed. "I was just thinking of you and wondering if I should see you before I went riding."

"I was going to speak to you about that," Arabella said, advancing into the room. "Say 'good morning,' Beulah," she said to the child she held by the hand.

"Beulah . . . want . . . peach!" the child announced, her greedy little eyes having seen the big bowl of hot-house peaches on the centre of the dining-room table.

"Why not give her one," the Marquis suggested.

"May she have it here?" Arabella enquired.

"Of course," he replied. "Turner, get a cushion for Her Ladyship."

The cushion was produced and Beulah was lifted by Turner on to a chair at the table. Arabella sat down beside her.

"She must have a bib," she said to the butler.

"I'll send to the schoolroom for one, Miss," Turner replied.

Arabella chose a peach and started to peel it on a Sèvres plate of blue and gold, using a gold dessert knife with a mother-of-pearl handle.

"You were about to say something to me," the Marquis prompted, his eyes on Arabella's face as she concentrated on the peach.

"Yes, indeed, My Lord," Arabella replied. "I was about to suggest that if you would permit it, I would like sometimes to ride."

"Of course," the Marquis answered. "How remiss of me not to have thought of it before! I am sure, Arabella, you ride exceedingly well."

"I like to think so," she said with a smile, which took away the conceit from her words. She had not forgotten her idea that she herself might ride to London, and first it was essential that she should have access to the Marquis's horses, so that the grooms would not be suspicious that she was going anywhere save in the park or on the Estate.

192

"When shall we ride?" the Marquis asked eagerly. "Now? Today?"

"I expect you have other plans," Arabella prevaricated.

The dining-room door to the pantry opened and Miss Matherson came in. She curtsied to the Marquis and came to the table, carrying a lace-embroidered bib.

"I regret to have been so long, Miss Arabella," she said, "but Her Ladyship's bibs had got mislaid when we brought the things down from the old schoolroom. But I have found one now and Rose is tidying the drawers so it will not take so long another time."

"Oh, thank you . . ." Arabella began, when suddenly the other door of the room was flung open and a man walked in.

Arabella stared at him and thought she had never seen anyone so splendidly attired. His riding-coat was of olive-green, his cravat was tied in the "waterfall" originally invented by Beau Brummel, his knitted breeches were without a wrinkle and his riding-boots were so highly polished they seemed almost to reflect the whole room.

"A record!" the gentleman exclaimed. "A record, my dear boy! Fifty-five minutes from Mayfair to Meridale! What do you think of that?"

"Richard!" the Marquis exclaimed, rising from his chair. "I didn't expect to see you!"

"I am well aware of that," Richard Huntington replied, "you wouldn't invite me, remember! But I am here with a message from the Great Panjandrum himself. None other than our dearly beloved Regent, who craves your attendance tonight at Carlton House to meet Paulo de Collalto at dinner and, later, to hear him sing."

"Now, who may he . . ." the Marquis began, only to be interrupted by a cry from Beulah.

"Hurting!" the child screamed.

Matty, who was tying the bib round Beulah's neck, murmured:

"I am sorry, Your Ladyship."

193

"Here is your peach," Arabella said, suddenly realising that she was staring almost open-mouthed at the new arrival and that Beulah was waiting for the plate.

"I apologise," the Marquis interposed, "I should have introduced you. But, indeed, Richard, your sudden appearance took me by surprise. Arabella, this is Captain Richard Huntington, a very dear friend of mine. Miss Arabella . . ." The Marquis stopped suddenly, an almost comical expression of dismay on his face, and Arabella realized that though it seemed an age since they had known each other and so much had happened between them, he had no idea of her real name!

". . . Russell," she added quickly, holding out her hand to Richard Huntington.

"And this is my sister," the Marquis said in an unnaturally loud voice.

Richard Huntington bowed but the expression on his face did not alter and Arabella watching him, thought: "He is not surprised by what he sees. He knew what to expect."

"And I must also introduce," the Marquis continued, "a very dear friend of the family, of whom I think you have heard me speak. Miss Matherson, who has been at the Castle ever since I can remember."

"Yes, indeed," Richard Huntington smiled, holding out his hand, "I have heard a great deal about you, Miss Matherson, but it would make you blush if I told you all the flattering things His Lordship said about you, when we were suposed to be fighting the Frenchies."

"Thank you, Sir," Miss Matherson said, dropping a curtsy.

"Now what's all this about?" the Marquis asked. "Turner, a place for Captain Huntington. I expect you could manage a trifle to eat."

"A trifle!" Richard Huntington ejaculated. "I could eat an ox!"

"And drink as well, I wouldn't be surprised," the

Marquis said. "Did you really reach here in fifty-five minutes?"

"I'm not roasting you," Richard Huntington asserted. "Fifty-five minutes—and that includes a slight delay when I stopped to enquire the way. I wanted to try out the paces of a horse I bought at Tattersalls' last month. If you recall you were disparaging about it, Julius. I've proved you wrong. It's a high-stepper, if ever there was one, a magnificent bit of blood!"

"You were saying something about Prinny," the Marquis prompted.

"Oh, yes, I musn't forget," Richard Huntington replied. "I saw Prinny last night and he sent you a most urgent command to dine with him tonight and meet this Italian chap."

"An Italian, dining at Carlton House? Is Prinny loose in the attic, or something?"

"Not at all, it's rather a romantic story, as it happens. Apparently this fellow, being an Italian, should have been fighting against us in the War but he hated Napoleon. So he became a spy."

"A spy!" the Marquis ejaculated.

"Yes. He found out everything he could that would assist us and somehow got the information to the British commanders."

"What an extraordinary tale!" the Marquis exclaimed.

"He was of a good family—he is actually the Duc de Collalto—but he felt his movements as a nobleman were restricted. So he took up singing professionally—apparently he always had a magnificent voice—and that ensured that he could go all over Italy, singing to the troops when they were in action, appearing in Rome before the Court and even journeying to France where he sang for the Empress."

"Must be a slap-up chap, one way and another," the Marquis said.

"They say he even came to England twice during the War," Richard Huntington went on. "Got himself smuggled in and smuggled out again and Napoleon never got a smell of it!"

"You must be gamming, it sounds a rum touch to me!" the Marquis scoffed.

"No, it signifies, for Prinny is going to decorate him," Captain Huntington replied. "Anyway His Royal Highness wants you at the dinner, and to listen to the singing afterwards. I must say, as far as I am concerned, I could do without the caterwauling!"

"You were always uncultured, Richard," the Marquis said with a smile. "My regrets, but you'll have to proffer Prinny my excuses. I'm too engaged here at the moment to go gallivanting to London.

"Taken to the country life, have you?" Captain Huntington asked. "There will be the devil of a dust at Carlton House but I don't blame you."

His eyes were on Arabella as he spoke and she blushed a little as she busied herself attending to Beulah, who was pushing pieces of the peach off her plate and on to the table-cloth.

The Marquis suddenly realise that Matty had been listening to Captain Huntington's conversation with rapt attention. She was no longer needed, having brought the bib Beulah required, but she appeared to be fascinated by what he was saying.

The Marquis's quiet—"I think that will be all, Matty," made her realise she was intruding and dropping a curtsy she went from the room.

"So you're not returning to the social bosom," Captain Huntington remarked, helping himself liberally from a dish of lamb cutlets.

"No," the Marquis said. "Now I am here I can't think why I found all those fah-de-lahs anything but a dead bore. You should try the country for a change."

"I've tried it often enough," Captain Huntington replied, "and found it depressingly dismal, especially when it rained."

He drank the wine the butler poured into his glass and added:

"If things go on like this, however, I shall be alone

among the high ropes. The Regent is talking of going to Brightelmstone and if there is one thing I detest it is that oriental sugar-crested edifice he is erecting there! Tony Lowther has posted away to his estates in Dorset and it is doubtful if we shall ever see him again!

"Tony has gone home, has he?" the Marquis said quickly. "That is excellent news."

"I thought it likely you would be pleased," Richard said. "But at the same time, my feeling about fresh air and frisky lambs is shared by one of your friends who has returned to the fold."

The Marquis's face hardened.

"Do you mean Lady Sybil?" he asked.

"Bull's-eye first time, old boy!" Captain Huntington exclaimed. "She's saying all sorts of disparaging things about you with that serpent-like sting for which she is so famous."

"I'm not interested," the Marquis said, frowning.

"She is even talking of getting someone to call you out," Richard Huntington continued blandly. "The last coxcomb she approached was none other than your old friend Sir Mercer Heron!"

The Marquis laughed somewhat bitterly.

"If ever there was a yellow-livered gabster, it's Heron," he said. "If anyone blows a hole through me, it won't be him!"

"That was what I thought," Captain Huntington said complacently, helping himself to tendertones of veal and truffles.

"Another glass of claret?" the Marquis suggested. "You will need all your strength, old boy, if you're to get back as quickly as you came. Are you staying for luncheon?"

"No, indeed," Captain Huntington answered. "I have to leave almost immediately. Anyway, I have no wish to thrust myself in where I am not wanted!"

"Oh, don't be cork-brained, Richard," the Marquis objected, "The reason why I didn't wish you to come here no longer exists."

He glanced for a moment towards Beulah.

"You shouldn't have secrets from your oldest friend," Captain Huntington said, especially when they are not of the least import."

"Not to you," the Marquis answered quickly, "but to some people."

, "Lady Sybil has been talking wide" Richard Huntington informed him. "We know she is a spiteful chatterbox of a female. But what she has said has made not the slightest difference to your real friends, Julius, and, if you think you haven't any, you are much mistaken."

Arabella felt a glow of affection for the young man who was saying all the things she liked the Marquis to hear. "This will cheer him up!" she thought. He had obviously tried to keep his sister's deformities hidden.

Beulah had now finished the peach and Arabella lifted her down from her chair.

"With your permission, My Lord," she said to the Marquis, "I will take Beulah for a walk."

"Yes, of course, Arabella," he said and there was an expression in his eyes as he spoke that she felt Captain Huntington would not fail to notice.

She led the child towards the door. As she passed through it she heard Richard Huntington say:

"Good God, Julius! That's the most lovely creature I've ever seen! Who the hell is she?"

She did not wait for the Marquis's reply. She took Beulah towards the hall wondering how she could get Captain Huntington alone so that she could give him the letter which she was carrying in her reticule. Here was a person, she thought with a sudden surge of thankfulness, who she had prayed would come to help them. By returning to London across the fields and byways which avoided the main road, Captain Huntington was unlikely to encounter the highwaymen.

They reached the hall. Beulah saw George on duty and tottered off towards him. He was always her favourite.

Arabella did not hear Miss Matherson approach until she was just beside her. Then she turned at the sound of her voice and saw she had a letter in her hand.

"Excuse me, Miss Arabella," Miss Matherson said, "but if you get a chance to speak to Captain Huntington again, will you ask him to take this letter to the Italian singer, Signor Paulo de Collalto?"

"Yes, of course," Arabella said in surprise, "but . . ."

"Tell Captain Huntington it is of the utmost urgency the gentleman should receive it as speedily as possible," Miss Matherson whispered.

Arabella took the letter in her hand.

"Yes, I will say that," she said, thinking that she would be able to give him this letter when she gave him her own to the Home Secretary.

"Do you know this gentleman . . ." she began and realised that Miss Matherson had already turned and walked away. She was moving very quickly down the corridor, and something told Arabella that she did not wish to be seen.

Eleven

ARABELLA lingered in the hall, feeling a trifle embarrassed as she made one excuse after another not to leave the Castle.

She sent George upstairs to ask Rose for another pair of shoes for Beulah, pretending she thought the ones the child had on were too thin. When they arrived, she spent a long time putting them on, playing with Beulah and making her laugh, so that the minutes crept by until, to her relief, she heard the voices of the Marquis and Captain Huntington as they came from the dining-room.

"I regret I cannot stay with you, Julius," Richard Huntington was saying, "especially since you have changed your tune and are warm with your hospitality; but Prinny will be seriously affronted if neither of us turns up at his dinner party."

"Make my peace with him," the Marquis begged. "I have no desire to be subjected to a fit of the sullen when I return."

"And when that will be?" his friend asked.

"I have no plans as yet," the Marquis replied, "but you can tell Mercer Heron I am ready to meet him where and when he desires."

'That would be enough to scare him across the Channel!" Richard Huntington laughed. "He knows you're a top fighter when it comes to aiming a pistol."

"It would give me great pleasure to blow a hole in

him," the Marquis said, "but my belief is that he'll never challenge me."

"You're right there," Richard Huntington agreed, "and now I must say goodbye. But first I want you to look at my mount. He's a fine bit of horseflesh, and, damme, well worth the two hundred guineas I gave for him."

"I certainly want to see him!" the Marquis exclaimed.

They moved towards the door and it was then that Arabella came from the foot of the Grand Staircase, where she had been standing out of sight.

"Forgive me, My Lord," she said to the Marquis, "but Miss Matherson asks if it would be possible for you to write a short note to Meridale House and ask them to send down some more of your clothes. Your valet has been complaining and Miss Matherson thought, as Captain Huntington was going back to London, he might be so obliging as to carry your instructions."

It was the only excuse she could think of on the spur of the moment to get the Marquis out of the way, and it made him frown and say rather crossly:

"Very well, but I cannot conceive why Matty cannot write to Timpson herself." He turned towards the Library, adding: "I'll not be a moment, Richard."

Richard Huntington would have followed him but Arabella touched him on the arm.

"One moment," she said in a whisper, "please wait."

He looked down at her in surprise. The Marquis disappeared and Arabella pressed the two letters into his hand.

"Would you be kind enough to convey these as well to Meridale House?" she said in a loud voice, knowing the footmen were listening. "They are both of great urgency and the posts here are slow and often sadly unreliable."

"Of course," Richard Huntington said accommodatingly. Then he glanced at the top envelope and Arabella saw his eyes widen when he saw to whom it was addressed.

"Open it when you are away from the Castle," she whispered almost beneath her breath, "but not here!"

He looked at her in perplexity as she said aloud:

"It is very important that they should reach their destination with all possible haste."

Richard Huntington stared at her as if he thought she was playing some joke on him, but when he read the expression on her face and saw that her eyes were desperate, he put the letters into the inside pocket of coat.

"They shall be delivered immediately," he promised, just as the Marquis came from the Library a piece of paper in his hand.

"It's dashed good of you to act as errand boy!" he said.

"Always glad to be of service," Richard Huntington smiled.

He bowed to Arabella and then, with his hand on his friend's shoulder, walked through the front door and down the steps to where his horse was waiting.

"Come and see the gee-gee," Arabella said to Beulah, picking her up in her arms.

She knew she was behaving in a most unconventional manner, but at the same time she was afraid lest Richard Huntington should say anything to the Marquis which would demand an explanation.

She therefore stood with Beulah at the top of the steps whilst the two men inspected the big bay on which Richard Huntington had made record time from London. The magnificent beast, with a touch of Arab in it, was prancing restlessly on the gravel, anxious to be off again.

"A fine bit of blood!" the Marquis commented. "I think you've got a bargain, Richard."

"I am persuaded that had you been at Tattersalls' that day you would have outbid me," Richard Huntington laughed. "There is another sale tomorrow— who knows what I may acquire without any competition from you!"

"I am going to add to my own stable during the

next month," the Marquis replied, "so don't snap up all the best blood before I get back."

Richard Huntington stood ready to mount and then he said:

"Oh! I nearly forgot! When I was on my way here, I enquired of a passing rider if I was heading in the right direction. He was a big, blustering chap, full of his own importance, and impressed on me that he was a Nabob in these parts! Said he had a step-daughter who was staying at the Castle. I thought that must be a bit of hum as he spoke in such a disparaging manner of you and your residence."

"What was his name?" the Marquis asked.

"Deane—Sir Lawrence Deane," Richard Huntington replied. "Do you know him?"

"I think not," the Marquis answered.

"Well, his step-daughter must be hidden somewhere in your ancestral pile," Richard Huntington laughed.

With those words he swung himself into the saddle, the groom released the bay and the horse instantly began to prance around. Richard Huntington looked down at his friend.

"Don't rusticate too long, dear fellow. London is a dead bore without you," he said and raised his hat to Arabella.

The Marquis, having watched him for a moment as he cantered down the drive, came up the steps, and Arabella knew from the expression on his face and the frown between his eyes that he was angry.

"I wish to speak with you, Arabella!" he said abruptly and walking past her crossed the hall towards the library.

Arabella handed Beulah to George.

"Will you please take Her Ladyship to Rose."

"Want . . . go out!" Beulah screamed.

"In a moment, pet," Arabella answered and ran towards the Library, with a feeling of apprehension in her breast.

She opened the door and saw the Marquis standing

203

at the window. She came towards him but he did not speak. Then as she waited he said sharply:

"Why didn't you tell me?"

"Tell you what?" Arabella asked.

"Do not pretend, Arabella!" the Marquis said sternly, turning to face her. "You're not as simple as that. You know full well what I mean. I must have been addle-brained not to have asked your name in the first place, but I thought . . ."

". . . I was some local girl of no significance," Arabella interposed. "I was well aware of that, but I thought it would not matter."

"Not matter?" he asked angrily. "You know it matters that I should compromise the step-daughter of Sir Lawrence Deane! How can you or anyone else explain your presence here, unchaperoned?"

"He need not know," Arabella answered.

"Arabella, don't be such a goof," the Marquis objected irritatedly, "it only needs one local resident to call at the Castle and, unless I am very much mistaken, your stepfather, having seen Richard, will suspicion that I am here. Have you a mother?"

"Yes, of course I have," Arabella answered. "After my father died three years ago, she married Sir Lawrence. I hate him! That is why she arranged for me to come here to companion Beulah."

"Pretending to be a child?" the Marquis queried.

"Doctor Simpson saw me when I was ill and thought that I was far younger than I was," Arabella explained. "It was a solution to my own problems, and so my mother sent me here to keep me away from Sir Lawrence."

There was so much pain in her voice at the thought of her stepfather, that instinctively the Marquis started to put out his hands towards her. Then he checked himself.

"This is a tangle which has to be unraveled," he said. "You should return home!"

"I will not do that!" Arabella declared.

"Then there is only one other alternative," the Marquis stated. "You must marry me. But I promise you, Arabella, that if you do so, you will never see me again! I could live in the same house with you and not make you mine. And that, as you well know, I will never do."

"I will not go home. I cannot!" Arabella cried. "I came away because I was afraid of him, because he intended to whip me and I was too weak to endure it."

"He beat you?" the Marquis exclaimed incredulously.

"Whenever he could find an excuse," Arabella answered.

"Oh, my darling! No wonder you are afraid," the Marquis exclaimed.

"I cannot go back. I cannot!" Arabella repeated with poignant fear in her voice.

"Then I must return to London," the Marquis decided.

"Oh, no!" Arabella exclaimed. "That is impossible! I could . . . could not ask it of you."

"Then what can we do?" the Marquis asked. "I had best marry you and have done. At least you will bear my name and I can see that you are provided for and guarded against ill-treatment for the rest of your life."

"I would not accept such an offer," Arabella said proudly. "No, I will earn my own living. It is I who must go to London, not you. I can find some sort of employment, perhaps as a companion or, indeed, a governess."

"Do you think anyone would employ you when you look as you do?" the Marquis said, with a caressing note in his voice. "You are too beautiful, Arabella. No woman would invite you into her house. It would spell trouble."

Arabella remembered her mother's words.

"Then what can we do?" she asked hopelessly.

"I don't know," the Marquis replied.

"Let us leave it for today," Arabella pleaded, thinking of the letters which Richard Huntington carried. If Gentleman Jack received his deserts, then the Marquis could go to London without her being afraid he would be shot down on the highway.

"No! We have to come to a decision," the Marquis insisted. "I realise it is for me to do something, Arabella! But, God knows, I am all at sea."

"Then let us do nothing," Arabella begged. "You were going riding. Why not go as you intended?"

The Marquis had come nearer to her and was looking down into her face. His eyes were on her lips and the blood rose in her cheeks as she felt as though he was kissing her.

"I must fetch Beulah," she said hastily.

"Wait!" he said. "Come with me to the stables. I have not inspected them since my return. Richard's mount has made me realise that I must buy some more horseflesh for myself. We will look at what blood I already have and decide what more is needed. Let us pretend, for a few hours at least, that we are ordinary people, Arabella, just a man and a woman who love each other."

"Or rather," Arabella corrected him, "a very distinguished nobleman and a local girl of no consequence!"

She was teasing, but the Marquis said sharply:

"It was insane of me, I realise now, to have been so blind. But you've bewildered and beguiled me ever since I first met you, Arabella! I am convinced it was you who mesmerised me into crediting such a nonsensical notion. But I swear to you, and you must believe me, that had you come from the humblest family in the land, I should still, had it been possible, have asked you to honour me by becoming my wife."

His voice dropped on the last word and all the misery which had been so obvious the night before when he had told her the story of his life came flooding back. It put a barrier between them that they both knew was insurmountable.

With a little smothered sob Arabella turned away.

"I will fetch . . . Beulah," she stammered.

"No, wait, Arabella!" the Marquis pleaded, but already she had left the Library and was out in the hall, sending one of the footmen upstairs to bring down her charge.

They went to the stables and Beulah was entranced by the sight of the horses.

"Doesn't she often come here?" the Marquis asked in surprise, as she gurgled and cried out to be lifted up so that she could pat the horses' noses and feed them with the carrots supplied by one of the grooms.

"I . . . I don't think Miss Harrison liked animals," Arabella said quickly.

She was well aware that the head groom was looking worried by the Marquis's surprise visit and she wondered apprehensively if anything was amiss. Surely the highwaymen would not be so foolish as to stable their horses at the Castle while the Marquis was in residence! Yet, as they moved from loose-box to loose-box, Arabella felt a kind of tension amongst those who accompanied them.

Suddenly the Marquis stopped in front of a grey mare.

"That's not one of my horses, Abbey!" he exclaimed. "Where did you get this animal?"

The head groom hesitated a moment.

"Mister Sheltham bought it, Milord."

"Sheltham!" the Marquis exclaimed. "I had no idea he was empowered to purchase horses for the Estate."

"You were . . . abroad, Milord, and he thought it . . . necessary," the head groom stammered.

He looked uncomfortable as he spoke and his eyes flickered.

"Is this the only one?" the Marquis enquired.

Again the head groom hesitated.

"No, Milord, there are . . . others."

"How many?" the Marquis asked sharply.

"Six, Milord."

Arabella held her breath. At the same time she could not help admiring the impudence of the highwaymen. These, of course, were their reserve mounts. No wonder they were always so swift to disappear if anyone gave them chase! No wonder they could reappear in so many parts of the country! What other highwaymen had horses in reserve, horses they could exchange easily and which were stabled without there being any suspicions concerning their ownership?

"I don't understand it," the Marquis grumbled. "I've never heard of an agent buying horseflesh on such a scale. He never mentioned it in his letters, and, as far as I am aware, all his correspondence reached me, wherever I may have been."

"One letter must have got lost, Milord," the head groom said. "I'm sure Mister Sheltham would have told Your Lordship."

"They're young horses, too," the Marquis ruminated. "They must have been but foals when he bought them."

He looked closely at all the horses, one after another. Then without saying anything he walked back with Arabella and Beulah towards the Castle.

"There's some mystery here," he said when they were out of hearing of the stable-hands. "I don't credit the story that Sheltham bought those horses! He's been dead some years and he was in ill-health before he died. That first animal can't be more than three years old now! I'm not such a gudgeon that I can't tell the age of a horse!"

Arabella did not answer. After a moment he went on:

"Have you any suggestions? I expect the truth is that you know far more about this than I do."

Arabella laughed.

"I cannot be held accountable for all the mysteries in your home, My Lord," she answered lightly.

"There's something going on here," the Marquis continued, speaking more to himself than to her. "First the Eastcotes, now these horses and, of course, the way Matty had let the Castle go to pieces before I returned. I don't understand it."

"It must be nearly Beulah's luncheon time," Arabella said quickly.

"You will lunch downstairs with me!" The Marquis spoke in a voice of authority.

"And afterwards will you go riding?" Arabella enquired.

"No," he replied. "I think I'll take you both driving. I noticed a curricle in the stables, which my father must have bought before he died. I have a notion to try it out. It will not be as fast as my Phaeton, of course, but more comfortable for a lady. Will you honour me with the pleasure of your company?"

Arabella smiled at him.

"It would be lovely for both of us!"

She took Beulah upstairs and changed her gown for luncheon. The child would miss her rest, she thought, but it would not matter for one day and she could go to bed early.

Arabella was thankful that the Marquis had decided to be with them, for she knew that were he riding alone she would be afraid for him.

She had a feeling that there was a new tension not only in the stables but in the Castle itself. It was almost as though a great cloud were approaching, which might envelop them at any time. The only hope was that Richard Huntington could do something quickly. If he had ridden back to London at the same speed with which he had come he would have arrived there long before now, she thought. Would he find it hard to get in touch with the Home Secretary, and would that august gentleman believe what she had written and send soldiers, as she had requested, with all possible speed to Hertfordshire?

She tried to work out in her head when help might arrive, but it was difficult to be sure of anything—Captain Huntington's reaction to the letters, how long it would take him to get in touch with the Home Secretary, what Military might be available, and whether anyone would take any action on the meagre information she had been able to convey in one short letter.

"Beulah . . . hungry!"

The child interrupted her thoughts.

"I know, my pet, we are just going to have luncheon with your brother. You will like that, won't you?"

"J . . . Julius!" Beulah said.

"That is right, Julius," Arabella repeated. She felt herself suddenly thrill at the name.

"Julius! Julius!" she whispered to herself beneath her breath. She loved him. She loved him so much that she could not contemplate a future in which he had no part.

Because she was afraid of the Marquis's curiosity about the horses and the Eastcotes, Arabella set herself out to amuse him at luncheon. She told him stories of the countryside and the people who lived there. She related to him how she had gone hunting, when she was a little girl, with her father, and how he had taught her to swim and to do many things which normally only a boy would do.

"He always wished I were his son," Arabella said, "and I wished it, too."

"I, on the contrary, am exceeding glad that your father had a daughter!" the Marquis asserted, and she blushed a little at the look in his eyes.

For the time being it seemed to her that they forgot all the horror around them and all the difficulties which, sooner or later, must separate them. The meal seemed touched with a sudden magic, and Beulah too was happy, chuckling to herself as she ate the dishes Mistress Coombe had cooked especially for her.

"Come along," the Marquis said as the meal finished. "Let us go out in the sunshine. My father used to say, 'Always make hay while the sun shines!' Well, that is my motto for today. Let us forget tomorrow, at least for a few hours!"

Arabella picked up her hat and Beulah's bonnet in the hall, and carrying them in her hand got into the curricle.

It was much lower and more trim than the Marquis's rather flamboyant vehicle, but it was drawn by his chestnuts driven as a pair, and she felt they looked very smart as they turned in front of the Castle and moved slowly down the drive and across the bridge.

I should go along the road to the forest, if I were you, Milord," the head groom had said as they were leaving. "They've repaired the road that way and it won't be so rough for the young ladies."

"Thank you, Abbey. I shall have to see to the roads, shan't I?"

"They're not in very good shape, Milord," the man warned him.

Arabella looked at Abbey and thought he looked ill. He was old; but even age would not account for the pallor of his face and an expression in his eyes which she recognised only too well. It was fear! Would he get into trouble with Gentleman Jack because they had been to the stables? she wondered. Was there some reason why he had suggested the road to the forest? She deliberately put such speculations from her. She was not going to spoil this afternoon, this golden afternoon with the Marquis.

He drove at a spanking pace along the forest road. Soon they had left the Castle behind and the road climbed a little to where, on the top of the hill, Arabella could see the dark fir trees, stretched in a long line for nearly two miles, ending where they protected the Castle against the winds which came from the North.

"When I was a child," the Marquis said, "I always used to believe there were dragons in the forest!"

"I too believed in dragons," Arabella smiled.

"And a knight to rescue you from them?" he asked. "I would like to do that, Arabella!"

"I wish you could," she answered.

"So do I," he said, and his voice was suddenly serious.

"Dra . . . gons!" Beulah cried, and they both laughed.

"She is getting much quicker-brained," Arabella said. "She picks up words you would never think she could understand."

"You're clever with her," the Marquis commended, but she knew he did not wish to discuss his sister now.

"Tell me what else you thought about when you were a little boy?" she asked quickly.

211

"I suppose because I was an only child I had to use my imagination," he began and suddenly stopped speaking as he looked ahead.

Arabella followed the direction of his eyes and gave a little gasp. She felt as though a cold hand had suddenly gripped her heart.

Coming towards them from the forest were six men on horseback—and even before she saw the leader, she knew who they were and why they were coming.

For a moment her voice strangled in her throat. Then, as the Marquis drew in his horses a little, she breathed:

"It is . . . the highwaymen!"

"The highwaymen?" the Marquis ejaculated. "What cursed luck! And I haven't a pistol upon me!"

"Be careful! Oh, Julius, for God's sake, be careful!" Arabella spoke with an anguish which he could not fail to understand. It was also, although she did not realise it, the first time she had ever used his Christian name to him.

"You must be mistaken," the Marquis said firmly, but already the highwaymen were upon them, one of them astride the road, blocking his way so that he had, perforce, to rein his horse to a standstill.

Gentleman Jack took off his hat with a flourish. He looked more evil and cruel than the last time Arabella had seen him.

"Good day, my Lord Marquis. It is a pleasure to meet you after all these years."

"Who are you and what do you want?" the Marquis asked coldly.

"I will tell you later who I am," Gentleman Jack said, "my men will escort you to a place where we can talk."

"And where may that be?" the Marquis enquired.

"It would save time if you would follow the horseman in front," Gentleman Jack replied.

"Why the devil should I?" the Marquis enquired angrily.

Gentleman Jack drew a pistol from his belt.

"I have no time to argue," he said. "Do as you are told or one of my men will take over the ribbons."

"Do as he says," Arabella whispered, her hand on the Marquis's arm.

She knew by the expression on his face that he dearly desired to argue with Gentleman Jack and refuse to obey him. But he was well aware that Arabella and Beulah were beside him and he also knew that single-handed and weaponless, he had little chance of fighting six armed men.

The highwayman on the road in front of them galloped ahead, while the others rode alongside the curricle. They were prisoners, Arabella thought despairingly, and wondered if Gentleman Jack would live up to his reputation and not shoot a defenceless man. At the same time she was afraid with a fear which made her tremble all over.

"Horses . . . more . . . horses!" Beulah said with relish and Arabella could only put her arm round the child and hold her close.

They drove off the road into the comparative gloom of the Forest along a track leading between the trees. They had not gone far before they saw ahead an ancient barn of the type used by farmers to store cattle-food in winter.

It stood in a small clearing and must have been there for many years. It was built of old beams between weather-beaten brick and had a thatched roof, greatly in need of repair.

"Come inside," Gentleman Jack said.

"I see no reason why I should obey your orders," the Marquis exclaimed angrily.

"You have little choice in the matter!" Gentleman Jack retorted with a twist to his lips.

Two of the highwaymen went to the heads of the horses. All six were unmasked, and Arabella could see that they were coarse, brutal men. Several of them were pock-marked, some had scars on their faces. They were all, however, well dressed and their horses groomed and in fine condition.

Still the Marquis was reluctant to leave the curricle.

"Shall I have to order my men to use force?" Gentleman Jack asked.

"Damn you!" The Marquis flung the words at him. But he got down nevertheless and held out his arms first to Beulah and then to Arabella. She looked up into his face as he held her.

"Careful!" she whispered.

"What else can I be?" he replied savagely.

They walked into the barn, followed by Gentleman Jack and three highwaymen. The other two remained outside with the horses.

The barn was half full of decaying straw. It had four strong black wooden posts supporting the roof, and from the smell of manure and leather Arabella guessed that this was yet another hiding-place for the highwaymen and their horses.

"What does this mean?" the Marquis demanded, facing Gentleman Jack.

There was an unpleasant smile on the highwaymen's sardonic face.

"We meet at last, my dear cousin," he replied.

"Cousin!" the Marquis ejaculated. "I am no relative of yours!"

"Indeed you are," Gentleman Jack answered, "and I have long wished to tell you of our relationship—a relationship of blood!" He laughed, an unpleasant jeering laugh, and snapped his fingers. "Tie him up!" he said to the men standing behind him.

They moved forward and seizing the Marquis dragged him struggling towards one of the posts which supported the barn.

"Curse you! Let me go!" Arabella heard the Marquis say, striking out with his fists and felling one man to the ground. But he was overpowered, and hatless, with his coat torn, he was dragged to the wooden post and tied securely to it with a rope.

Then, before Arabella realised what was happening,

the men having secured the Marquis seized her too and tied her in the same way to another post. The rope which encircled her waist was strong and cut into her bare arms.

"Let her go, you swine!" the Marquis shouted to Gentleman Jack. "She has done you no harm!"

The highwayman ignored him, merely snapping his fingers once again and pointing to Beulah. Now the child was picked up and carried to a third post. For a moment she thought it a game; then she began to whimper and call to Arabella.

"Hurt . . . they hurt . . . Beulah!"

It was a piteous cry, but Gentleman Jack, standing in the centre of the barn, ignored it.

"Now the hay," he ordered, and his men brought from the corner of the barn some bales of hay that could not have been more than a year old; for they were fresher and less mildewy than the rest stacked about the place.

They threw the hay in great armfuls at the Marquis's feet and around Arabella. Then they encircled Beulah in the same way.

The child, no longer crying, was watching their movements in an almost fascinated manner. Arabella felt that she, too, was unable to speak because she had a suspicion so dreadful, so terrifying that she dare not put it into words, even to herself.

"What the hell are you doing?" she heard the Marquis ask, and knew that that was the question to which she, too, longed to know the answer.

The men had finished distributing the hay and they looked to Gentleman Jack for instructions. He made a gesture which sent them to the door.

"Go to the Eastcote's farm," he said. "I'll meet you there in half of the hour. Leave me the curricle—take my horse and ride through the forest. Let no one see you!"

"We won't be seen," one of the men answered in a hoarse voice.

It was the first time that any of the highwaymen

except Gentlemen Jack had spoken, and Arabella thought that perhaps their silence had been more frightening than any action they had taken.

"Now, my game-cock!" Gentleman Jack sneered. "Not feeling so perky, I imagine!"

"What the hell are you playing at?" the Marquis asked furiously.

"It's no game," Gentleman Jack replied.

"When we do not return to the Castle," the Marquis said, "my servants will come looking for us."

Gentleman Jack smiled unpleasantly.

"I have given my instructions to the Castle staff."

"You have given instructions? Why the devil should they accept an order from you?" the Marquis asked in genuine astonishment.

"The Castle is mine already in everything but name," Gentleman Jack replied. "Now, my dear Coz, I am contriving that it shall become my possession in Law!"

"You're crazed! I cannot comprehend what you're saying!" the Marquis retorted.

"Let me first explain our relationship," Gentleman Jack suggested, and Arabella knew by the way he spoke that he was relishing every moment of this verbal exchange.

"Your uncle—your father's younger brother—seduced my mother. She was a pretty wench, not of any import, of course, to the Belmonts, with their high-nosed airs and graces. But undoubtedly bedworthy. I was the result of your uncle's philanderings, and naturally he was gentleman enough to pay for his pleasure in gold. What else could he offer to the daughter of a common inn-keeper?"

Gentleman Jack spoke in a sarcastic, cynical voice, which told Arabella more clearly than any words how deeply he resented the fact that he was illegitimate.

"What was your mother's name?" the Marquis asked.

"Wilder. Surely you remember old Wilder who used to keep the 'Dog and Duck' in the village? He was my grandfather."

216

"I am distressed if my family served you ill," the Marquis said.

"I should, of course, be honoured that the blood of the Belmonts runs in my veins," Gentleman Jack replied, "and humbly grateful for the golden guineas that your uncle provided for my education. Yes, indeed, I am educated, Coz, which is why they call me 'Gentleman Jack'."

"Gentleman Jack!" the Marquis ejaculated. "Why, I've heard of you. So yours is the gang that has been terrifying Hertfordshire!"

"The gang that has found it very convenient to use your Castle as its headquarters," Gentleman Jack replied.

The Marquis gave a gasp.

"The horses!" he said. "And you mentioned Eastcote just now. So that is why he gave notice to leave."

"He won't leave when I'm at the Castle," Gentleman Jack replied. "I'll need good farmers to run the land as it should be run, and not neglect it as you have seen fit to do, my smart young blade, who prefers Carlton House to Meridale!"

"I have now returned," the Marquis said, "and I am here to stay!"

"It is indeed distressing that you are too late and your desires cannot be granted," Gentleman Jack said sarcastically. "Tonight, when the noble Marquis of Meridale is dead, I shall claim my inheritance—the inheritance that is mine by birth, although I had the misfortune to be born on the wrong side of the blanket!"

"You're mad as Bedlam!" the Marquis said sharply. "You cannot claim the Castle! No court in the land would listen to such an impertinent presumption."

"I am well aware of that," Gentleman Jack replied. "There's no justice for bastards—the by-blows of the nobility. No, give me credit for a few pigeons in the loft! What I shall produce is your will, my dear Coz, made out in my favour, because you wish to right the wrongs of your ancestor perpetrated against the inno-

217

cent village maiden who, I am fully persuaded, made every effort to entice him into her bed."

"Will? What will?" the Marquis asked.

"Oh, it will be very convincing," Gentleman Jack said with a smirk. "One of my men who helped tie you up is a clever forger. We found your signature, several examples of it, in Sheltham's office. It would take a very astute attorney, briefed by you, to refute the signature. And you, my dear relative, will unfortunately not be there to brief anyone!"

There was a moment's silence.

"What are you going to do with me?" the Marquis asked.

"I intend to set fire to the barn," Gentleman Jack calmly replied.

"Oh, no! You cannot do such a thing!" Arabella cried. "It is too cruel . . . it is inhuman!"

At the sound of her voice, shrill with fear, Beulah began to cry. She had been whimpering quietly, now, as if a sudden panic overtook her, she began to scream —ugly screams which came with difficulty from her throat.

"You cannot mean it," the Marquis said in a low voice.

"Stop that loony's ear-splitting bellow!" Gentleman Jack shouted in a sudden irritation.

"Beulah, do not cry, my pet," Arabella pleaded. The child, thoroughly frightened by now, only screamed the louder.

"Blast the crackpot! I can't hear my own tongue!" Gentleman Jack exclaimed, and wheeling round he fired directly at Beulah. The noise of the report seemed to shake the whole barn!

The child hung limp, only prevented from slipping to the floor by the ropes that encircled her.

"God damn your soul!" the Marquis cried, as Arabella shut her eyes against the horror of what she had seen.

Priming his pistol again, Gentleman Jack merely smiled.

"I have wanted to do that for a long while," he said. "The brat always disgusted me! And now, my Lord Marquis, I will show you one last act of mercy, not because I care a fiddle whether you suffer or no—in fact it would give me intense pleasure to hear you scream as this old barn burns to the ground—but because I have no time to waste and wish to join my men at Eastcote's Farm. Tonight they are to be disbanded, they will be paid off from the treasure I have accumulated against this very moment."

"The treasure in Beulah's room!" Arabella gasped.

"So you've found that, have you?" Gentleman Jack snarled. "I should have strangled you that first morning when I found you snooping round the stables. But it does not signify. My men will disperse each with his share of the spoils of many pleasant encounters with the nobility and gentry on the King's Highway! And then, my dear Coz, Gentleman Jack will become Jack Wilder, Gentleman, the owner of Meridale Castle."

"You will not escape retribution!" the Marquis cried. "You will swing for this!"

"I think it very unlikely that anyone will challenge my ownership," Gentleman Jack answered. "And so, my Lord Marquis, if you have said your prayers, I will blow a hole through you. But first, I am convinced, you would wish me to dispatch your ladybird. It is best for you to watch her die, rather than let her see you weak and helpless, robbed of your manhood by death!"

"Let her go!" the Marquis shouted hoarsely. "For God's sake let her go, Wilder. Your quarrel is not with her!"

"And have her blabbing all over the countryside?" Gentleman Jack asked sneeringly. "No, she shall die. Time presses, I have no further time for argument."

He raised his pistol and Arabella shut her eyes.

"Dear God," she whispered, "let me be brave."

Then suddenly from the door a voice rang out:

"Wait! There is something you have forgotten!"

The highwayman turned round sharply, and Arabella opening her eyes saw a lady standing in the dooway wearing an exquisitely cut red riding-habit, her black hat trimmed with a scarlet veil.

For a moment there was only silence until, in a strangled voice and with staring eyes as if he beheld a ghost, the highwayman ejaculated one word:

"Miriam!"

Then she shot him, with the small, ivory-handled pistol she held in her hand. At first it seemed as though the bullet had not touched him; for he stood there, stupidly, his own pistol limp in the hand which had fallen to his side. Slowly, he swayed, toppled over and fell with a crash to the ground.

The lady, without looking at the highwayman, came further into the barn. In a voice that was almost too hoarse to be recognisable the Marquis exclaimed:

"Mother! It is you, isn't it!"

"Yes, darling," the lady replied. "And thank God I was here in time! I was afraid, terribly afraid, that something would have happened before I arrived. When Matty told me at the Castle you had gone driving towards the forest I guessed where he would take you."

She had drawn near to the Marquis as she spoke, and now she reached up and kissed him as he stood bound to the roofpost

Arabella could see how beautiful she was, no longer young but beautiful in a manner that was ageless, with perfect features and a grace which was indescribable.

"I must untie you," the Marquis's mother said. "Ah! I see! The knot is at the back."

Turning to the ropes she managed to loosen them and the Marquis with a struggle freed himself.

He put his arms round his mother, and held her close. Then he moved across to Arabella, and as he released her he said, speaking over his shoulder:

"I can't believe that I'm not dreaming! They told me you were dead! Sheltham wrote to me of the funeral and your—grave."

"I know, darling," the Marquis's mother said, "and when you hear what I have to relate you will understand why."

She looked across the barn and said softly:

"Poor, poor little Beulah! I was not in time to save her but—perhaps it was best that she should die!"

"Mother, how can you say such a thing!" the Marquis asked. "He shot her down in cold blood! I know too well what I used to feel about her, but to see any child treated in such a way . . ."

"I know," his mother answered, "but there were reasons for his hatred of her."

Free of the ropes which had bound her, Arabella ran to Beulah. She pulled the child loose and took the limp body in her arms, wondering wildly if there could be any chance of resuscitation.

"She is dead," she heard the Marquis say, and looked up to find him standing beside her.

"Y . . . you are s . . . sure?" Arabella faltered.

"There is nothing you can do," he said quietly, and drew her to her feet.

Arabella could feel the Marquis drawing her away, but still she hesitated, reluctant to leave the still, strangely silent little figure on the floor. The Marquis laid his lace-edged fine linen handkerchief on Beulah's face. Then almost forcefully he led Arabella back towards his mother, who was waiting for them, her eyes on her son's face.

"Come," she said, as they approached, "let us go into the other part of the barn. I cannot bear to look at that man lying there. I have prayed so long for his death, but even now he still seems to exude evil."

As she spoke she picked up the red velvet skirts of her riding-habit and led the way to the end of the barn where they were screened by some high stacks of rooting hay from the two bodies.

"Why do we not go back to the Castle?" the Marquis asked.

"There is no time," his mother replied. "I have to return to London and, Julius, make no mistake, I am dead!"

"Dead?" he repeated as if he did not comprehend what she was saying.

221

"To everyone but you and Matty. Darling, it is better that way."

"But I don't understand," the Marquis said.

"I know," she replied, "and I have treated you ill. But indeed, there was nothing else I could do. You see, because of Jack Wilder I had to die—for everyone's sake."

"He threatened you?" the Marquis asked.

"Worse than that," his mother replied.

She sat down on some bales of hay and motioned the Marquis to sit beside her. Then, with an exquisite gesture, she held out her hand to Arabella.

"You are very lovely, child," she said gently. "I think perhaps you have a tenderness for my son."

"We cannot speak of that, Mother," the Marquis interposed quickly.

His mother just smiled at him and taking Arabella by the hand drew her close so that they sat side by side.

"Now listen," she said, "for there is very little time to tell you all that has happened. As you know, Julius, your father and I were exceedingly happy together. He was much older than I and I married him when I was very young. But I loved him deeply and he loved me.

"When you were away at Oxford, your father had to leave me for a few days to deal with some pressing business in London. I did not want to accompany him, so I stayed on alone at the Castle. That night, Jack Wilder came to my room."

"How dare he?" the Marquis cried. "Why didn't you have him thrown out?"

"I slept alone in the West Wing, as you well know," his mother replied. "I struggled and fought against him until I fell unconscious. When I came to, I was alone but . . . he . . . had taken his . . . pleasure of me!"

"Mother!" the Marquis ejaculated, and Arabella saw that his mother's hand was bloodless beneath the strength of his fingers.

"I knew who he was, of course," his mother went on. "It had been whispered for some time that old

Wilder's grandson was one of the highwaymen who were beginning to be notorious on the roads into London. Naturally, I would not demean myself by relating what had happened to any of the servants. I waited for your father's return."

"And you told him?" the Marquis enquired.

"He was brought back to me a dying man," his mother answered. "He had had that terrible carriage accident and the doctors despaired of his life! I told myself that I would confess what had happened as soon as he was well enough to hear me. Then, to my horror, I found I was pregnant!"

"Oh, my God!" the Marquis exclaimed brokenly.

"At first I wanted to die," the soft voice went on. 'Then I knew that I must try to save your father's life, and that if he learnt what had happened it would kill him."

"And so it was Wilder's child you bore," the Marquis said, and his voice was almost inaudible.

"Wilder's child," his mother repeated, "and it was born two days after your father's death."

"How you must have suffered!" the Marquis murmured.

"I didn't believe it was possible to live through such hell as I experienced all the time I was carrying Beulah," his mother answered. "You see, Wilder came and went in the Castle as he wished. I tried to stop him, but already the servants were afraid and he threatened me that if I informed the Justice, he would tell them that he was my lover!"

"If only I could have killed him!" the Marquis cried.

"There was something else he told me, too. He told me that he had fathered several children and that every one of them had been deformed or crazy! There was a long line of madness in his mother's family. His mother, whom he says was seduced by your uncle, died in Bedlam; her mother—Wilder's grandmother, was witless and drowned as a witch. A number of his other female relatives were all insane. It was a curse, he told me, that he had inherited, so that he loathed the female children he fathered and wanted only to destroy them."

The Marquis suddenly put his hands up to his face.

"Oh, my darling!" his mother said gently. "I know what you must have felt when you saw the baby. I understood why you had left without saying goodbye. When I learned you had joined your Regiment, I thought it was the wisest thing you could do."

"I believed that I could never marry for fear that I, too, could produce a child like that!"

The words seemed to come stammering between the Marquis's lips and his mother gave a little cry.

"I had not thought you would feel that way," she said. "Oh, how wrong and thoughtless of me, Julius! I should have told you the truth before now. But you must understand it was very difficult. You see, when your father died, Wilder told me that he intended to marry me. He had one obsession . . . to live at the Castle and be master there. And he thought an easy way would be to become my husband. Then he would doubtless have disposed of you!"

"I would have shot him down like a dog if I had known of this," the Marquis said.

"I suppose in a way I panicked but I was also nearly insane with fear and worry," his mother went on. "I flew to London, where I found an old friend—the Duc de Collalto. He had been smuggled into England on a secret mission. Your father and I had stayed with him when we had visited Italy, and because I had always known that he loved me, I told him of my desperate plight."

"So he helped you," the Marquis said.

"He married me," his mother replied simply. "But first he decided that I must disappear. We both knew that Wilder was a madman without a vestige of decency. He could have made a terrible scandal by claiming Beulah as his own child, the honour of the family would have been called in question and that, with the love I had had for your father, I could not countenance!"

"No—I understand," the Marquis murmured.

"It was Paulo who arranged everything with dear Matty," his mother went on.

"She has always known you were alive?" he asked.

"Yes, indeed. And she has kept in touch with me whenever it was possible. She had written me some months ago that you had not returned to the Castle. That is why I did not try to communicate with you, thinking that perhaps you were content living your own life. And, of course, while the War was taking place, it was impossible for me to return to England."

"But you have come now!" the Marquis exclaimed.

"Strictly incognito!" his mother smiled. "You see, although Paulo goes to Carlton House tonight, I must remain behind! No one must see me, Julius darling, no one must suspect that the Marchioness of Meridale is not interred in the family vault beside her husband!"

"I never questioned your death," the Marquis said, "and even now I cannot believe that you are alive!"

"I am alive, but I am married to an Italian. In Italy people are very kind to the English-born Duchessa de Collalto. But there is no suspicion, I assure you, that she had a strange history before she became the wife of their most popular singer."

"And your husband . . ."

"We are very happy," Julius's mother said softly. "He loves me deeply and I think, Julius, that you will like him too. He is a very brave man. The information he was able to give to the Allied Armies during the War was of inestimable value. It was so clever of him to become a professional singer. The Italians, and also the French, will permit anything of a man who sings like an angel!"

She paused a moment, then added: "Tonight Paulo is to receive a British Honour from the Prince Regent. I am glad for his sake, but I shall be happier when tomorrow we leave for Italy!"

"Mother! Am I not to see you again?"

"Not before I leave," his mother replied. "But I have a feeling, Julius, that you might soon be planning a honeymoon and we would be delighted if you and your wife would come and stay on my husband's estates in Southern Italy."

She rose as she spoke, put her arms round the Marquis's neck and drew his face down to hers.

"My darling son!" she said. "I have always loved you, believe that! And try to understand how, because I loved you so deeply, I tried to save you from the knowledge of my humiliation and suffering. Perhaps I did wrong, perhaps I should have trusted you. But you were so young!"

"How I wish you had told me!" the Marquis exclaimed.

He held his mother close to him, and then she gently disengaged herself and turned towards Arabella.

"Forget all that has happened, my dear," she said kindly. "Jack Wilder is dead and, please God, his evil dies with him."

She moved across the barn, the Marquis followed her, while Arabella remained behind. She heard their voices and the sound of a horse galloping away. Then he came back to her.

He did not speak but lifted her up in his arms, and she hid her face against his shoulder as he carried her through the barn, past the dead bodies and out into the forest.

She opened her eyes to see the sunshine through the branches of the trees and there was the sound of birds. Still holding her in his arms, the Marquis said:

"There is a great deal we have to do. We must, of course, make no mention of how my mother saved our lives. I will say that I killed the highway man after he had shot Beulah."

"I have a better idea," Arabella announced as the Marquis set her down on the ground.

"What is that?" he asked.

"Why not do as Gentleman Jack intended and burn the barn to the ground? It would save so many explanations. The bodies will never be recovered and there will be no doubts or queries as to how you could have

226

shot the highwayman when you had no pistol with you, or why he killed Beulah."

Arabella paused. The Marquis was listening intently.

"The story will be that he meant to burn us all," she continued, "but somehow you got free and struggled with him, leaving him in the fire while you carried me to safety."

"You are right," the Marquis said. "That tale will require far less complicated explanations."

Without arguing further he went back into the barn. A few moments later Arabella smelt smoke. It grew stronger and suddenly she was aware of flames like yellow tongues leaping through the open door.

For a moment with a sudden fear, sharper almost than anything she had known before, she thought that the Marquis was trapped inside, until, as she waited transfixed, she saw him coming towards her.

Then the ground seemed to rise up and the trees fall down on her head, covering her completely, and darkness enveloped her.

Twelve

ARABELLA opened her eyes. For a moment she wondered where she was; then seeing Matty hovering anxiously at the foot of the bed, she remembered.

She had come back to consciousness to find the Marquis's arms round her, and even the horrors of what had happened inside the burning barn seemed unimportant beside the fact that his face was close to hers.

He had lifted her up in his arms and carried her to the curricle.

"We have to get back to the Castle," he said.

"Of course," she answered. "I am all right."

"Hold on tightly," he said. "I am going to put the horses through their paces."

She was still too bemused from her faint to wonder why he was in such a hurry. She was only vaguely aware that the horses, tied by their bridles to a tree, were moving restlessly and whinnying with fear at the smell of smoke and the crackle of the flames.

The Marquis, having loosed and calmed them, turned the curricle and set off towards the Castle. Now he was driving, it seemed to Arabella, like a madman, and yet he had a magic touch on the reins which kept the horses under control and the wheels of the light curricle on the ground.

Soon they were nearing the Castle, and only as it came into view, standing there grey and impregnable, did Arabella suddenly realise the reason for their haste.

A quick contraction of her heart told her all too clearly that the Marquis was not yet out of danger.

They swept along the drive and the Marquis drew up at the Castle door with a flourish. As the grooms came running he gave curt instructions:

"I want a riding-horse immediately, the fastest in the stable!"

A groom ran to do his bidding whilst two others went to the heads of the chestnuts. The Marquis put his arms round Arabella and lifted her to the ground. She turned to him, aware of a sudden weakness which made her feel her legs would not carry her.

As if he understood instinctively what she was feeling he carried her up the steps and set her down gently in the hall. But at the same time his air was distant, as though his mind were on other things, and she felt that for the moment she was of no consequence.

"Where are you going?" she asked as he turned from her, knowing the answer before he spoke.

"To see that those other accursed murderers do not escape!" he replied.

"But you cannot go alone!" Arabella cried. "There are five of them and they will shoot you down. Oh, Julius! Wait! I have sent for the soldiers."

The words arrested him in sheer astonishment.

"You have sent for the soldiers?" he repeated. "What do you mean?"

"Captain Huntington carried a letter from me to the Home Secretary," she said. "I have known for some time what has been going on, but I could not tell you about it. Gentleman Jack had intimidated everyone, the servants in the Castle, the people on the Estate."

"Yes, I can understand that," the Marquis said impatiently, "but the soldiers! Is there any likelihood of their getting here in time?"

"I do not know," Arabella replied, "but I told Captain Huntington to read my letter. Perhaps he will take action."

"I cannot wait on the chance that the Military will come to our assistance," the Marquis said. "As soon as

229

these scoundrels know that their leader is dead, they'll be off! You can be sure of that!"

He turned towards the butler.

"Bring me my pistols!"

Turner stared at him. Then in a slow, grave voice he asked:

"Your Lordship will pardon the presumption but did I understand you to say that the leader of the highwaymen was dead?"

"Yes," the Marquis replied, "Gentleman Jack, if that is what you call him, lies dead in the forest."

"That is indeed great and welcome news, Milord," the butler said, and Arabella perceived the excitement on the faces of the footmen who were listening.

"There are, however, five highwaymen alive and at Eastcote's Farm," the Marquis announced. "I intend to capture them. If any man is courageous enough to come with me, I would welcome his assistance."

Turner gave his orders.

"George," he said, "run at once to the stables and tell Mister Abbey what His Lordship has said. I warrant there will be no lack of horsemen to accompany you, Milord! There's no one here as has not suffered from the threats and cruelty of Gentleman Jack and his gang."

"It's a pity no one had the courage to speak of them before," the Marquis said drily. Almost before he had finished speaking, the footman standing nearest the front door gave an exclamation.

"They're a'coming, Milord, I be seeing 'em!"

"See who?" the Marquis enquired.

"Soldiers! They be coming down the drive. That be an army wagon they're a'driving."

Arabella gave a gasp of relief. Now the Marquis would do nothing so foolhardy as tackling the highwaymen without proper support.

In the excitement of the moment convention was forgotten. The Marquis hastily went out onto the steps of the Castle, accompanied by Turner and three footmen. Arabella followed them, standing a little in the background, regretting as she had regretted so often before that as a mere woman she could take no part in what was essentially a masculine adventure.

The army wagon, drawn by four stalwart horses, was rattling over the bridge. An officer on horseback came riding ahead up to the door of the Castle.

He was a splendid sight in his red coat. He saluted the Marquis punctiliously but at the same time he wore a broad grin on his face.

"Here we are, Meridale," he announced, "come to the rescue with the greatest possible push!"

"Gerald! I've not been so glad to see your ugly phiz since you rescued me at Waterloo! But you cannot have got here from London so swiftly."

"No, indeed!" the officer replied, dismounting. Richard knew we were on manoeuvres at Hatfield and persuaded the Colonel that you were in dire and immediate need of help. So I have brought eight of our best men. Some of them served with you in France."

"We will reminisce as soon as we have captured the enemy!" the Marquis said. "Don't let them down from the wagon, Gerald—my horse will be here at any second. I will lead you to where the highwaymen are in hiding."

As he spoke the grooms came from the stables, one leading the Marquis's stallion, four others mounted and carrying pistols of all types and sizes. Their faces fell when they saw the soldiers.

"We are obviously a formidable force by now," the Marquis remarked as he swung himself into the saddle. "The important thing is not to let any of the rogues escape. If they do, they might choose to take their revenge on some of the defenceless people I understand they have threatened for so long. So, Gerald, this must be a concerted attack from all sides. We must encircle them."

"You tell me what you suggest," the officer replied. "You always were a dab hand at deploying your troops."

The two men rode off together, while the wagon-load and the mounted grooms followed them.

"Let them drive as far as they can," Arabella heard the Marquis say, "it will be quicker. And then we will surround the farm."

Further words were lost in the sound of the horses' hooves and the rumble of wheels. Arabella, with a curious feeling of loneliness, moved away from the front door and turned towards the Grand Staircase.

He had forgotten her, it seemed. Like all men when there was fighting to be done, he had no further thought for a woman.

She felt her spirits drop and a feeling of complete exhaustion creep over her. She held on to the banisters and then Matty was at her side, helping her up the rest of the way.

They reached her bedroom and Matty said quietly: "What happened to Her Ladyship?"

It was then the tears came, tears that suffused her eyes and streamed down her cheeks.

"Gentleman Jack killed her," Arabella whispered. "Oh, Matty! It was horrible. Poor little thing, it was not her fault."

"He always hated Her Ladyship," Matty said. "But don't you cry over her, Miss. Her Ladyship is with God. She could never have been normal, however much anyone tried to teach her. And indeed, you did try, Miss Arabella."

"It was horrible, horrible!" Arabella sobbed. She cried all the time as Matty helped her into bed and brought her a hot drink. Soon, utterly exhausted by the dramatic events of the day and the lack of sleep the night before, she knew no more. . . .

Now Matty brought her some warm soup and she sipped it, more to please the solicitous old woman than because she felt in need of sustenance.

"What is the time?" she asked.

"It is nigh on five o'clock," Matty replied.

Arabella sat up firmly in her bed and pushed aside the cup of soup.

"What has happened?" she asked. "Oh, Matty, how could I have fallen asleep when so much was happening?"

"You were worn out," Matty said, "but the rest has done you good."

"But what has happened?" Arabella repeated.

"They were all accounted for, every one of them," Matty replied. "One of the highwaymen was killed and two of the soldiers were wounded, but I understand it was not very difficult to capture them. They were like a lot of sheep now that Gentleman Jack was no longer at their head."

"They have been taken to London?" Arabella asked.

"Yes, the soldiers have taken them away and they will be hanged at Tyburn," Matty said with satisfaction. "I hear the people are cheering themselves silly down in the village and Mister Turner thinks there'll be celebrations all the way to London. News travels fast and so many people who have suffered from the highwaymen will be ready to go down on their knees and thank God Almighty that their misery is all over and done with!"

Arabella got out of bed.

"I wish to go downstairs and hear all about it," she said.

"That is exactly what His Lordship wants you to do," Matty replied. "He asked that you should come to him as soon as you were well enough."

"Well enough!" Arabella ejaculated. "He must think me a feeble creature to take to my bed like some vapourish female."

She started to slip off her nightgown then stopped dead. In the centre of the room was a round-topped, leather travelling-trunk and beside it her own meagre, rather old-fashioned piece of baggage. The tops were open and Matty had obviously been packing. There were still several gowns on a chair.

Arabella did not ask any questions. There was no

need to. She knew without being told what was happening. The Marquis was sending her away!

She was not foolish. She knew it would be impossible for her to remain at the Castle. The county people would learn what had occurred and they would come to offer the Marquis their congratulations. They would also be full of curiosity to see what he looked like after such a long absence.

There would also be explanations to be made, lawyers to be faced, and the Justices of the Peace to be told that Beulah had died in the fire, as well as Gentleman Jack.

Yes Arabella thought, she would have to go. She only prayed that the Marquis had not arranged for her to return home, for she could not face Sir Lawrence again and endure his brutality.

She did not notice until she was dressed that Matty had helped her into a new gown. It was a lovely creation in white batiste, trimmed at the edge of the skirt and on the sleeves with valuable Venetian lace.

"Her Ladyship always wore a very special pendant with this dress," Matty said, "and I know she would like you to wear it today."

"She is very beautiful," Arabella said and saw that her words had made Matty happy.

"The most beautiful person in the whole world as far as I am concerned," Matty answered.

"It is all due to you that both the Marquis and I are alive, you realise that, don't you?" Arabella said.

Matty nodded.

"Yes, His Lordship told me what happened," she replied. "I knew, when I wrote, that Her Ladyship would not fail us! It was only through Captain Huntington coming here at breakfast time that I learned she was in England."

As she spoke, Matty took from a velvet box an exquisite pendant of diamonds and pearls which glittered in the light of the candles. She turned it over to show Arabella that on the back of the pendant was a miniature of a little boy.

"Is that His Lordship?" Arabella asked.

Matty nodded. She slipped the pendant round Arabella's neck, fastening the necklace of pearls from which it hung by the pearl and diamond clasp.

"It is too grand for me," Arabella protested. "I am not sure Her Ladyship would wish me to wear it."

At the same time she knew that the gleaming jewel became her. It did indeed seem to be a part of the gown itself.

"Wear it, Miss, while you go downstairs," Matty suggested.

"Yes, I will do that, and then I must give it back to you before I leave," Arabella said.

Even as she spoke the words she felt that they struck like a note of doom against her heart.

"There is a cape trimmed with marabou and a bonnet to match the gown," Matty announced. "I will bring them downstairs with the baggage."

Arabella shut her eyes against the agony of knowing that she must go away. Then pride, something she had never lacked, made her lift her little chin high as she went from the room without another word and down the Grand Staircase to the hall.

At the sight of her, a footman hurried to open the door of the Library and she passed through it, hearing it close behind her and feeling a sense of relief that the Marquis was alone.

He was sitting at his desk signing papers, and so intent on what he was doing that for a moment he did not hear her and she could take in his handsome countenance, a faint smile as if of happiness on his lips, the elegance of his blue satin coat and snowy cravat. Then he looked up and sprang to his feet.

"Arabella!" he exclaimed. "You have come at precisely the right moment, I have just finished.

She came a little further into the room and it seemed to her as though he deliberately looked not at her but at the papers which were on his desk.

"I have made a lot of plans," he said in a low voice. "I hope you will give them your approval."

Still Arabella did not speak. She was indeed fighting for control of herself, wondering if she could remain quiet and dignified when she must say "goodbye".

"We must leave immediately!" the Marquis said.

"We?" Her voice sounded strange even to herself.

"Yes," he replied, "for Turner tells me that already people are going up to the forest to see what is the mighty conflagration against the skyline. Soon there will be callers and I have no inclination to endure their questioning or the endless recital of what has happened in the past. It is the future with which I am concerned."

He paused for a moment, but still he did not look up as he continued:

"I had thought that, if it met with your wishes, we should leave here immediately and drive to High Wycombe. My godfather lives there and would, I am convinced, be delighted to act as our host tonight. He is, incidentally, a Bishop. He is retired but I am sure it would give him great pleasure to marry us this evening in his private Chapel. You will of course wish to inform your mother what has occurred, and I have arranged for a groom to carry her a note, as soon as you have written it."

Arabella drew in her breath but she did not speak. The Marquis went on:

"Tomorrow my travelling-coach will join us from London and we will proceed to Dover, where my yacht will carry us across the Channel. I have a great desire to show you France, Arabella, and Italy will be a new place of exploration for us both. Finally, of course, we will reach my mother and the Collalto Estates in the South. Does all this meet with your approval?"

His voice died away. Then Arabella said in a low voice speaking very slowly:

"There is no need for you to feel obliged to marry me, My Lord! My relatives will not know that I have played any part here, save that of a child. I am also persuaded that my mother would consider Miss Matherson to have been sufficient chaperon for the very short time you have been in residence. I would, however, be obliged if Your Lordship could convey me to London and not to my stepfather's house!"

Arabella stopped. The Marquis had come from behind the desk and was standing very close, looking down at her with a smile on his lips and a twinkle in his eye.

"Oh, Arabella!" he said softly. "You darling, foolish little goose. Didn't you realise that the reason I was laying my plans before you so formally was that if I dared to look at you they would never be told at all!

"I don't feel obliged to offer for you, Arabella. I don't care a damn for all the conventions and all the proprieties in the world! I want you for my wife because I love you, and if you refuse to marry me, I shall compel you by main force because, my dearest dear, I cannot live without you!"

Arabella raised her eyes to his and the Marquis felt as though suddenly the room was lit with a thousand tapers.

"That is the truth, Arabella," he said with a note in his voice that made her heart turn over in her breast. "When I thought that brute was about to kill you, I knew then that if you died I had no wish to go on living. I love you, Arabella, as I never thought it possible to love any woman! Do you understand?"

She could not answer him, for although her lips parted no sound came. Then he said:

"There is still one thing I would say to you. My secret fear, which has haunted me all these years, is dispelled. But what of yours, Arabella? More than once you have told me that you could not bear to be touched. For one glorious moment I overcame that fear. But has it gone for ever? For if you marry me, however much you pleaded with me, however much you tried to escape from me, it would be impossible for me not to hold you, not to touch you, not to kiss you, Arabella. I want you. And this, my little love, is your last chance to escape."

He opened his arms wide.

"If you want to go you are free, and I swear that I

will not stop you. But once you are mine—then I will never let you go."

They stood looking at each other and Arabella saw the sudden anxiety on his face, a fleeting fear that after all he might lose her.

Then, as her heart beat within her like the thundering of waves on the shore, she felt suddenly as though she could fly to the stars.

He held out his hands towards her and the sheer excitement and elation of the moment seemed to tingle over her body like the warmth of the sun.

"Answer me! Arabella!" he said masterfully, with the note of command in his voice she now knew so well. "Answer me, because for me the whole world hangs on your answer."

Suddenly Arabella felt desperately shy of him. He was a man, who once she had thought in her ignorance she despised but who now held her whole heart. But she could not now admit it.

She looked down, her eyelashes dark against the purity of her skin, and the Marquis saw she was trembling.

"Are you frightened of me, Arabella?" he asked gently.

"A . . . little. I . . . think," she answered, her voice so low he could hardly hear the words.

Yet even as she spoke she knew it was not the Marquis of whom she was afraid but the esctasy rising within herself at the thought of his touch.

"I would not frighten you, my darling," the Marquis said tenderly. "But I must know if you are mine and that you will not resist me."

There was a silence in which Arabella felt he must hear the passionate beating of her heart.

"Arabella! Answer me!"

It was a cry of desperation from a man in an agony of suspense.

Then Arabella, with the blood rising in her cheeks and the breath coming quickly from between her lips, answered softly:

"I had thought . . . perhaps . . . that when we were
. . . married . . . we might go . . . together . . . to the
little . . . pool in the . . . forest . . . and . . . swim there."

The Marquis made a little sound that was half
laughter and half a note of triumph and swept her into
his arms. Then his lips were on hers, holding her mouth
utterly captive, and she felt as though the world whirled
around them and knew they were free—free of fear and
free of everything save their love and their need for
one another.